The Ghoul

The Ghoul

FRANK KING

COACHWHIP PUBLICATIONS
Greenville, Ohio

The Ghoul, by Frank King
© 2025 Coachwhip Publications edition

First published 1929
Frank King, 1892-1958
CoachwhipBooks.com

ISBN 1-61646-611-1
ISBN-13 978-1-61646-611-4

Chief Inspector Dransfield pulled a wry face at his visitor.

"You've got me on the hip, old man," he confessed. "The fellow's a mystery to me. We want him for nearly every crime on the calendar—and most of 'em more than once—and I'm ashamed to admit that we know nothing about him. I can't help you in the least."

"You're frank enough about it, anyway," laughed Paul Grendon, glancing round the severely furnished office of the police chief. "I hardly expected such candor from Scotland Yard."

"Oh, Scotland Yard doesn't suffer from swollen head. We've sense enough here to know our limitations. Of course, I shouldn't be quite so indiscreet with anyone else. But I learned long ago to tell you the truth; any prevarication only brings out that confounded grin of yours."

Paul Grendon laughed again. Though, in a way, they were rivals, he and the Inspector remained stanch friends; they understood and appreciated one another.

"Well, tell me who christened him 'The Ghoul'?" he asked.

"Search me! The name's just attached itself to him, and it's deuced appropriate. He is a murderous devil, a regular bloodsucker.

"As to his identity, we're in the dark about that. Just look at these!" Dransfield pulled a sheaf of papers from a drawer and flung them on the desk in front of his visitor. "Recent reports by some of my best men."

Grendon glanced at the first sheet, quickly reading the brief precis of the report which headed the page:

THE GHOUL?

James Laverack. Address: unknown. Age: about 30. Occupation: footman or butler. Height: five-foot ten. Build: slim. Complexion: florid and freckled. Color of eyes: uncertain. Hair: reddish. Distinguishing peculiarities: snub nose.

Remarks: often seen in public houses in Marylebone district with men known to us. No records, but was certainly concerned in the Esher Murder.

He turned to the next:

THE GHOUL?

Walter Frant, known as "the man from Leeds." Address: The Grange, Fixby Park, Leeds. Age: about 65. Occupation: retired (ironmaster). Height: five-foot four. Build: rotund. Complexion: pale. Color of eyes: uncertain. Hair: almost bald, white mustache and beard. Distinguishing peculiarities: slight limp left foot.

Remarks: pays frequent visits to Town. West End bars and clubs. Often in company of well-known confidence men. Leeds police know nothing, and no records found. Had some connection with the Millionaire's Check Fraud.

The third was as follows:

THE GHOUL?

Count Arliesno, supposed to be an Austrian nobleman. Age: about 45. Height: five-foot six. Build: powerful. Complexion: dark. Color of eyes: uncertain. Hair: black and wavy; small mustache. Distinguishing peculiarities: warts on nose and right ear.

Remarks: seldom in London, but each visit has coincided with some crime attributed to the Ghoul. Holds passport to Denmark. Copenhagen police know nothing. Vienna police state no such title as Arliesno.

He grinned as he handed the papers back to Dransfield.

"Seems to be a protean sort of gentleman, this Ghoul of yours," he remarked.

"Protean!" The Inspector snorted. "Why, every report I get about him is different. And, you know, my men are not fools. There's something fishy in each one of these cases. I'll wager that every one of these suspects has some very definite connection with the Ghoul. He seems to control a large gang of crooks, each a specialist in his own particular line."

"And you think these people—Laverack, the man from Leeds, and Count Arliesno—are subordinates, members of his gang?"

"I don't know. One—or more—of them may be the man himself. I'm told he's a wonder at disguise. So far as I can make out, no one has seen him in his natural self."

"A violet born to blush unseen, eh? Well, your information does seem a trifle vague."

"Vague? Of course it's vague! I told you I couldn't help you."

"Can't you get to know something from members of his gang?"

"Oh, we keep roping in the smaller fry, but they won't squeal. Not a word! They're scared stiff of him. And I'm not surprised. He's got a hellish reputation. You've heard about him, of course. A perfect fiend. I don't see how any normal human being could perform cold-blooded atrocities as he is capable of. By the way, what are you after him for? Blackmail, I suppose?"

"Yes, blackmail. I'm acting for the usual terrified couple, who daren't call in the regular police."

"They'd be just as safe with us if only they knew it," mused the Inspector. "Funny, isn't it, how they get it into their heads that publicity necessarily dogs the footsteps of Scotland Yard?" He chuckled reminiscently. "We could tell 'em a tale or two, eh, old man? Still, it's perhaps as well for you that people feel like that about blackmail. There wouldn't be much work for a private detective if they didn't."

"Professional jealousy!" smiled Grendon. "I believe you're really envious of my clients."

"Well, perhaps I am," admitted Dransfield, unable to resist the infection of his friend's smile. "I sometimes wish I'd gone in for the unofficial side, as you've done. You've such a soft job compared with mine. No superiors barking at you because you can't locate The Ghoul. No press raging and blaspheming at the inefficiency of your methods. Quiet, homely little cases of blackmail to deal with. And whenever you're in difficulties, a friend at Scotland Yard to fall back on for help and advice."

Paul Grendon rose from his chair and extended his hand.

"You're an ill-used man," he said solemnly. "And the help and advice you've given me this morning are of incalculable value."

The Inspector shook the proffered hand warmly.

"You're welcome, old chap," he grinned. "Honestly, I wish I could have told you more. But we're up against a big problem in The Ghoul, and heaven knows whether we shall ever solve it. Anyhow, the best of luck! Give us the nod if you get on his track, won't you? If you find yourself in a tight corner—and you certainly will if you get anywhere near him—remember that we're ready to help. But don't use that SOS code I told you about unless you're really in danger. It's supposed to be for official use only."

"Thanks, I'll remember. You said it would be understood anywhere?"

"Yes. Any police station in England will act promptly on it. It may help you out of a hole. But watch your step carefully, for the love of Mike! Don't make any mistake about The Ghoul! He's dangerous—damned dangerous; and he sticks at nothing. If it's a question of one of you shooting, see that you get yours in first."

"Thanks again," said Grendon. He paused with his hand on the door, and his gray eyes twinkled. "I'll let you know when I've caught him," he added; and went out.

Chief Inspector Dransfield whistled.

"Impudent young devil!" he muttered with a smile as he returned to his papers. "Shouldn't be surprised if he does catch him. He has cheek enough for anything! . . ."

1

The Inheritance

The short November afternoon was fading into premature dusk. Thin, silent rain fell drearily. A dank, clinging fog had risen from the river, and was creeping furtively over the city. Through this gray pall the familiar roar of London's traffic penetrated, persistent, yet with an eerie, muffled effect.

Betty Harlan turned away from the window with a grimace of disgust. She shivered, as she drew the thick curtains and switched on the light. The day had seemed very long and depressing. The yellowish, misty light had made any work impossible, and Betty had idled the dull hours away in great discontent.

She was usually a cheerful little soul, looking out on a friendly world with laughing blue eyes. But to-day an unaccustomed sense of loneliness had seized upon her. It seemed that everything was wrong.

"I wish I had a regular job like Sally," she muttered, lighting the spirit stove under the kettle. "I wish I had a lot of money. I wish I could have a change, get away from here for a while. I wish—oh, I'm a fool!"

The room—Betty called it her studio—was large and warm and comfortable. A log fire hissed and spluttered in the old-fashioned grate. Bright-hued rugs were scattered in profusion on the polished floor, and the chintz covers of the easy chairs were cheery and colorful. A large easel bearing an uncompleted canvas stood near the window, while the many sketches and studies tacked on the walls were further witnesses to Betty's industry.

She glanced at these drawings as she searched for the toasting fork, and a wistful smile curved her red lips.

"I'm afraid I'm no good," she sighed. "I'm nothing but an amateur dauber. Though the Heartful Magazine *nearly* bought that last cover I did for them."

It was, perhaps, lucky for Betty Harlan that her bread and butter was not dependent on the earning-power of her pencils and brushes. In an overcrowded market her work was overlooked. But though she had not as yet shown any promise of attaining to the Academy, there was no doubt that she made an extraordinarily attractive picture as she knelt before the fire with the toasting fork, her slender figure curved with youthful grace, her soft cheeks flushed with the heat, and her bright eyes dancing with the reflection of the flames.

"I'm wasting my time," she murmured disconsolately, quite unconscious of the fact that some man would one day consider her very existence an achievement. "I ought to be *doing* something, doing something worthwhile. Instead, I'm just fooling about—vegetating. I'm wasting my life."

A cheerful singing from the kettle brought her to her feet. She made tea, and spread butter on the toast with generous hand. As her little white teeth met in the first piece, a low, discreet knock sounded on the door.

Visitors to the studio were usually members of a small Bohemian circle of friends. They were not treated with any great degree of ceremony.

"Come in!" called Betty, munching away at her toast.

The door opened softly, and a gentleman entered. No other word could justly be used to describe him, because he was so immaculate and resplendent in his frock coat and top hat, so important and dignified with his large mustache, so stately in his entry into the room. He had, too, such a polite, ingratiating smile; and when he removed his hat, his scanty hair was brushed so carefully across the top of his white, shining head.

"You are Miss Elizabeth Harlan, I presume?" asked this gentleman, smoothly.

Betty stared at him in surprise, a piece of toast held aloft in the air.

"I am," she murmured at last. "But I don't know— Who are you?"

"My name is Everard Broughton. I am—"

"Then it's you who sends me the money every month?" interrupted Betty, her eyes wide and astonished. "How is it you've never been here before? Why do you—"

The gentleman coughed, and raised a neatly gloved hand in mild deprecation.

"All in good time, Miss Harlan. All in good time. The purpose of my visit to you this afternoon is to explain the matter fully and in detail."

Through Betty's surprise and excitement flashed the realization that she was neglecting her duties as hostess.

"Please sit down," she exclaimed, dragging up a chair. "You'll have a cup of tea, won't you? And I'll make some more toast in a jiffy."

"Thank you very much," said Mr. Broughton, carefully lifting his coat tails. He sat down and peeled off his gloves. "The inexorable march of Time permits me now to reveal to you a secret which had to be hidden before."

And so, while Betty made more toast, her visitor explained, in his somewhat pompous tones, the mystery that had always puzzled, sometimes worried her.

For as far back as she could remember she had known of the existence of this Mr. Everard Broughton. Ever since the death of her mother, so many long years ago, he had been a constant, though never understood factor, in Betty's life. She had never seen him before, but his vague and shadowy influence had always colored her environment. It was Mr. Everard Broughton who had placed her in the convent school where she had spent a happy childhood. It was Mr. Everard Broughton who had paid the fees at the expensive finishing school near Paris. It was Mr. Everard Broughton who still paid the rent of the studio, and sent her each month crisp Bank of England notes which amply provided for her modest wants. He was, so to speak, Providence personified, a figure almost mythical in his attributes. Yet here he was in the flesh!

She had tried often to discover the identity of her mysterious benefactor, and the reason for his interest in her welfare. But all her inquiries had brought her to a blank wall of bland courtesy which she could not pass, so that eventually she had come to accept the situation without further question. Her curiosity, of course, had never been less than dormant; and now she listened entranced to the story of an old romance, the rather commonplace details of which sounded very wonderful to her.

Mr. Broughton, it seemed, was only an intermediary. He was a solicitor, acting on behalf of a client who had strictly insisted on anonymity.

Years ago, long before Betty was born, Edward Morlant had loved her mother. He had loved her and lost her. But though she had treated him none too well, his kindly, sympathetic nature was such that he had never lost his love for her.

Mr. Broughton was careful to expatiate on the many excellencies of Edward Morlant's character. Betty received an impression of a lonely, lovable old man who had found an altruistic happiness in providing for the daughter of the woman he had loved.

"But why didn't he tell me all about this right at the beginning?" she asked. "I'm sure I should love him and make him happier. Why didn't he take me to live with him as soon as Mother died?"

"I do not know," replied Mr. Broughton, flicking an imaginary speck of dust from his immaculate spats. "I have no instructions on that point. Pray allow me to continue."

The marriage of Betty's parents, he went on in his suave fashion, had been disastrous. When Gerald Harlan deserted his wife and child, Edward Morlant had come to the rescue. He had provided for them, always anonymously, until the death of Elizabeth, the mother. And then he had taken little Elizabeth, the orphan, under his wing, and done everything for her that was possible.

"It's funny," mused Betty, her blue eyes bright with sympathy for the secretly cherished romance, "funny that he has always kept so much in the background. When Mother was—left alone, why didn't he—"

"On that point, also, I have no instructions," said Mr. Broughton smoothly. "You will, I am sure, understand that I am merely conveying to you certain details which my client confided to me. Unofficially, I might remark that Mr. Morlant was rather eccentric in his—"

"Was?" echoed Betty. "Is he—dead?"

"He died on Sunday last. He was buried yesterday."

"Oh, why didn't you let me know before? I ought—"

"I am fulfilling his wishes precisely, Miss Harlan. It was not Mr. Morlant's desire that you should attend his funeral. He was very definite that you should not be informed of his death until the day after his interment."

"Had he—other relations there?"

"None. I was the only mourner."

"Oh, I wish I had known. After all he has done for me, it seems such a shame that he should die as lonely as he lived."

"Such sentiments do you credit, Miss Elizabeth. As I have said, however, Mr. Edward was always eccentric, and his solitude was probably of his own choosing. But no useful purpose is served by discussing this. We must get to business."

Betty stiffened in her chair, and the brightness faded from her eyes. Bad news was on the way. She knew what was coming. With the death of her benefactor, of course, her allowance would cease. This was the business that brought her visitor.

She watched him as he drew a large envelope from his breast pocket, and carefully extracted and unfolded the contents. She wondered if all solicitors were so glib and pompous as Mr. Everard Broughton, and decided that they couldn't be. It seemed to her that his manner was deliberately cultivated. There was a suggestion of insincerity about him that colored all he said. He probably meant quite well, but she felt that she didn't like him.

Having adjusted his *pince-nez*, Mr. Broughton looked round the studio.

"You have some very meritorious drawings on the wall," he observed. "Does your artistic work bring in any appreciable income yet?"

Betty shook her curly head ruefully.

"I haven't earned a cent with it."

"But you are still interested?" he went on. "You are comfortable here, and will not like to leave?"

So she had guessed aright. Betty's mouth drooped as she glanced round the cozy room. She had been so happy here with Sally.

"I suppose I shall have to?" she sighed. "My allowance will stop now?"

"On the contrary, Miss Elizabeth. Very much on the contrary! You are the sole legatee under Mr. Edward's will."

"I'm what?"

"He has left the whole of his estate to you. And appointed me the sole executor."

"Does that mean—"

"I will read you the will." Mr. Broughton flourished the paper in his hand. "No, on second thoughts, that will take too long. It is a rather complicated document. You may peruse it at your leisure. For the moment, I will confine myself to telling you the most important provisions."

"Please do." Betty nodded her curly head vigorously. "And make everything very simple, because I'm far too excited to understand anything difficult."

"Very well. As I have said, you are sole heiress to Mr. Edward's wealth. So far, I can congratulate you. There are, however, certain conditions to be observed. And I, as executor, must see that they are carried out."

"Well, hurry, please. What are the conditions?"

"In the first place, you must live at Hameldon House for the six months immediately following the testator's death."

"Where is Hameldon House?"

"In Yorkshire. It has been the home of the Morlants for generations."

"All right. Go on."

"In the second place, you must take up residence there at once. To-morrow."

"But, Mr. Broughton, I couldn't possibly—"

"The conditions are very explicit, Miss Elizabeth. You will see for yourself when you read the will. I must insure that they are followed out in every detail. Unless you return with me to Hameldon House by to-morrow at the latest, you forfeit the inheritance."

"But I've no clothes, no—"

"I am afraid we cannot take such things into consideration."

Betty turned her head away and grimaced. She was sure now that she didn't like Mr. Broughton. There was too much of the heavy hand about him.

"Are there—any other conditions?" she asked, after a while.

"Nothing of importance. You will understand, of course, that a good deal is left to the discretion of the executor, and that for a while you must regard me as your—er—guardian."

There was another pause while Betty readjusted her thoughts to this new viewpoint. The idea of being responsible to Mr. Broughton did not appeal to her.

"I am assuming that you will not be so foolish as to throw this inheritance away," went on the solicitor, stroking his heavy mustache. "But you must make up your mind at once."

"What sort of a place is Hameldon House?" asked Betty, wondering why Edward Morlant should insist on her living there.

"It is old—very old. To be absolutely frank with you, Miss Elizabeth, it is not a particularly delectable residence. It is situated in a very lonely spot, surrounded by wild moorland. It is several miles away from the nearest town. It is—er—somewhat depressing."

"You wouldn't make a good house agent, Mr. Broughton."

"I should not care to live in the place myself."

A peculiar tone in the solicitor's voice made Betty glance at him in surprise. There was a significance in it that sounded almost like a warning. Or could it be a threat? In either case, it seemed to her that he would not be at all displeased if she refused to obey the conditions of the will.

She watched his fat, expressionless face, trying to read his thoughts. It came to her at that moment that she not only disliked him, but that she also distrusted him; and she made up her mind at once. She had never been in any real doubt about what she would do, and now her vague suspicion that there was some motive underlying what he said strengthened her decision.

"I shall go, of course," she said, a hint of defiance in her voice. "I can't afford to miss anything, however lonely the house may be."

If her visitor was disappointed with her decision, he showed no sign of it.

"Of course not," he agreed smoothly. "You would be very foolish if you allowed anything to jeopardize your chances of such an inheritance."

It suddenly occurred to Betty that she knew nothing of the extent of Edward Morlant's wealth.

"You have not yet told me," she remarked, "how much I have inherited."

Mr. Everard Broughton spread out his white, plump hands as though he had just performed a miracle.

"Taking all sources of income into consideration," he replied unctuously, "the estate will probably be worth some five thousand pounds per annum."

2

In the Fog

Betty gasped. She had not expected that her inheritance would exceed a fifth of the sum named.

"It sounds like a fairy tale," she murmured. "You're quite real, aren't you? I'm not dreaming?"

Apparently Mr. Broughton could not smile except when it suited his own purpose.

"It is no dream," he said solemnly, stroking his mustache. "You will find that Hameldon House, at least, is very real."

Again the warning note sounded in his voice, and Betty wondered if he were trying to frighten her.

"Why don't you want me to go there?" she asked abruptly.

She had hoped that the unexpectedness of the query might elicit some symptom of uneasiness or a slip of the tongue which would confirm her suspicions. She was disappointed. No sign of emotion showed on the solicitor's broad, fleshy face, and his glib reply held no more than a tinge of asperity:

"That is an extraordinary question, Miss Elizabeth. Indeed, I might almost say, a foolish question. I have traveled up from Yorkshire for no other purpose than to take you back with me. I sincerely hope and trust that you intend to conform with the conditions of the will."

"Oh, yes, I'm coming. I've made up my mind about that."

"Good. Then we can start immediately?"

"Immediately? Good gracious, no! I must see Sally first, and tell her all about it."

"And who, might I ask, is Sally?"

"Sally—Miss Poulter—shares the rooms here with me. She's my best friend. She'll be delighted when she hears of my good luck." A shadow crossed Betty's flushed face. "I—I shan't like leaving Sally, even for six months."

"She is not on the premises at the moment?"

"No. She's out at work all day. She runs a little beauty parlor just off the Strand."

"It is really necessary, in your opinion, that you should see Miss—er—Poulter before you leave?"

"Of course it is!"

"Then I will not press the point." Mr. Broughton rose to his feet and meticulously straightened his coat. "I can occupy myself with various business details this evening. I must insist, however, that you meet me at Euston station to-morrow morning at ten. To comply with the conditions of the will, it is essential that you reach Hameldon House before to-morrow night."

"I can't understand why—"

"Nor can I, Miss Elizabeth. But facts cannot be altered by any amount of discussion. We must accept things as we find them. Mr. Edward, doubtless, had his own reasons for the stipulations he made. The least we can do is to respect them. Is it understood that you meet me at ten to-morrow morning?"

Betty was not accustomed to being hectored, and she didn't like it. But it hardly seemed worthwhile to quarrel with Mr. Broughton just now, though she made a mental note of the fact that he must be dealt with severely on some future occasion.

"All right," she agreed. "I'll be there."

"Very good." The solicitor drew a bulky wallet from his pocket, and extracted several Bank of England notes. "I shall take the liberty of advancing you this small sum in case you are short of ready cash. I shall also leave Mr. Morlant's will with you, so that you can study its provisions at your leisure during the evening."

He placed the document and the notes on a table, and held out his hand.

"I must hurry away now, Miss Elizabeth. By this time to-morrow we should be at Hameldon House."

Betty extended her slim fingers, and found his clammy, nerveless grip as disagreeable as she had expected.

"Good evening, Mr. Broughton," she said. "I hope I shall find the house brighter and more cheerful than you have pictured it."

"I hope so, too. I sincerely hope so. But you will soon be able to decide."

Mr. Broughton picked up his hat and gloves, and marched majestically to the door. After opening it, he turned and bowed stiffly, showing the top of his bald head again. Then he carefully adjusted his top hat and went out, closing the door noiselessly behind him.

For quite a while after he had gone, Betty sat still in her chair, gazing into the fire with dreamy eyes. Most of the toast remained uneaten, and occasionally she nibbled at a piece, oblivious of the fact that it was cold and greasy.

She was not a greedy girl, nor was her horizon bounded on every side by money. But few normal people could receive the news of such a legacy without a certain amount of pleasure.

Indeed, it all seemed too wonderful to be true. Only a few minutes ago she had been discontented, wishing for a change, wishing for wealth, wishing for anything that would make a break in the monotony of life. And, presto! In the twinkling of an eye all her wishes were granted.

There was a sense of unreality about the whole business. Betty felt almost as though she must have been dreaming. But when she thought of him, really, Mr. Broughton had none of the attributes of a fairy godmother. And besides, there was the money lying there on the table.

This, at any rate, was real and tangible. Betty rose from her chair and picked up the notes. She was astonished to find ten of them, each to the value of £5. She crinkled them in her fingers; they were genuine enough. It was not a practical joke carried out by some of her friends.

The will, too, appeared quite convincing to her. She glanced at the superscription: "Last Will and Testament of Edward Morlant," and idly ran her eyes down the typewritten sheets without taking in any details. She noticed that it had been executed only a month ago, and that Everard Broughton and one Charles Bidgood had witnessed the signature.

Everything was in order, then. She was not dreaming. Incredible though it might seem, she was rich. She had an income of five thousand pounds a year. She did a little mental arithmetic, and realized that the money on the table represented her income for less than four days. . . .

It was rather a shock. Betty walked slowly about the room, trying to comprehend just what it meant to her. She would be free to have what she wanted, to do what she wanted. She could buy beautiful clothes and jewels. She could have a car—two if she desired. After the six months, she could travel, see all the wonderful sights of the wonderful world. She was not tied down to any place or occupation.

A wonderful prospect, with all her life before her! Betty knew that she ought to feel very elated. But at the back of her thoughts was a vague, ill-defined uneasiness. She did not feel entirely comfortable about this inheritance. There was something strange about it, something not quite straightforward, something that affected her almost unpleasantly.

Mr. Broughton, for instance. She did not like him and she did not trust him. He was so very suave, so very—oily was the word that came to her mind. He gave her the impression that he was playing a part. And she was sure that, for some reasons of his own, he did not want her to enjoy her stay at Hameldon House.

Why had he tried to prejudice her against the place? What possible reason could Edward Morlant have had for insisting that she should go there so hurriedly? Betty could not avoid the feeling that there was something hidden and mysterious behind this inheritance of hers. There was something in the nature of a menace. She experienced a definite shrinking from the idea of traveling to Hameldon House in Mr. Broughton's company.

And yet, of course, she must go. It would be the height of folly to throw away her inheritance just because she did not understand everything connected with it. Besides, if Mr. Broughton had some underhand little schemes of his own—well, to Betty's way of thinking, this was all the more reason why she should not hesitate.

"I'll go and see Sally," she decided. "It'll be two hours yet before she comes home. I can't possibly wait so long to tell her all about it."

She washed up the plates and teacups, and put on her hat and coat.

"Dear old Sally!" she murmured, placing another on the fire. "She'll be ever so bucked about it." She turned out the lights. "But I don't know how I shall manage without her for six months."

The landing at the top of the stairs was very dark. As Betty pulled to the door of the studio behind her, she suddenly started, and stood rigid. Her heart missed a beat, then raced on again. For something had moved in the darkness, something almost noiseless, something stealthy and furtive.

After a moment of tremulous searching, she found the electric switch and snapped on the light. There was no one but herself on the landing. She drew a big breath of relief.

"It must have been a cat," she told herself, nevertheless descending the stairs rather hurriedly. "I'm a little fool, developing nerves like that."

The street outside was not inviting. With the coming of night the fog had grown denser. The lights from the glaring shop windows extended no further than the edge of the greasy pavements. The road was a tangled, hopeless confusion of hooting taxis, lorries and buses. The thin drizzle of rain was becoming heavier, hurrying belated shoppers to the warmth of their own firesides.

Betty decided that on such a night she could walk to Sally's tiny shop as quickly as a bus would take her. Fastening the collar of her raincoat, she crossed the main road and plunged into the maze of side streets that fringed the river.

Here the fog seemed worse. The infrequent gas lamps, each with its halo of greenish, yellow light, did little to dissipate the gloom. The streets were almost deserted. From the nearby river, anxious sirens sounded almost continually, calling to one another, mournful and wailing as the cries of lost souls.

Before long, Betty grew decidedly uncomfortable. Though she knew the way quite well, it was not too easy to be sure that she was taking the right turnings. It was certain that, if she once went astray, she would be lost completely. The fog was getting into her throat, and that thin place in her shoe was letting the wet in at last. She began to wish that she had stayed at home with the warm, bright fire, and occupied herself with packing until Sally's arrival.

And, naturally enough, she began to think again of the fright she had had on the landing. It was easy to tell herself that a cat had been the cause of it, but more difficult to believe it. Because she had felt sure that, for the fraction of a second, she had seen the dim, shadowy figure of a man in the darkness; sure that she had not imagined the quick intake of his breath as he disappeared.

"He might have slipped in any of the other rooms," she thought, glancing uneasily over her shoulder. "I ought to have looked in all the doors. And then I should have known for certain instead of feeling silly about it like this."

The dark, deserted streets were not reassuring when thoughts began to take such a line. Betty was no more nervous than the average girl, but she found her heart beating more quickly than usual. Suppose the unknown man had followed her! Suppose he was waiting his opportunity, waiting until they reached a still more lonely spot!

She hurried forward, looking back frequently. She could see no more than a yard or two in any direction. It seemed to her that the thick wall of fog cut her off from all comfort and security. She became aware that the tapping of her shoes on the pavement sounded very loud; and as she listened to them, she thought she could hear a fainter footfall, almost like the echo of her own, only a little way behind her.

She grew definitely uneasy. Now that she had once noticed them, the faint footfalls were unmistakable. Tap, tap, tap, they came on, keeping time with her own. She felt sure that someone was walking cautiously in her wake, almost within reach, yet making every endeavor not to be heard.

To test her conviction, she stopped abruptly, listening. Quite distinctly, she heard one footstep behind her; then silence. She moved forward and, in a moment, stopped again. The phenomenon was repeated.

There was not a soul in sight. The fog was thicker than ever, and no sign of life came from the huge silent warehouses that lined the street. Betty clenched her teeth hard, and ran. She knew, without a shadow of doubt, that someone was following her through the darkness.

She ran until she was brought up sharp by a high, blank wall. She halted, panting, striving to peer into the acrid blanket that encompassed her. She saw at once what had happened. In the fog she had missed her way and run into a *cul de sac*.

Close at hand, over a low parapet, she could hear the oily swirl of the river past the piles of a wharf. The sirens of the groping shipping were startlingly near. But though she held her breath and strained her ears, she could catch no sound of her pursuer.

She was trying to calm her agitation, congratulating herself on her escape when suddenly, without the slightest warning, a figure loomed up out of the fog.

A scream rose to her throat. Before she had time to utter it, a firm hand was placed roughly over her mouth. Another seized her shoulder, and pushed her backwards towards the low wall which guarded the river.

She could distinguish no detail of her assailant's dress or appearance. It was a moment or two before she realized his intention. Not until she felt the wall at her back and heard the swirl of the water immediately below her, did she guess that she was in the grip of a calm, deliberate murderer.

The man did not speak a word. He asked no question and offered no explanation. There was something in this horrible, unnatural silence that petrified Betty, so that she was helpless in his grasp, unable to make any effort to escape. He did not even look at her but, with head averted, remorselessly pushed her back.

Back—further back—until she felt that her spine must snap across. Her clutching hands caught at his coat and gripped it despairingly; until the relentless, irresistible pressure of steely muscles forced the wet fabric to slip through her fingers.

The hand over her mouth and nose pressed more closely. She was almost suffocated. Vivid, scintillating lights danced before her staring eyes. There was a rushing, roaring noise in her ears; and penetrating through it, as though from a great distance, the unceasing lap-lap of the water just below her head.

Her helpless, sliding fingers caught on a large pin in the lapel of his coat, tearing the flesh. The pain acted as a stimulus, rousing her from her stupefaction. Full realization of her danger came home to her. Desperately seizing the pin, she thrust it into his body with all her strength.

Surprised by the unexpected sting, he started back. Betty slipped from his momentarily relaxed grip, and tried to run from him.

Before she had taken a couple of strides away from the wall, he was upon her again. His arm closed about her shoulders in a steely embrace. The relentless hand covered her mouth and nose as before.

No longer stupefied with horror, she kicked and struggled to escape. Her sharp little teeth bit wildly at the suffocating hand. But her efforts were of no avail. And gradually they grew weaker.

He was choking her where she stood. Another second, and all would be over. She felt him brace himself for the task of carrying her to the wall and throwing her over. Dazed, almost unconscious, she knew that she was done. And then, startlingly near at hand, a raucous voice broke into song:

> *"Awa-ay out in the desert,*
>   *My mouth feels full of cotton.*
> *Gee! But I feel thirsty!*
>   *I wish I had a drink."*

Still in the same unnatural silence, the murderer relaxed his grip, and Betty could breathe again. Gasping painfully, she tried to call out and failed. There was a sound behind her. Glancing over her shoulder, she saw that a young man had materialized out of the fog, and was standing between her and the river.

"I shay, Mister," he said, in an unmistakably alcoholic voice, "I'm lost in an im-impenetrable forest, I shay. I wanna go to Tooting, an' I'm lost in an—"

Betty suddenly slid to the ground. Without word or warning, her assailant had released her and vanished.

The young man stood watching her for a moment, swaying unsteadily on his feet.

"It'sh very wrong to be drunk so early in the day," he admonished her. "If you can't shtand on your feet now, what'll you be like later on in the day?"

"I—I'm not drunk," said Betty feebly. "He—he was trying to kill me."

"Kill you?" The young man exploded. "Kill you? The dirty dog! I'll go and catch him."

"No! No! Don't leave me!"

"Musht leave you, me dear. Musht go an' catch him. Make him come back and apologize."

Before Betty could speak again, her savior had staggered away into the fog. She listened breathlessly until the sound of his footsteps died away, then burst into a fit of helpless, hysterical laughter.

After a while she dragged herself to her feet. She was sore and shaken, but she must waste no time on self-pity.

The sooner she was away from here the better. Her assailant might still be lurking within reach, awaiting another
opportunity to attack her. She shuddered as she looked
down at the dark, oily water, swirling rapidly past. Then,
cautiously and silently, she began to feel her way out of
the *cul de sac*.

3

Sally's Decision

In a side street off the Strand was a tiny shop, tucked away between two blocks of offices. Its satin-lined window was filled with a dainty assortment of goods and devices for the use of young-old ladies, ranging from simple lipsticks to fearsome mechanical contrivances for straightening the nose. A card announced that no kind of massage was undertaken on the premises, but that superfluous hair could be painlessly removed within.

The sign over the shop said merely: "Beaute D'Yvonne." There was no indication that the business had been founded and was being successfully carried on by Miss Sally Poulter.

Miss Poulter was a rather extraordinary young woman. Her business rivals and enemies were wont to say that she was no advertisement for the goods she sold. And it cannot be denied that, in feature at least, Sally was far from beautiful. She had an impertinently snub nose, and the suspicion of a cast in one eye gave her an expression of great impudence. But her complexion was perfect. Her health was perfect, as was her figure. Her friends—and they were many—said that the upward tilt to her nose was as piquant as the slight convergence of her eyes. Her gay, lighthearted disposition made her a joy forever.

Sally did pretty well out of "Beaute D'Yvonne." She did, perhaps, even better out of a side line of which no mention was made outside the shop. For Sally was "psychic." Tables danced under her fingers, and planchettes simply raced at her bidding. She was an ardent spiritualist. She was an adept in crystal gazing and fortune telling.

To speak truthfully, Sally had no great belief in her powers as a clairvoyant and prophet. But the practice was really very profitable; and the fact that she was a confirmed believer in spiritualism was no reason, so her native common sense told her, why she should not turn an honest penny from wealthy clients who went further in their beliefs than she did.

"I expect I'm a bit of a fraud," she would say to Miss Webster, her second in command. "But I don't really know. I *do* see things, sometimes, and I *do* hear 'em. I don't say they're true. People can believe 'em or not, as they like. Anyhow, they're just as likely to be true as not. And you know how people *will* pay to be told 'em. They'd be hurt if I wouldn't go into a trance for 'em."

This was no more nor less than the truth. Sally knew that she had psychic powers such as are granted only to the few. But she did not know how far to trust them. And so she fell in with her clients' wishes, prospered thereby, and suffered her conscience to trouble her not at all.

At present, however, the little gold mine was not working. Business was very slack. "Beaute D'Yvonne" had been empty most of the day, and the hours had dragged incredibly. Sally was deep in a fit of the blues. She was both surprised and delighted when Miss Webster entered her little sanctum to announce that Miss Elizabeth Harlan had called.

In her hurry to greet the unexpected visitor, Sally almost fell down the narrow stairs.

"This is lovely!" she cried, bursting through the swing doors. "You never told me— Good Lord! What's happened, Betty? Been in a smash?"

Betty certainly looked as though she might have been mixed up in a motor accident. Her face was pale. Her hat was crushed out of shape, her raincoat muddied and torn.

"No," she replied, forcing a watery little smile. "I've not been in a smash. Let me clean up a bit, Sally, and I'll tell you all about it."

Seeing that she was shaken, Sally asked no more questions, but led her up the stairs and into the sanctum. Here she prepared a cup of tea while Betty made herself more presentable.

"Now," she said, adding a spoonful of yellow liquid to the tea, "just drink this and you'll feel better. I've always to keep some whisky about the place in case any of my clients suffer from—er—faintness."

Betty gratefully sipped at the tea; and as the color slowly crept back to her soft cheeks, she told the whole story from the moment of Mr. Broughton's entry into the studio.

Sally listened wide-eyed and without interruption until Betty reached the point where she had been rescued so opportunely by the drunken man.

"Gosh!" she exclaimed. "It's a funny business, isn't it? And—horrible, too. That devil—saying nothing! No wonder you were upset. What did you do next?"

"Well, I didn't feel like walking any more—"

"I should think you didn't!"

"So as soon as I got out of those back streets, I found a taxi and came straight on here."

"You didn't see any more of that—that ghoul who tried to murder you?"

"No."

"Well, it's a funny business." Sally looked at her friend thoughtfully. "This Broughton man's a queer customer, from what you say. It seems almost as though. . . . Betty, do you think—was it him who attacked you?"

"I don't know. I couldn't tell at all. You see, he grabbed me so suddenly that I never caught a glimpse of him. And I'd no time to wonder about—" Betty shuddered. "It all happened so quickly. It was lucky for me that drunken man came along, wasn't it?"

"Lucky? I should say it was lucky! And mighty strange that he should be wandering about in such a place."

Betty nodded. "Just what I was thinking in the taxi. But it would be silly to imagine that he had any connection with what happened, wouldn't it? I mean, he couldn't—"

"I know what you mean," said Sally. "But we mustn't start making any wild theories like that." She rubbed her nose meditatively. "And yet—I don't know . . .

"And so you're wealthy now," she continued, after a while. "I'd almost forgotten about that in all this excitement. Do we celebrate to-night?"

"I'm afraid we can't." Betty smiled ruefully. "If I'm to meet Mr. Broughton at ten in the morning, I'll have to chase round to-night to get ready."

"You're still intending to go up to this place in Yorkshire, then?"

"Of course. Wouldn't you?"

"I don't know. Seems like I'm a fool. I don't want you to lose the inheritance. But it looks as though this attack on you had something to do with it, doesn't it?"

"Well, I thought so. I thought it looked as though someone was trying to put me out of the way. And that's one reason why I'm determined to go. I'm not going to be frightened out of my rights. If that's their game, whoever they are, they'll be disappointed."

"You've plenty of pluck, anyhow, Betty," cried Sally, catching her in her arms and hugging her. "If someone had just tried to kill me, I'm afraid I'd be thinking twice about going, to say the least of it. But perhaps we're jumping to conclusions. Perhaps there's no connection in all this. Let's go home and read that will carefully. We may learn something from it."

"Meaning that you'll shut the shop up?" asked Betty, delighted. "It isn't closing time yet."

"Never mind. There's nothing doing to-day. It's only a waste of electricity to keep the place open. Come on. There's nothing to wait for. Miss Webster'll see that everything's locked up."

The fog outside was as bad as ever, and the taxi crawled along as though feeling its way through the maze of bewildered traffic. The two girls were unusually silent. Despite her attempt at composure, Betty caught herself continually glancing out of the window. She would not have been surprised, at any moment, to see a horrible face leering in at her through the glass. She had tried to show a brave front to Sally. In reality, the murderous attack on her had left her nervous and shaken.

Sally, too, was apprehensive. She knew that Betty was neither fanciful nor apt to exaggerate. It seemed clear to her that her friend had escaped death that evening by something approaching a miracle. The murderer, apparently, knew a good deal concerning their movements. It was not beyond the bounds of possibility that he might return to make a second attempt.

They were both rather reluctant to leave the company of the friendly taxi-man. It was not too pleasant to be returning to their rooms where, for all they knew, further nasty surprises might be awaiting them. They kept close together as they ascended the stairs, not too brightly lit, and shrouded in fog. There was quite a moment of suspense while they unlocked and pushed open the door of the studio.

Once inside, however, much of their discomfort vanished. The cold, clinging fog, with its terrifying associations, was left behind. The fire blazed cheerily, and the studio with its comfortable, homely furniture and softly shaded lights, looked very cozy.

"It was good of you to come back with me," said Betty, dropping into a chair with a sigh of relief. "I don't mind confessing to you now that I'd have been scared to death crossing that landing alone."

"I felt a bit queer myself," admitted Sally, sitting cross-legged on the hearthrug. "I'm not at all sure, you know, Betty, that you ought to go to Hameldon House. It looks like asking for trouble. Let's have a squint at that will, anyway, and see if it tells us anything."

Betty fetched the will from the table, and the two of them puzzled through it together. The legal phraseology was perhaps unnecessarily complicated, but eventually they managed to get the sense of it.

There was really very little in it beyond what Mr. Broughton had already indicated. The whole of Edward Morlant's estate—which was described in some detail—was bequeathed to Elizabeth Harlan. There were two provisos; first, that the said Elizabeth Harlan should take up residence at Hameldon House within two days of the testator's funeral; second, that she should continue to reside there for six months without a break. In the event of her failing to comply with both or either of these conditions, the estate should be wound up, and the proceeds allotted to certain specified charities. Everard Broughton was appointed executor; and the testator expressed a desire that, in the case of any difficulty arising, the legatee would be guided by the opinion of the executor.

"It sounds all right, doesn't it?" asked Betty when they came to the end.

"It does," agreed Sally. She studied the signature thoughtfully. "He seems to have been a decent old boy," she added.

"He must have been." Betty's blue eyes grew tender. "Think of all those years, Sally! Years when he did everything possible for the woman who had rejected his love. I'm sure he must have been good."

"I think you're right." Sally suddenly rose to her knees.

"Betty, I wonder—"

"Well?"

"Well, he trusted this man Broughton, didn't he? He must have trusted him. Doesn't that sound as though Broughton must be straight; as though he couldn't have had anything to do with what's happened this evening?"

"It does, when you put it that way. Unless, of course, Edward Morlant was deceived in him."

"After all, Betty—" Sally jumped up, eagerly following her own line of thought. "After all, the attack on you may have been a coincidence. It may be that you crossed the path of a madman, that the same thing might have happened to anyone else who chanced to be there."

"But the landing, Sally? I'm sure that he was on the landing, and that he followed me."

"Yes, there's that. I suppose it's possible that your nerves played you a trick, just then? We've never looked round to see if there are traces of anyone being there. Let's investigate now."

"All right. I ought to have done that at the time. But I—I was rather scared."

They went out together onto the landing, leaving the door of the studio wide open. The space at the top of the stairs was bare and empty, and they were soon satisfied that nothing was to be found there. They opened the other doors which led to their bedrooms and the kitchen, and searched thoroughly without making any discovery. It was not until they came to the last door—of a store cupboard—that Sally uttered a little exclamation and picked something from the floor.

"What is it?" cried Betty. "What have you found?"

Sally kept her hand tightly clenched. A growing gravity was apparent in her excited eyes.

"Had Mr. Broughton a mustache?" she asked.

"Yes, yes. Why do you ask that?"

For reply, Sally slowly opened her hand, disclosing what lay in the palm. It was a wisp of crêpe hair, such as actors use, fashioned into the form of a heavy mustache.

"Anything like this?" she whispered.

"J-just like that," answered Betty.

The two girls stared at one another for a while in frightened silence.

"Well, that seems to settle the question, doesn't it?" said Sally at last. "It may not be conclusive evidence, but it's good enough for me."

"You think it was Broughton who tried to kill me?"

"I do. Even if it wasn't him, it's quite certain that you were followed from here, and that the attack on you was not just a coincidence. Betty, you mustn't go to Hameldon House."

Betty's firm little chin rose up in determination.

"I shall go, Sally! Edward Morlant intended me to have his money, and I won't be scared out of it in this way. It's not the money itself that matters so much; but after all he's done for me, it's only right that I should try to respect his wishes."

"You're an obstinate child. Honestly, Betty, I don't like the idea of you going to such an outlandish place when we don't know— What about telling the police?"

"I don't think that would be much good, would it? It isn't as though I were staying on here. There'd be such a lot of fuss and bother, too. But if anything happens up there—"

"Yes! You'd lock the stable door when the horse is stolen. You're not fit to— Look here, Betty Harlan! You're not going up there alone. I'm coming with you!"

Betty's eyes sparkled.

"Oh, Sally, if only you could! I'd love that. But you can't leave the shop."

"I can. There's nothing much doing there just now. Miss Webster'll manage all right for a few days. I'll come with you."

"Hurrah! I'll be frightened of nothing now." Betty caught Sally in her arms and waltzed her round the landing. "You really mean it? You're sure you can manage?"

"Of course, I mean it. I'd never sleep if I let you go up there alone. Come on. We've a lot to do. Let's make a start on that packing."

4

HAMELDON HOUSE

The large clock outside Euston pointed to five minutes to ten when Betty and Sally alighted from their taxi. It was not an ideal morning for traveling. The fog had vanished during the night, but rain still fell with dreary persistence.

As they hurried into the noisy station, Betty caught her companion's arm.

"Look, there he is!" she whispered. "By the bookstall. Top hat and frock coat all complete."

Sally looked with interest at the tall, dignified gentleman, in immaculate though somewhat old-fashioned attire, who was patiently pacing to and fro in front of the bookstall.

"Like a bridegroom, rather, isn't he?" she murmured with a smile. "Seems ridiculous to suspect him of trying to murder anyone. He's so prim and proper. A relic of Victorian days, I should have said, who considers all women angels and smoking a crime. And we've been thinking that he might— Just shows that you never can tell. He didn't say whether he's married or not, did he?"

"He did not," laughed Betty. "For Heaven's sake, don't start vamping *him*, will you?"

Sally, however, would make no promises. She was an incorrigible flirt, and was never so happy as when she had a new victim to torment.

"Let's show ourselves," she said. "And watch him carefully in case he gives anything away."

They had approached to within a few yards of Mr. Everard Broughton before he saw them. After a moment's indecision he recognized Betty, and his broad face expanded into a bland smile, while the top hat came off with a flourish.

"You are punctual, Miss Elizabeth," he said, showing his shiny head in a stiff bow. "It is a virtue I greatly admire."

"I've brought Sally with me," announced Betty. "Miss Poulter—Mr. Broughton."

The solicitor extended his large white hand.

"I am delighted to make your acquaintance, Miss Poulter," he said glibly. "Miss Elizabeth refused to accompany me up North until she had consulted you. I am sure you advised her that it would be the right—nay, the only—course to pursue."

"Oh, yes," replied Sally, smiling at him very sweetly. "I advised her to come with you. I'm sure she can't go wrong if she follows your advice."

A hint of a frown wrinkled Mr. Broughton's smooth forehead. It was evident that he was not quite sure whether Miss Poulter meant what she said.

He glanced at his watch, fidgeting like a schoolboy.

"I think, perhaps, it is time we found our seats, Miss Elizabeth. The train is in, and I have our tickets." He turned to Sally. "Good-by, Miss Poulter. I hope at some future—"

"Oh, but Sally's coming with us," interrupted Betty.

The solicitor raised his thick, bushy eyebrows.

"I beg your pardon. Did you say that Miss Poulter—"

"I said that Sally is coming with us."

"But that is impossible. Quite impossible, Miss Elizabeth. Mr. Edward desired that you—"

Betty stopped him with an imperious gesture. She had decided last night that she would not be hectored, and this seemed a suitable occasion for revolt.

"I have read the will through very carefully, Mr. Broughton," she said. "There is not a single word in it which could be construed into a wish that I should live alone at Hameldon House. I do not intend to live there alone."

A trace of confusion disturbed Mr. Broughton's serenity. He was obviously surprised at Betty's firmness.

"But there is no accommodation prepared, no servants," he protested, fingering his heavy mustache. "There is only one bedroom available, and no arrangements have been made for the reception of more than one person. It is quite impossible that Miss Poulter should accompany you to-day. Later on, perhaps—"

"Look here, Mr. Broughton!" Betty drew herself tip to her full five feet three inches and wagged a finger at him. "Is the house yours or mine?"

"My dear young lady, it is yours, of course."

"Very well, then. Don't let's argue about it any more. Sally's coming with us."

The ultimatum was crude, perhaps, but it served its purpose. Mr. Broughton knew when he was beaten.

"Just as you like, Miss Elizabeth," he capitulated gracefully. "I hope, if Miss Poulter suffers any temporary inconvenience, she will remember that I am not responsible. If you will excuse me a moment I will see about a ticket for her."

The two girls stood watching in triumph as he marched to the booking office.

"That's the stuff to give 'em!" observed Sally. "You can come to the point when necessary, Betty. It looks real enough, doesn't it?"

"You mean his mustache? Yes, it does."

"And his greeting was quite natural. He didn't seem at all surprised or disconcerted to see you. I'm beginning to wonder if he does know anything about last night."

"I'm wondering why he doesn't want you to come," said Betty. "It's funny, isn't it? I got such a very definite impression last night that he didn't want me to come, either. Perhaps he wants to keep the house empty for some reason."

"Well, he's in for a disappointment in that case. Anyhow, it's no use puzzling about it until we've seen the house. We'll keep quiet about last night, shall we? If he does know anything, he'll be expecting us to mention it, and he'll perhaps let something out."

Mr. Broughton returned with the ticket, and with difficulty they found seats in the train which was now on the point of departure. He showed no sign of resentment over his defeat, and was very attentive and affable to both girls.

The journey was long, and the sodden landscape through which they sped not inspiring. Lunch-time came as a welcome break. They transferred to the dining car, and Sally watched Mr. Broughton curiously as he attacked the first course.

"I'm sure it's real now," she whispered to Betty. "He wouldn't dare risk soup if it wasn't."

In the afternoon, the weather grew worse and the journey more uncomfortable. They had to change stations at Leeds, and wait an hour for a local connection which pottered along as though to-morrow would do. It was quite dark when they reached Blackshaw, the terminus of the branch line, and the nearest station to Hameldon House.

"We have a six-mile drive before us," announced Mr. Broughton as he helped them out of the dingy, ill-lit carriage. "I made arrangements for a conveyance to await us here. If you will please come this way. . . ."

The station at Blackshaw was not a cheerful place on such an evening. In the dim light of the infrequent oil lamps, the two girls could hardly see to follow their guide. The exposed platform was swept by a strong wind which rushed in from the moorland, driving a stinging rain before it.

"I'm glad you came with me," said Betty, slipping her arm through Sally's. "I'd have been in a blue funk by now if I'd had to come alone."

Sally looked round and wrinkled her snub nose in disgust. Below the station could be seen a few pin points of light, the lights of the village almost obliterated by the rain. But beyond these there was nothing but the mysterious, impenetrable blackness of the moors, a blackness filled with wind and rain, a blackness which seemed to extend forever, isolating the girls completely from the world they had known.

"It's pretty awful, isn't it?" she replied, pulling her coat more closely about her. "Simple life, of course. Back to Nature, and all that kind of thing. But give me the good old Strand on a night like this!"

Outside in the road a remarkably decrepit old taxi stood waiting. Mr. Broughton opened the door with a flourish, and helped the girls to climb in.

"It is not a Rolls-Royce, ha, ha!" he said with unexpected levity, as he squeezed himself in opposite them. "But it is the only public conveyance Blackshaw can boast—except the hearse."

The driver with difficulty started up his wheezy engine, and they were soon chugging and panting up a long, steep hill. The lights of civilization were left behind almost immediately, and nothing was visible in the surrounding darkness but the rough, stony road ahead, fringed on either side by a narrow strip of moorland, ever alternating between black, naked peat, straggling heather, and piled, weirdly shaped rocks.

When they reached the top of the hill, they were exposed to the full fury of the storm which was racing over the bleak uplands. Impetuous gusts tugged at the old taxi, so that the two girls were expecting it to overturn at any moment. The rain pattered like a fusillade of peas upon the rattling windows, and they could hardly hear themselves speak.

"Delightful weather," shouted Sally, straightening her hat which had been forced down over her eyes by a tremendous lurch of the car. "Entrancing country. Most enjoyable excursion."

"I regret that your welcome should be so inauspicious," apologized Mr. Broughton gravely. "I am afraid this part of Yorkshire is not seen at its best towards the end of the year."

Since leaving the village they had not passed a single human habitation. They traveled more than half an hour along the wild, desolate road before they reached their destination. Even then they could see little or nothing of Hameldon House; the outline of a straggling building loomed up vaguely before them, but not a light showed anywhere in its black bulk.

"Is there no one in the place at all?" cried Betty, looking at the uninviting house in some dismay.

"Bidgood is here," replied Mr. Broughton, hurrying them into the shelter of a stone porch, after telling the driver to wait. "Bidgood is always here. But his quarters are at the back."

He pulled at a knob beside the door, and the two girls could hear the hollow echoes of a bell reverberating through the house. After a little delay there came the muffled sound of feet shuffling over a stone floor, and the metallic clang of a bolt pushed back. A moment later, the massive door swung slowly open, disclosing a shriveled old man with a candle in his hand.

"Good evening, Bidgood," said Mr. Broughton. "I have brought Miss Elizabeth with me, and a friend who has come to share her solitude."

"A friend? I have heard naught of any friends."

The old man raised the flickering candle, and his dim, sunken eyes fixed on Betty, ignoring Sally altogether.

"You are welcome to Hameldon House, Missie," he said, as though forgetting that he had spoken before. He opened the door wide. "Pity 'tis that you did not come in Mr. Edward's time."

Without further speech he turned and led them across a spacious stone-flagged hall, peopled with shadows, and pushed open the door of a room leading off from it.

"Mr. Edward called this the library," he went on. "He always had his tea in here, and I reckon you'll do the same."

The room was reasonably illuminated by two well-trimmed lamps, and a cheerful fire blazed in the wide, old-fashioned hearth. Betty noticed the heavy shutters over the windows, and realized why they had not seen a light from outside.

"Well," she said, feigning a satisfaction she was far from feeling, "it's warm enough in here, anyway."

"I think you should be comfortable now," said Mr. Broughton. "I will leave you in Bidgood's care—unless there is anything more I can do for you."

Betty was surprised.

"Are you going straight back?" she asked. "Isn't there—haven't we a lot to talk about?"

"In the morning, Miss Elizabeth. In the morning. I have been away two days, and various matters require my attention. I must return to Blackshaw immediately. But I will arrange to place the whole of to-morrow at your disposal."

He extended his large, white hand to each of the girls in turn. There was a curious haste in his movements that could not be overlooked. He caught the old man, who was shuffling towards the door with his candle, by the arm, and impatiently pushed him out of the room.

"He seems to have taken a sudden dislike to our company," remarked Sally as the door closed behind the two men. She took off her hat and coat and flung them on a chair. "Well, this is a queer sort of place, if you ask me. Still, we're here!"

Betty's wandering gaze, after traveling slowly round the room, had fixed on a large oil painting which hung over the carved oak chimney piece. It represented a man in the prime of life, with pale, studious face. A book was in his hand, indicating his favorite occupation, but his head was raised so that his oddly colored eyes looked out of the picture as though in surprise.

"Come and look at this, Sally," she said. "It's a fine painting, isn't it? I wonder if it's Edward Morlant?"

Sally came and stood by her side, studying the picture critically.

"I expect it is," she nodded. "Though it's not unlike our friend Mr. Broughton, in a way. Whoever it is, he's got a kind, appealing sort of face, hasn't he? And yet there's something I don't quite like—"

She broke off as the door opened and Bidgood returned. He stood on the threshold and peered into the room, his wrinkled old features barely visible in the shadow.

"You'll have some tea now, I reckon, Missie?" he asked, addressing Betty.

"Yes, please," she replied. She looked up at the picture again. "Tell me, is this—"

"Aye, that's Mr. Edward," interrupted the old man hastily. "If you'll excuse me a two-three-minutes, I'll bring in the tea."

He shuffled away without waiting for a reply, and they heard a distant door bang to behind him.

"He doesn't want to talk," said Sally sapiently. "That may be a point in his favor. On the other hand, it may not. He's a queer old stick, isn't he? Not a bit pleased to see me." She sat down and lit a cigarette. "Well, what do you think of this bit of Hameldon House? It's yours, you know."

"I'm not greatly impressed so far," admitted Betty with a rueful smile. "It—it was rather like coming into a dungeon, wasn't it? And as for this room—"

She glanced round again wistfully. The library was comfortable enough in a solid, stodgy way, but not at all the kind of a room a girl would choose to live in. It was lined with books from floor to ceiling, except where the fireplace, windows and door intervened. The furniture was heavy and substantial, dark carved oak that gleamed dully in the lamplight. The carpet was thick and expensive, but somber. The tapestried curtains over the narrow, mullioned windows were of the same cheerless color. The general effect of the whole was gloomy and depressing.

"If it looks no better by daylight," she concluded, "I—I'll clear the whole lot out!"

"I'm with you there," agreed Sally enthusiastically. "We'll have a spring cleaning. That's one thing in favor of the place. You can do as you like with it all, can't you?"

Betty made no reply. Sally saw that her intent gaze was fixed again on the oil painting over the chimney piece.

"Wondering if your benefactor would mind?" she asked. "He looks one of the old-fashioned kind, doesn't he? Rather a darling, I should think. Though he reminds me of Mr. Broughton. But aren't his eyes queer? Almost as though—"

"Ssh!" interrupted Betty abruptly. "Listen!"

Outside, the storm was still raging. The wind whistled about the old house, and the rain drummed loudly on the shuttered windows. The two girls were motionless, straining their ears for any sound beyond the fury of the elements.

The fire hissed and spluttered, tormented by the rain-drops that fell down the wide chimney. Apart from this, there was dead silence in the library. But as the girls listened, they suddenly looked at one another and drew closer together. For in a lull of the storm they both distinctly heard a soft, shuffling noise—the sound of stealthy footsteps very near at hand.

5

FOOTSTEPS IN THE NIGHT

For a few moments the two girls stared at one another without speech or movement; and in those moments, the stealthy sound was repeated, this time unmistakably nearer than before. It seemed, almost, to be within the room; certainly it could be no further away than the door.

Sally's eyes were wide with excitement. Her cheeks had paled a little, and her breast rose and fell unevenly. She crept closer to Betty who was equally agitated, and together they stood mute as though held in a very fascination of dread, waiting for some evil thing to appear.

It was Betty who first broke through the spell of sudden, irrational fear that had bound them. Nerving herself to the ordeal, she tiptoed quickly to the door and flung it open.

Neither of them knew what they expected to see, whether some grisly specter or a threat in more material form. But through the open doorway they could glimpse nothing but the silent blackness beyond. Even when, greatly daring, they carried a lamp from the library, there was nothing more terrible than shadows in the draughty, stone-flagged hall.

They returned to the room and shut the door, uneasy, yet half inclined to laugh at their fears.

"I didn't imagine that noise, did I?" asked Betty, setting down the lamp upon the table.

"You did not. I heard it, too. Quite plainly."

"It couldn't have been the old man, Sally. There wasn't time for him to—"

"Of course there wasn't. Whoever it was must have been standing just outside that door when you went to it. Only a very active person could have got away so quickly."

"Perhaps our nerves are—well, jumpy. I shouldn't be surprised. After last night, you know. Still, there is something queer about the house and—"

"There's something queer about the whole business," said Sally emphatically. "I'm glad I came with you."

Shortly afterwards, there was a discreet rap on the door, and Bidgood entered with a heavily laden tray which he deposited on a small table close to the fire. Betty watched his gray head with its thin, scanty hair closely as he bent over the tray arranging the plates and teacups.

"Bidgood," she asked abruptly, "who is there in the house besides us?"

The sugar tongs dropped from the old man's hand and fell clattering in the fender.

"Besides us?" he echoed, his voice shaking a little. "Why, no one, Missie."

"No one at all?" persisted Betty. "No servants?"

"We three are alone in the house," said Bidgood, more firmly. "There's Rover in the kitchen, of course, but you don't reckon him, I suppose?"

"Who is Rover? A dog?"

"Yes, Missie. Mr. Edward's dog. A fine creature but heart-broken just now, mourning his master."

"Poor old fellow. We'll try to console him to-morrow. I expect he's getting no exercise. But, Bidgood, surely you don't mean to say that you run this place without any help?"

"There's a widow woman comes in each day. Name of Clayton. But she leaves each evening before dark, because she's scared of the walk home."

"Then we shall be completely alone—just the three of us—until morning?"

"Yes, Missie."

"All right. That will do for the present. Is there a bell in case we want anything?"

Bidgood indicated the old-fashioned bell-pull hanging beside the hearth, then shuffled from the room. Betty waited for a while after the door had closed behind him, then turned to Sally.

"I think he's lying," she said thoughtfully. "He was startled when I asked him who else was in the house."

"That's true," agreed Sally. "But I shouldn't attach too much importance to it. It was a funny question to ask, you know. Besides, he's had the house to himself for the last few days, and perhaps he's had a few pals in on the quiet to keep him company. Anyhow, we'll soon find out if he's lying. He can't keep up a pretense of that sort. Funny, isn't it, how we've suddenly developed a habit of suspecting everybody we meet?"

Betty laughed. "We've had a certain amount of reason, if you ask me."

"Well, there's no reason why we should suspect this tea, is there? It looks mighty good to me, and I'm peckish above the average."

The tea was mighty good. It was a Yorkshire "high tea," with cold ham and tongue, hot toasted muffins, heaped platefuls of bread and butter, and a varied assortment of cakes and pastries. The two girls discovered that a little fright does not necessarily affect a healthy appetite, and they thoroughly enjoyed the good fare.

"This man Bidgood may be a liar," remarked Sally appreciatively. "But he knows how to toast a muffin."

"He does," admitted Betty. "It's quite evident we're not going to starve at Hameldon House, whatever else happens."

Before long, things seemed considerably brighter. They lingered over the tea and cigarettes, enjoying the cozy warmth of the fire. Eventually, Sally rose lazily to her feet and strolled round the room, examining the titles of the books on the shelves.

"I say, Betty," she exclaimed, as she reached a section near the window, "here's a queer lot! I've never seen such a collection of weird books. *The History of Sorcery; Lycanthropy; The Practice of Magic; Vampires and Were-wolves;* stacks of 'em, all of the same kind. And here's Madame Blavatsky's *Isis Unveiled.* Edward Morlant must have been a student of the occult."

"A kindred spirit, Sally."

"I don't know about that. I'm interested, of course, but I've never been much of a student."

"You'll have a good opportunity while you're here."

"Oh, I'll dip into this lot sometime. I like to read something that makes me feel goosey. But not tonight, Josephine—not to-night."

Betty smiled as she pulled at the bell.

"I hope you won't be seeing any spooks here, Sally. That would be about the limit."

Sally became serious at once.

"There's nothing psychic about Hameldon House," she said with conviction. "No spirits or ghosts, I mean. I always know, Betty. Somehow, I can always sense the presence of anything like that. And I've not had a single queer feeling since I entered the door."

"I can't understand you believing in spirits," mused Betty. "It all seems so impossible to me."

"I can't understand it myself," said Sally ruefully. "Sometimes I think I'm a fool. A fine, healthy girl like me with such neurotic ideas, as some people call 'em. I wish many a time that I never saw things. And yet—"

Her confession of faith was cut short by the entry of Bidgood. The old man silently busied himself in rearranging the disordered tray.

Betty watched him curiously, then made another attempt to break through his reserve.

"That was a very nice tea, Bidgood," she said. "We both enjoyed it immensely."

"Thank you, Missie," he replied. "I'm glad."

"You must find catering rather difficult with no shops nearer than—"

"Blackshaw is the nearest village. I go there twice a week."

"Six miles away! Surely you don't walk?"

"At present I must. Mr. Edward sold his horse and trap just before he died."

"Well, we'll soon have that put right. Six miles! What a tragedy if you happen to run out of anything!"

"I've learned not to do that, Missie," said Bidgood, a grim smile softening his wrinkled features. "I've got used to it."

"You've lived here a long time, I suppose?"

"All my life." The smile faded from his face. "I served Mr. Edward's father before him."

There was a simple dignity in the old man's tone that touched Betty.

"That's something to be proud of, isn't it?" she said sincerely. "And you were in Mr. Edward's confidence. I know that because you witnessed his signature to the will."

"He trusted me, Missie."

It seemed to Betty that she was doing very well, that she was making friends with the old servant.

"I wish you would tell me, Bidgood," she went on, "why he wanted me to live here."

A shadow passed over the old man's wrinkled face.

"Of that I know naught, Missie," he said, gathering up the tray. "You should ask Mr. Broughton when he comes in the morning."

"Does he know? He told me he didn't."

"Then no one knows," muttered Bidgood, shuffling to the door. "No one will ever know."

The two girls sat in silence for quite a long time after he had gone.

"I thought you were going to get something out of him," said Sally at last, stretching herself. "But he shut up like an oyster, didn't he? There's some sort of mystery in all this, Betty. Edward Morlant had some curious confidants. Mr. Broughton—and Bidgood. I wouldn't trust either of them an inch!"

Betty's blue eyes were thoughtful.

"I—I rather liked this old man," she said slowly. "He struck me as being the real, old-fashioned family servant. Don't you think he seems genuine?"

"Oh, yes, he *seems* genuine," agreed Sally. "But so does Mr. Broughton's mustache." She lit another cigarette and made herself comfortable in front of the fire. "I suppose the noise we heard might have been the dog?"

"I suppose it might."

"But you know jolly well it wasn't!" Sally laughed shortly. "You're a fraud, Betty Harlan. No dog would make a noise like that, and you know it. You know as well as I do that we're up against something we don't understand. And though you won't admit it, you're probably just as scared as I am."

Betty knelt down on the rug beside her, and slipped a hand into hers.

"I am scared, Sally," she admitted. "Or at least I should be if you weren't here with me." She shivered. "I can't imagine what I should have done if you hadn't come. I'd never have dared to sleep alone here. I—I think last night upset me a bit."

Sally flung motherly arms about her.

"Of course it did, you poor darling!" she exclaimed. "And, like a fool, I'm not helping you a bit. Whatever I may feel about this place, it must be a hundred times worse for you. Let's try not to talk about it any more just now, but make some plans for the future."

So they sat together on the hearthrug, and built wonderful castles in the glowing fire. But try as they would to concentrate on other things, some mention of their present position could not be avoided. A chance remark would bring back some recollection of the episode in the fog last night, of the wild drive to Hameldon House, or of their unpleasant experience since their arrival. Neither Broughton nor Bidgood could be driven entirely from mind. And eventually they gave up the attempt and settled down frankly to discuss their fancies, theories and fears.

At the end of two or three cigarettes, they found themselves no nearer an understanding than before. Why Edward Morlant had insisted that Betty should live at Hameldon House; whether the attack on her was connected with her inheritance; whether Everard Broughton had anything to do with it; whether Bidgood were friend or foe; whose was the step they had heard so near to them; all these queries were raised and discussed *ad nauseam*.

"Let's go and unpack," suggested Betty at last. "We're getting nowhere now; and perhaps we'll learn a little more from Mr. Broughton in the morning."

"Or from Bidgood," said Sally, poking the fire. "I'm sure he's hiding something."

Betty rose to her feet, her gaze fixed again on the painting over the chimney piece.

"I don't like this room, Sally," she said slowly. "It gives
me the creeps. All the time we've been talking, I—I've
felt as though we were not alone, as though someone were
watching us."

Sally looked at her with some concern. She knew that
her friend was not apt to be fanciful.

"I expect that picture's got on your nerves a bit," she
said, soothing. "I've heard of 'em doing that kind of thing.
And those eyes *are* queer. Seem to be staring right through
you. I could imagine all sorts of things if I looked at 'em
for long. Let's go up and investigate our bedroom, shall we?
I don't suppose you want to explore the house to-night?"

"I do not!" agreed Betty with emphasis. "I think that
can very well be left until morning."

She rang the bell, and a few moments later Bidgood
shuffled into the room.

"We're going to bed now," she told him. "I suppose you
know that Miss Poulter is staying with me?"

"Mr. Broughton told me." The old man showed none
of the confusion that had affected the solicitor at Euston
station. "But I've only one room ready, Missie, with the
sheets aired and so on. Mr. Broughton said, perhaps for
one night, you wouldn't mind—"

"That's all right, Bidgood. We'll share the room for
to-night, at any rate."

On a little table beside the door stood an array of
candlesticks. Bidgood lighted one for each of them. They
picked up their hats and coats and followed him across the
cold, stone-flagged hall, and up a wide, thickly carpeted
staircase.

The upper floor of the house seemed a maze of corridors, dark and gloomy, peopled by the restless, grotesque
shadows thrown by their lights. Up here, too, the noise

of the storm outside was accentuated, and sudden wailing drafts brushed their faces and plucked at the flickering flames of the candles.

Both Betty and Sally were glad, when at last they reached the shelter of their bedroom, to find a cheerful fire blazing in the hearth.

"I hope you'll sleep well, Missie," said Bidgood, addressing himself as always to Betty. "I reckon you'll like a cup of tea first thing in the morning?"

"Yes, please," she replied with a smile. "It's nice of you to think of it."

As soon as the old man had gone, Sally flew to the door and examined it.

"Thank Heaven there's a bolt!" she exclaimed, fastening the door securely. "I've never seen anything so bogey as those corridors in all my life!"

The room itself was not particularly reassuring to two girls inclined to be nervous. It was large and shadowy, only dimly lit by the two candles and the flickering firelight, and full of cupboards in any one of which someone might be lurking. The bed was a huge, four-poster affair, solidly constructed in carved mahogany, and hung with thick tapestried curtains voluminous enough to hide a dozen evildoers. But heavy shutters, which could be opened only from the inside, covered the windows, and the door was bolted. When Betty and Sally had made a tour of inspection of the cupboards, they felt that they were safe from intruders until morning.

They unpacked leisurely, and arranged their belongings in the cupboards or the capacious drawers of a tallboy.

"You might as well settle down permanently and make yourself at home in this room," said Betty. "Because you'll get no other while you're here."

"I don't want another," rejoined Sally. "I wouldn't sleep by myself in this house for ten thousand a year!" Eventually they blew out the candles and tucked themselves up in bed. They didn't expect to sleep, of course, for they told one another that they were far too excited to close an eye. They lay watching the dancing firelight on the ceiling, occasionally exchanging some thought or impression.

But the day had been long and tiring, and both girls were healthy and conscience free. It was not very long before a concert of soft regular breathing announced that they were sound asleep. . . .

The fire burned lower. A log fell with a subdued crash, sending a shower of sparks up the chimney. The red glow gradually died away, and the room was left in darkness.

The storm outside had spent its fury. The drumming of the rain on the shutters slackened, then ceased entirely. The wind sank, muttering, to rest. In the room was a silence complete but for the even breathing of the sleeping girls.

Suddenly Betty sat bolt upright in bed. A noise had penetrated through her dreams and wakened her. As she listened, she heard it again—the creaking of boards in the corridor outside, and slow, careful footsteps such as she had heard from the library.

It was all she could do to stifle a scream. But she clenched her fists and gritted her teeth until the impulse had passed. She would get to the bottom of this, she told herself. She would find out who was wandering about her house in the middle of the night.

With heart beating wildly, she slipped out of bed and crept to the door. In the darkness, she fumbled until she found the bolt, and slid it back without a sound. Cautiously she opened the door and peered out.

The corridor was a well of inky blackness and she could see nothing. For the moment, too, the house was silent as a tomb. But as she stood there trembling, holding her breath, she sensed that something was approaching. And then, quite close to her, she heard the stealthy pad-pad of the footsteps returning.

6

BIDGOOD TELLS A LIE

Betty felt herself unable to move hand or foot. As she stood there in the darkness, tense and terrified, waiting in frozen immobility for the approach of whatever was coming, a low, sibilant whisper reached her from the bed:

"What is it, Betty? What's the matter?"

The knowledge that Sally was awake brought her back to reality. At least she was not alone. Silently sliding the bolt again, she tiptoed back to the bed.

"It's here!" she breathed. "Just outside the door!"

"What's here, Betty?"

"I don't know. What we heard before, I suppose. There's someone or something moving about in the corridor."

Sally shivered, and slipped back under the bedclothes.

"Then get into bed," she whispered. "For the love of Mike come back to bed, and let it go on moving about."

"I'm going to see what it is," replied Betty, putting on her dressing gown.

"You're what?" Sally sat up again, aghast.

"I'm going to get to the bottom of this."

"Oh, you little fool! Come back to bed. You mustn't go. It's one thing to be brave, another to be foolhardy."

Betty, groping for her slippers, made no reply, and Sally knew that further argument was useless.

"You're a pig-headed little fool!" she groaned, throwing off the bedclothes. "You don't know what risk you're running. And I'll have to come with you because—because I don't dare stay here alone. Here, where's my bag? There's a flashlight of sorts in it, though I don't suppose the thing will work."

A moment later the two girls stole to the door, armed with a tiny pocket torch in the shape of a pencil. Betty cautiously pulled back the bolt and turned the knob. As she opened the door, a rasping sound and a faint ray of light came from the end of the corridor.

Someone had struck a match and, probably, lit a candle. They could not see who it was, for the light was hidden from their view by the corner; but the monstrous, distorted shadow flickering on the wall bore some slight resemblance to a human being.

"Thank Heaven for small mercies!" muttered Sally. "It's a some *one,* and not a some *thing!"*

By the movements of the shadow, and the fact that it grew gradually larger and less distinct, they gathered that their quarry was walking towards the top of the stairs. They followed as quickly and as noiselessly as possible, finding their way without much difficulty by the light in front of them.

It was not until they reached the top of the stairs that they caught a glimpse of the night walker. Betty uttered a little exclamation as she recognized the frail figure moving across the hall, candle in hand.

"Bidgood!" she cried loudly. "What are you doing?"

The old man stopped abruptly. He looked round, obviously startled out of his wits. The candle dropped from his hand and was extinguished on the stone floor.

Betty pressed the catch of the tiny electric torch, and by the help of its feeble rays they descended the stairs and confronted the old servant.

"What are you doing here?" she asked again, angrily, flashing the light full in his face. "Why are you wandering about at this time of night?"

Bidgood's wrinkled features worked convulsively, and his gnarled fingers trembled as he attempted to relight the candle.

"I—I remembered that I had left the front door unfastened, Missie," he stammered, avoiding her eyes. "I came down to attend to it."

His explanation carried no conviction, and Betty's anger increased.

"If that was all you came down for," she asked sternly, "why did you sneak past our door like a criminal, silently and without light?"

"I—I didn't want to disturb you, Missie."

Sally had taken the candle from his trembling fingers and lighted it. She went now to the front door and examined it.

"It's locked and bolted," she announced. "And chained up, too. Like the door of a jail."

"You hear that?" said Betty shortly, turning to Bidgood again. "Can't you think of a better story?"

The old man was hopelessly confused and bewildered. His gnarled hands fidgeted in distress.

"I think I—I must have been dreaming," he faltered.

Betty realized that, whatever the truth might be, he did not intend to tell it.

"I think you'd better get back to bed," she snapped.

"Yes, Missie," he acquiesced, humbly.

He seemed older than ever when he tottered up the stairs in his red flannel dressing gown, his thin gray hair ruffled and untidy. Betty was very disappointed with the turn events had taken. She sighed as she got into bed with Sally.

"I was rather inclined to like Bidgood," she said. "But I'm afraid he's a liar."

"There's one thing in his favor, though," rejoined Sally, pulling the bedclothes about her neck. "He's a rotten liar!"

Liar or not, Bidgood brought them an excellent cup of tea in the morning. He also cooked a remarkably good breakfast. And as the day had dawned bright, clear and frosty, with no further interruption to their sleep, the girls felt that their nerves might have magnified the importance of last night's happenings.

Hameldon House, with shutters thrown back, and patterned sunlight streaming through the mullioned windows, seemed very different from their first impression of it. The small, cozy room in which breakfast was served had none of the depressing effect of the library. A large bunch of early chrysanthemums on the table gave it a home-like touch which both Betty and Sally were quick to appreciate.

"Perhaps things won't be so bad now, after all," said Betty hopefully.

"They're cheering up a bit," agreed Sally, finishing her coffee. "Anyhow, I won't catch the first train back to Town."

Soon after breakfast, Mr. Broughton arrived. In him, too, a very definite change was apparent. His frock coat and top hat had been laid aside, and he looked much less immaculate but much more comfortable in a well-worn tweed suit.

"It is a beautiful morning, ladies," he greeted them as soon as he entered the door. "I propose we take a walk round and view the house and grounds."

Betty, however, had other plans. She had decided to tackle the question of Bidgood without delay.

"Tell me, Mr. Broughton," she began, indicating a chair, "is Bidgood trustworthy?"

"Absolutely, Miss Elizabeth! Absolutely! I wonder why you ask that?"

"Because he tells stories, for one thing. He was wandering about in the middle of the night, and he couldn't give a reasonable explanation of his actions. I suspect that he is hiding someone in the house."

The solicitor smiled tolerantly as he sat down, stroking his heavy mustache.

"But that is impossible, I am sure," he asserted. "Bidgood is too old and faithful a servant to do anything of that nature. I have known him for years, and I cannot imagine him taking such a liberty."

"Well, I believe there is someone in the house who shouldn't be here— We heard someone walking about, and—"

"Ah! That is a different matter." Broughton's voice sounded surprisingly human and sympathetic as though he understood perfectly. "I warned you that Hameldon House is not an ideal residence. I feared that something of this kind might happen."

"Something of what kind?"

"I mean that you should—er—hear things. I myself have heard many strange and inexplicable noises here. The house is very old, you must remember, and has the usual disadvantages of all old places. I do not believe in ghosts—"

"Neither do I," interrupted Betty.

"I am relieved to hear that. I feared perhaps you might. I feared that these weird noises which are audible from time to time might make you uncomfortable. I assure you that there is no cause for alarm. I am convinced that some natural explanation, such as warping woodwork—"

"I am not alarmed," said Betty shortly. "But neither do I imagine footsteps. Before I do anything else, I intend to search the house from top to bottom."

"An excellent idea," agreed the solicitor heartily. "A really excellent idea. You will feel more comfortable when you have demonstrated the impossibility of your suspicions."

He seemed just as eager, this morning, to allay any fears as they had thought him ready, yesterday, to arouse them. Betty was puzzled, and rather angry because she could not understand him. Without saying any more, she led the way upstairs.

They started at the top of the house and worked gradually down. They visited every room, poked into every corner and cupboard. Both Betty and Sally were surprised, not only at the unexpected size of the house, but also at its cleanliness, and the solid comfort with which every part of it was furnished. Remembering Edward Morlant's lonely bachelor state, they had quite expected to find some rooms empty and shut up, given over to dust and decay. Instead of which, the whole place seemed ready for immediate occupation.

"It is Bidgood who is responsible for this," explained Broughton, in reply to some remark of Sally's. "When Mr. Edward became a recluse, he lost all interest in his goods and chattels, and would have allowed everything to rot in its place. But Bidgood's whole heart is bound up in the house. It is wife and child to him. He has slaved night and day to keep it from ruin and decay."

"He has succeeded wonderfully well," murmured Betty, gazing at the highly polished front of a wardrobe which had not been used for years. "He—he is a strange, contradictory creature."

Though their search was exhaustive, they found no trace of any illicit occupation. As it became evident that Betty's suspicions were unfounded, the solicitor began, in rather laborious fashion, to chaff her about them.

"You are very gay to-day, Mr. Broughton," remarked Sally, surprised at his levity.

"I—I am very happy, Miss Poulter," he replied, with unusual simplicity.

"Happy? Is it a birthday or something?"

To the amazement of the two girls, a slow flush spread over his broad face.

"No, it is not a birthday," he explained. "But, to a lonely bachelor like myself, the society of—er—two charming ladies is—er—well, a very pleasant change."

After such a naïve declaration, neither Betty nor Sally felt any nearer to an understanding of Mr. Broughton's true character. They did feel, however, that he was perhaps more human than they had thought him.

They came, eventually, to the kitchen, where they made the acquaintance of Mrs. Clayton and Rover. Mrs. Clayton was a stout, motherly body who obviously stood in tremendous awe of Bidgood. She had little to say for herself, and disappeared unobtrusively at the first opportunity. Rover was a beautiful collie who immediately, without fuss or ceremony, attached himself to Betty as though he had never known another master.

Quite satisfied, now, with the negative result of the exploration, Betty still felt that the events of last night required some explanation. However, it was no use questioning Bidgood again at the moment, so she declared that they would carry out Mr. Broughton's original suggestion. They put on hats and coats, and went out into the garden for their first view of Hameldon House and its surroundings.

In the pale sunlight of the November morning, the old house had a very definite charm of its own. Of Elizabethan architecture, its weather-beaten walls, mellow with age, accorded well with the wild austerity of the heath around it. Situated at the head of a deep rift in the moorland, it showed a brave face to any wind that blew. So far as the eye could reach in every direction, it stood alone, miles from its nearest neighbor, an outpost home of man set in the heart of the barren waste.

"It's very lonely, isn't it?" murmured Sally, looking round at the rolling stretches of heather and peat.

"Yes, it's lonely," replied Betty. "But I—I like it. There's something very wonderful about this moor country. And the house seems to suit it, doesn't it? Though I do wish we'd arrived here by daylight. We should have got such a different impression."

Mr. Broughton suggested that they should climb the nearest hill and get a better idea of the country. It was an ideal day for walking, and they made a good pace, with Rover trotting sedately behind. On the way, the solicitor with questions concerning Edward Morlant and his mode of life.

He could tell them little more than they already knew. Beyond a guarded statement that the deceased was eccentric in his habits, he would pass no opinion on him. Despite Bidgood's hint that he was the only person likely to know, he professed complete ignorance of the reason why the will required Betty to live at Hameldon House for six months.

"I wish I knew more about him," said Betty, as they reached the top of the hill. She found herself talking quite confidentially with Broughton, feeling much more at her ease with him than she had ever done. "I wish I had known him before he died. Where is he buried?"

"In Blackshaw cemetery. And that reminds me." The solicitor fumbled in his pocket. "I have a photograph here. . . . Mr. Edward ordered the headstone some few days before he died. He described what he wanted very minutely. I received a photograph from the sculptors for approval this morning."

Betty glanced at the proffered photograph with some distaste. It represented a massive plain stone, without decoration, carrying the usual pious formula and, in much larger type, the words: "He is not dead, but sleepeth."

"Evidently he was a religious man and believed in an afterlife," she remarked. "I suppose it is what he wanted?"

"Exactly. He was particularly anxious that the last words should be prominent."

"Well, no one is likely to miss them."

"Shall I tell the sculptors, then, to complete their work and set up the stone in Blackshaw?"

"It's all right so far as I am concerned."

Having admired the wide-flung view from the top of the hill, they retraced their steps towards the house. Seeing that Sally and Mr. Broughton appeared interested in one another, Betty set herself the task of rousing Rover from his melancholy. She succeeded so well that before long they were racing wildly together down the hillside.

The two of them reached the house long before Sally and Mr. Broughton, who were loitering, apparently engaged in a very mild, attenuated kind of flirtation. Betty's soft cheeks were flushed with the exercise, and Rover was frisking around her happily enough. As they entered the hall, Bidgood came forward with a card on a salver. He was apologetic in manner, as though striving to efface the bad impression he had created last night.

"A young gentleman waiting in the library to see you, Missie," he said.

Betty picked up the card in surprise and read the few words engraved on it: "Mr. Clarence Knight. Representing Messrs. Lepage & Co."

"Surely you don't get travelers coming right out here, Bidgood?" she exclaimed. "Whoever can it be?"

"I don't know, Missie. He came about half an hour ago, and said he would wait until you returned." He peered at her anxiously. "I hope I did right in allowing him to wait?"

"Quite right, of course. I'll see him at once."

"Thank you, Missie."

Obviously relieved, the old man shuffled away to the kitchen. Betty crossed the hall towards the library.

As she approached it, a curious thing happened. Rover, who had been following close at her heels, suddenly dashed forward and pawed frantically at the closed door, sniffing and whining in great excitement.

Betty could hear someone moving swiftly about in the library, as though agitated. Fearing lest the dog might annoy or attack her unexpected visitor, she stooped and slipped her hand under his collar. Then she opened the door.

"You needn't be frightened," she called reassuringly. "He won't hurt you. I've hold of him and—"

She stopped abruptly, and her blue eyes opened wide in astonishment. Her precautions for the visitor's safety were wasted. There was no one in the room.

7

Mr. Clarence Knight

Betty stared round the library, hardly believing her eyes. Where was this Mr. Clarence Knight whose card she held in her hand? She had heard his movements so distinctly just before she opened the door. And in the space of a few seconds, he had apparently vanished into thin air.

The dog broke loose from her grasp and dashed into the room, galloping around it, whining in excitement. After a couple of circuits, he came to a stop in front of the hearth, leaping up towards the oil painting over the chimney piece, giving tongue in a series of sharp, staccato barks.

A moment later, Bidgood hurried in. His hands were shaking and his voice trembled.

"Missie! Missie!" he cried. "I forgot to tell you that you mustn't bring Rover in here."

Betty couldn't help noticing his obvious consternation, and wondered at the cause.

"Whatever are you talking about, Bidgood?" she asked coldly.

The old man made an effort to calm himself.

"It's the dog, Missie," he explained, humble appeal in his dim eyes. "Mr. Edward never allowed him in here."

"Why?"

"Because of the painting. For some reason, it always upsets him. He nearly goes mad whenever he comes anywhere near it."

Betty glanced at the dog, who was still jumping up and barking. There was no doubt that he was strangely excited.

"I see," she said thoughtfully. "I suppose he recognizes his master." She turned back to the old servant. "Where's the visitor?" she asked abruptly.

Bidgood started. "Haven't you seen him, Missie?"

"No. You said he was in here."

"I left him in here. I—I don't know—"

"Well, he's not here now, is he? Just before I opened the door I heard someone moving about and—"

Betty stopped short. Unmistakable fear showed in the old man's wrinkled features.

"You know something about this, Bidgood," she cried, seizing him by the shoulders and shaking him. "You know something about this mysterious visitor."

"No, I don't, Missie!" Bidgood's trembling voice rose into a wail. "I don't, Missie! I don't! I swear before God that I don't know anything of him!"

There was an earnestness in his tone that carried conviction. Whatever lies he had told before, Betty felt sure that he was speaking the truth now, that he was as worried about Mr. Clarence Knight as she herself.

Sally and Mr. Broughton came in just then, and she explained the position to them. The solicitor's white forehead wrinkled as he listened.

"What was this young man like, Bidgood?" he asked sharply.

"He—he was just an ordinary young man, sir. Quite pleasant spoken."

"And you left him alone in here?"

"Yes, sir. I was busy getting lunch ready."

"You're a fool, Bidgood. I thought you had more sense than to leave strangers alone in the house. And whatever's the matter with that dog?"

"I was just telling Missie," said Bidgood quickly. "It's Mr. Edward's painting. He never could abide it. He'd tear it to pieces if he'd half a chance."

"Well, we'd better get him out before he goes quite crazy about it."

Mr. Broughton, clearly very disturbed, crossed to the frenzied dog, and dragged him out of the room.

"It's my fault Rover went in there," said Betty, following him into the hall. "He heard someone moving about, just as I did, and he—"

"Tut-tut, Miss Elizabeth. I have warned you about strange noises in the house. You must not pay attention—"

"You mustn't treat me like a child, Mr. Broughton. I'm not without a certain amount of intelligence. Whoever this man may be, he was in the library immediately before I opened the door, and—"

"I can't understand that at all," interposed Sally, joining them. "He couldn't have got out by the windows, could he? It seems to me there must be some other way—"

"That is very foolish, Miss Poulter," interrupted Broughton, turning on her with a frown. "There cannot possibly be another room."

Betty received the impression that he was trying to stifle any discussion of the matter, even if it meant quarreling with them.

"Foolish, is it?" she exclaimed, resenting both his tone and the implication in his words. "You think both the dog and I imagined what we heard?"

"Well—er—Miss Elizabeth, I would hardly say that. I am quite sure you must have heard something. But, clearly, if this Mr. Knight was not in the room when you opened—"

"Pardon me." A soft, pleasant voice broke in, "I think you mentioned my name."

They turned to the door in surprise. A fair-haired, smiling young man had just entered the hall from outside.'

"Clarence Knight, at your service," he continued, advancing towards them. "I'm a peaceful sort of fellow myself. But you seem to be quarreling about me.

"We are!" snapped Betty. "How did you get in?"

"I walked in, lady."

"And how did you get out of the library where the servant left you?"

"By the same simple mode of locomotion."

"Oh, don't be a fool, man. You know what I mean. Were you in the library just before I opened the door?"

"Unfortunately, no; or I should have seen you earlier. So many precious minutes wasted. And all because I took a walk round your garden to pass the time."

Evidently Mr. Knight would have them believe that he knew nothing of what had happened. Betty scrutinized him carefully. He was a good-looking, clean-shaven young fellow, something over thirty years of age, with fair, wavy hair, and gray eyes which somehow conveyed the impression of strength. But there was a facetiousness in his manner, and a foolish smile on his clear-cut features which irritated her intensely. Moreover, she didn't believe his story.

"Well, you've been waiting for me, I understand," she said. "What do you want?"

"I want to sell you some furniture," replied Mr. Clarence Knight promptly.

"You want to—what?"

"To persuade you to refurnish this house. Very excellent stuff you've got here, of course, but slightly out of date, don't you know? Whereas I can supply you—"

"I don't want any furniture."

"Ah, so you think, perhaps, lady. But do you know what I mean by furniture? I represent the firm of Lepage, known all the world over. We don't furnish houses, lady; that's an idea of the past. We furnish homes—nests. None of these cumbersome antiques, but up-to-date modern creations, artistic and labor-saving. If you will look through this catalogue—"

"I don't want any furniture," repeated Betty. "So please don't trouble about the catalogue."

The young man grinned cheerfully at her. Apart from this, he took no notice of her remark.

"I must explain to you," he went on, with extraordinary rapidity, "that we have most accommodating terms in case you wish to pay out of income. No deposit, no obnoxious inquiries, no references. Monthly amounts to suit your convenience. No payments when sick or out of work. It isn't that we don't want your money, though it may appear so. The fact is that we trust you. Every customer a friend—that's our motto. Free life insurance. Free fire insurance. Goods delivered in plain vans, and all linoleum laid without extra charge. Established fifty years and never a complaint. The only firm in the world that can give you all these advantages—and the goods."

He paused to draw a long breath. Betty seized the opportunity of stopping his flow of eloquence.

"Please understand this," she said, speaking slowly as though to a child. "I do *not* want any furniture. You are wasting your time."

"On the contrary, I'm improving the shining hour," he replied, quite undaunted. "I'm in no hurry. You see, I like talking to you, whether you buy anything or not."

Betty felt like smiling at his impudence, but decided that it would not be wise.

"I think you'd better go," she said coldly, turning away.

Mr. Knight accepted this definite dismissal without any loss of cheerfulness.

"Thank you for seeing me, lady." The foolish grin appeared on his face again. "You'll appreciate me more when you know me better. I'll call again."

He made a profound bow, and walked towards the door. Halfway across the hall, he slipped and fell with his leg twisted beneath him.

"Damn!" he ejaculated; and a moment later: "Pardon me, lady. It's very wrong to be drunk so early in the day."

Betty started. In a flash of recollection, she saw enacted again a scene in the fog, horrible and terrifying. She felt again the murderous pressure of a rough hand over her nose and mouth, heard the sullen swirl of water immediately below her helpless head. And she pictured the half-seen figure of the young man who had saved her, swaying unsteadily on his feet, and telling her with the utmost gravity that it was wrong to be drunk so early in the day.

Was it possible that the man seated on the stone floor of the hall, tenderly rubbing his ankle, was indeed he who had come to her rescue two nights ago? Was he, by means of an apparent joke, secretly claiming acquaintance in a way no one but herself would understand? Had he come to Hameldon House deliberately and of set purpose to protect her from some further and as yet unsuspected danger? And if so, who was the person from whom their acquaintance must be kept secret?

It seemed incredible that the words he had used should be a mere coincidence. And Betty felt, too, that the fall had been a fake, that Mr. Clarence Knight was not so badly hurt as he pretended to be. Was the whole thing a plan to get into the house? It was true that he seemed too foolish to make a plan of any sort. But then, his foolishness might be assumed.

Betty was very puzzled. Unquestionably, there was some mystery about this young man. It was difficult to believe that he was not lying about the library. She looked at him as he sat there, gingerly rubbing his leg, and wondered what she should do. No one had moved to assist him.

"Sprained my jolly old ankle, I think, lady," he said. "You don't mind if I sit on your not too comfortable floor for a while?"

"Of course not," replied Betty absently. She could not make up her mind whether to trust him or not. "Can I help you at all?"

Mr. Broughton stepped forward, an impatient frown on his broad face.

"This house is not a hospital, young man," he said roughly. "You must clear out—quick."

Mr. Knight grinned at him and disdained to reply.

"No one asked you to come here," went on the solicitor, growing more annoyed. "You pushed your way in, and the sooner you remove yourself the better.

"You wouldn't turn a poor cripple out into the cruel world," said Mr. Knight with a sublime confidence. "I know your kind heart too well to think that."

He glanced at Betty, and she glimpsed an urgent appeal in his gray eyes. For some reason, he wanted to remain in the house. She did not understand his motive, but she felt that she ought to support him. Moreover, she didn't like the way the solicitor had interfered in a matter which did not concern him.

"I think you forget yourself, Mr. Broughton," she said. "I told Mr. Knight he could stay."

"But, Miss Elizabeth—"

"Don't let's argue about it," interrupted Betty. During the last few minutes all her uneasiness and uncertainty about the solicitor had returned. He knew more than he had admitted and his very anxiety to get rid of this stranger was suspicious. "Mr. Knight will stay until his ankle is better if it takes a week!"

So that was that. Mr. Knight did stay; and for the rest of the day he limped about the house annoying everyone with his fatuous remarks and idiotic grin.

His cheerfulness was not infectious. He got on Sally's nerves, and she frankly told him so. Mr. Broughton was gloomy. Even Miss Poulter's tentative advances could not rouse him. He might have been meditating some evil, or he might have been just sulking. Betty didn't know, and she didn't care. She was beginning to think that the situation at Hameldon House was beyond either her comprehension or her control.

It was not a bit of use pretending she was comfortable. Everybody in the place seemed to be secretive, and to have hidden thoughts and plans of his own. She felt sure about no one but Sally. She could trust neither Bidgood nor the solicitor. And she really didn't know what to think about Mr. Clarence Knight.

He gave her no further hint as to his identity, and she shrank from asking him outright, in case she should be wrong. It was clear to her, however, assuming him to be the man who had saved her from the murderer, that there was some strange mystery surrounding her, a mystery, moreover, which held a threat of very definite danger. If he was playing a game, it was a deep game. She didn't understand it in the least, and her ignorance annoyed her more than anything else. She hated the feeling of baffled helplessness which met her at every turn.

The episode at the library door had made a strong impression on her. She was convinced that both Broughton and Bidgood could tell her something about this if they would. There was not the slightest doubt in her mind that someone had actually been in the library while she was in the hall. If not Mr. Clarence Knight, who could it have been? And how had this elusive personage managed to get out of the room before she opened the door?

With Sally, she had, of course, jumped to the idea that there might be some secret way out of the library. The house was very old, and such things were not unknown. During the afternoon, she had overcome her distaste for the room, and made a solitary but careful search of it. She had found nothing to support the theory of a secret passage.

She was compelled to admit herself beaten. She had her suspicions, it is true, but they were too absurd to breathe to anyone. She would not mention them even to Sally, though they puzzled over things together. Selly, just at the moment, was not very helpful. In her, excitement over the adventure was paramount. Betty was excited, too. But growing up in her now, and resisting every attempt to stifle it, was a definite foreboding of disaster to come.

There was an atmosphere of strained expectancy about this house. She could not avoid the feeling that something more was going to happen; and, remembering the attack on her two nights ago, she feared that this something would be very unpleasant.

Dusk came, and with it an exacerbation of her discomfort. The old house was lonely enough by daylight, but when the shutters were closed there seemed to be no escape from it. She was surprised at her reluctance to lose Mrs. Clayton's motherly presence.

Tea in the library was not a cheerful meal, and Mr. Knight's pleasantries served only to set everyone's nerves on edge. He was still limping, and appeared in no hurry to get away. Betty began to wonder if he intended to stay the night, and what she should do if he suggested it.

She could not eat. Having drunk her tea, she got up from the table and wandered about the room. She wished

she could make up her mind about him. If it were he who
had saved her, she owed him a deep debt of gratitude. She
was strangely annoyed that he should act so foolishly.

After a while, she stopped by an old bureau in a distant
corner of the room, furtively watching him. His gray eyes
were fixed on the painting over the chimney piece, and
she thought they looked very keen and intelligent. His
face was unsmiling, and she was impressed by the strength
suggested by his clear-cut features.

Why did he grin so much? She fidgeted impatiently.
Her fingers came in contact with a piece of carving on the
bureau, and idly traced it out. Suddenly, there was a click-
ing sound behind her. A protuberance of the carving had
given way beneath her finger and a small secret drawer in
the bureau had shot out.

Startled by the noise, the others turned inquiringly.
Betty looked at the drawer. There was nothing in it but a
small book bound in red leather. She picked this up and
opened it.

Her eyebrows lifted in surprise as she turned the pages.
Then an eager flush tinged her soft cheeks.

"Look!" she cried, running back to the others. "Perhaps
we'll learn something now. Edward Morlant's private
diary! In a secret drawer in his bureau!"

8

THE DIARY

Sally jumped up from her chair in great excitement.

"What a lucky find!" she cried. "It ought to tell us quite a lot. Oh, do let me have a look at it."

"Who's the old bird," asked Mr. Knight, "whose memoirs are so thrilling?"

Betty frowned at him. For a moment she felt like slapping his impudent face. Then, remembering that he knew nothing of the circumstances, she changed her mind.

"Mr. Morlant has just died," she explained. "He left his money to me under rather strange conditions. We are hoping that this diary will give us some explanation of those conditions."

"Then read to us, lady. We'll be as quiet as mice while the mystery is unfolded."

Mr. Broughton rose slowly to his feet. His eyes, under their shaggy brows, were uneasy.

"I do not think you—we ought to look into that diary, Miss Elizabeth."

"Why?"

"Because it may contain matter which Mr. Edward did not intend us to know."

"It may explain a lot of things that puzzle us."

"I think, at least, you should allow me, as Mr. Edward's solicitor, to look through it first."

Betty hesitated. The request sounded reasonable.

"Didn't you know of its existence?" she asked.

"No."

"Then evidently Mr. Morlant had some secrets from you, too. I don't see why—" She paused, frowning thoughtfully. "I wonder if Bidgood knows anything about it."

She rang the bell, and they waited in silence until Bidgood shuffled into the room.

Betty held out the little red book towards him.

"Have you seen this before, Bidgood?"

The old man started. "I—I think so, Missie."

"You know what it is?"

"Mr. Edward's diary. I thought he had destroyed it. He always said he would."

"I've just found it in that bureau. In a secret drawer. I'm going to read it."

Sudden alarm sprang up in Bidgood's sunken eyes.

"But, Missie," he protested. "Mr. Edward did not—"

Betty stopped him with a gesture. His obvious concern had helped her to decide. If both he and Broughton were so reluctant that she should read the diary, it could only be because it might contain something they didn't want her to know. And she very much wanted to know this elusive something.

"I'm going to read it," she repeated. "Now. You'd better stay. I may want to ask you some questions. Sit down."

She opened the book again. The others sat watching her without further speech, waiting for her to begin. The solicitor and the old manservant could not hide their uneasiness. Sally was boiling with curiosity, while Mr. Knight seemed to be enjoying the situation thoroughly.

The diary went back for many years. Most of the entries were brief. They had not been made with any regularity, but only when something of outstanding importance had occurred, or perhaps when Morlant had been seized with a fit of industry. There were long gaps in the time sequences, extending on several occasions to over twelve months.

The first entries in the book were full of a girl, a girl named Elizabeth; and Betty realized, with a little spasm of pity and pain, that she was reading about her mother.

These, apparently, had been joyous days for Edward Morlant. He loved, and was loved in return. The diary told the tale of a happy, uneventful courtship, of Elizabeth's holidays at Hameldon House, and the visits the writer had paid to the home of her parents. There was an ecstasy in the few, glowing words which showed that Edward's love had been deep and tender; yet running through it all was a vein of melancholy, a suggestion of sadness as though he had a foreboding that his happiness could not last.

Betty did not read these idyllic entries aloud. They were of no interest to anyone but herself and the lover who had just died. She briefly explained the circumstances to her listeners, and passed on until a few words scrawled on a page to themselves caught her eye.

"'*Elisabeth has found me out,*'" she read. "'*She has discovered my secret. God help me! What can I do?*'"

She looked up at Mr. Broughton.

"What was this secret?" she asked. "Do you know?"

"I do not, Miss Elizabeth," he replied earnestly.

"You've no idea at all?"

"Not the slightest." His tone carried conviction. "I have never known what came between Mr. Edward and your mother. It happened before I knew him."

"And you, Bidgood? Do you know anything about it?"

The manservant slowly shook his head. There were tears in his dim old eyes.

Their ignorance was exasperating, but Betty felt that they were both telling the truth. Evidently Edward Morlant had kept a good deal to himself. She turned to the diary again, hoping to find some further details. But the writer had not shared his trouble even with this silent and discreet friend.

"*To-day, Elisabeth married Gerald Harlan,*'" was the next entry, dated over a year later. "*I pray that she may be happy. The future holds nothing for me now that I have lost her, but I cannot blame her. She did right to break our engagement. I am not fit to care for so precious a flower.*'"

"I don't know, after all, that I ought to go on," said Betty when she had read this. "It seems almost like—well, sacrilege. We were never intended to see this. And yet, if we could find out about that secret. . . ."

"Suppose you just glance through it," suggested Sally. "And don't read anything aloud unless it seems to have some bearing on what we want to know."

"Yes, carry on, lady," chimed in Mr. Knight. "Don't worry about us. We'll be as quiet as mice."

Betty opened the book again. The entries now were more numerous, and every one of them was about Elizabeth. Her blue eyes grew misty as she realized how completely the man's life had been bound up in her mother.

She read on without speaking, forgetting for the moment the others who were watching her. Soon, pain crept into the diary, helpless sorrow, and fierce anger. For Gerald Harlan was not treating his wife well, and the heart of the man who loved her was sore.

There was a note of little Betty's birth, and a hope that things would now improve. Later entries showed how this hope was slowly dissipated; until there came the simple phrase: "*Harlan has deserted her*"; followed by a sudden outburst of fury: "*May his soul rot in Hell!*"

A long break now, extending over almost two years. Not a word about all that Betty knew the writer had been doing at this time for his Elizabeth and her daughter; not a word about the state of his own mind during this period.

Though this, perhaps, was sufficiently indicated by the isolated sentence at the bottom of the page:

"It's no use thinking of asking her. She couldn't come to me. The barrier between us still persists."

Betty turned the page sorrowfully. She had not fully appreciated before the tragedy of Edward Morlant's life, the long years devoted to a hopeless and despairing love.

Though she had known that she must find it somewhere, the stark simplicity of the next entry came as a shock to her:

"Elizabeth died to-day. Why do I live?"

She did not read through the pages that followed.

They contained the outpourings of a broken heart, the passionate grief of one who had lost all he held dear. But the few sentences she noticed showed that the writer was not accepting his loss with submission. His soul was filled with bitterness, and he reviled and stormed at Fate with a wild abandon that rather frightened her.

These entries, though not very numerous, extended over several months. Then, it seemed, pain began to be dulled and resignation to take its place. There were many allusions to the little Elizabeth, and all that Morlant intended to do for her. Mention was made, at long intervals, of her progress at the convent and at the finishing school near Paris.

One of these Betty read aloud:

"'I saw little Elisabeth again to-day, though of course she did not know me. She grows more like her mother each time I see her. I wish to God I could bring her here to cheer up this old house. But I dare not—I dare not!'"

"Mystery again," she said irritably. "What was there to prevent him bringing me here, Mr. Broughton?"

"I do not know, Miss Elizabeth. I myself suggested it on several occasions, but he would not hear of it."

"Why didn't he dare do it, Bidgood?"

"I don't know, Missie. He was always talking about it, but he—he seemed frightened of something happening."

"What could he have been frightened of? Surely nothing could happen to me? Unless—" Betty turned to Broughton again. "It wasn't my father, was it? He wasn't frightened that my father would cause trouble?"

"Whatever the reason, that, I think, is out of the question," replied the solicitor. "I was in Mr. Edward's confidence so far as Gerald Harlan was concerned. In fact, it was part of my business to keep an eye on his progress. According to our information, your father was killed in a drunken brawl at some foreign port, long before this time."

"I wish we could find out what he was frightened of," murmured Betty, absently fingering the pages of the book. "It might be so very important."

The allusions to herself in the diary grew less frequent. In their stead were queer, incoherent entries which she could not understand at all. Several consecutive pages, too, had been torn out, as though the writer had later regretted some of the things set down.

There was a growing suggestion of wildness in these private confidences that made Betty wonder if Edward Morlant's mind had been unhinged by his troubles.

There were strange boasts and prophecies, much involved discussion about the nature of the soul, and veiled references to subjects such as Gupta Vidya, the Wisdom Religion, and Mahatmas, of which she knew nothing.

"What are all these things?" she asked, reading the names out. "Sally, you ought to know. They're something to do with spiritualism, aren't they?"

"Not spiritualism, exactly," replied Sally. "Theosophy. Don't you remember, I found a lot of books over there by the window dealing with it?"

"Yes, I remember. But what's it all about?"

"Can't tell you properly. It's a kind of secret science. You've heard of Madame Blavatsky, haven't you?"

"She was a charlatan, wasn't she?"

"That depends on whether you're a skeptic or a believer," interposed Mr. Knight, "Many people still think she was an inspired prophetess and teacher."

"But what did she do?"

"She was a sort of High Priestess in this cult," explained Sally. "It's supposed to be the oldest in the world, and has numbered all the world-teachers, such as Buddha, Confucius and Christ, among its initiates. The Mahatmas are the very top dogs, incarnate intelligences which are not limited by the ordinary bonds of humanity. I mean, they can do miracles and things. They're mostly Indians, I believe. If you are initiated into the Wisdom Religion, and study and train yourself properly, there's no end to what you can do eventually. You can transport yourself from place to place as though you had a magic carpet; you can live without eating or drinking; and you never die. Some of the Mahatmas, Adepts or Masters as they call them, have been living for centuries."

"Me for a Mahatma!" grinned Mr. Knight. "I'd like to be able to go to Brighton or Blackpool whenever I wanted without paying railway fare or hotel bills."

"Sounds a lot of rubbish to me," said Betty practically. "But apparently Mr. Morlant believed in it."

She dismissed the subject and returned to the diary. Almost immediately, she came to another entry which puckered her brow.

"*I'm frightened about James,*'" she read. "*If ever he should learn— But how can he learn? And yet— I tell myself that I am safe. And yet—*'"

"Do either of you know who James was?" she asked. "And why this fear of him?"

Both Broughton and Bidgood shook their heads in silence. Mr. Knight shook his in sympathy.

"They're not very helpful lady," he remarked. "Perhaps Jimmy was a Mahatma."

"I wish you'd be quiet," flashed Betty. "You seem incapable of realizing that this is important."

The first entry on the next page caught her eye, and she uttered a startled little cry.

"I say!" she exclaimed. "Just listen to this: *'I have discovered the secret of immortality! I have become an Adept! All power and wisdom are mine! I cannot die!'*"

"Poor old fellow!" murmured Sally. "And all his troubles are over now."

"But listen!" cried Betty. "Listen how he goes on: *'When my time comes, it will seem to all that I am dead. My earthly frame will go down into the grave, but I—I shall not die. My soul, with all its accumulated knowledge and power, will still live. And the wonderful secret of life to which I have been admitted will enable me to reanimate the poor mortal tissues, so that my body itself shall rise from the grave and carry me where I will.'*"

"Gosh!" muttered Sally. "Remember the grave stone, and how keen he was about the words 'He is not dead, but sleepeth'? I wonder if—"

"*'On the third day,'*" Betty went on, her voice trembling a little, "*'I shall return. I shall return secretly, for no one must know of this wonderful achievement except initiates. I shall take a last farewell of Hameldon House, and depart to some distant clime there to begin my second life. On the third day after my burial I shall return to burn this diary, for all trouble and strife will then be ended.'*"

There was a long silence in the library when Betty ceased reading. Though no one really believed in Edward Morlant's words, they were characterized by a solemn

sincerity that made the listeners uneasy. For there was no
doubt that the man himself believed in what he had written; and, after all, no one knew that he was wrong.

Sally, in particular, was deeply moved. She knew that
she possessed psychic powers such as are not common
property. She knew that many things at which the unbe-
liever scoffs are real and vital. Her investigations in the
spirit world, crude, shallow and mercenary though they
had been, had convinced her that there was much in life of
which most people are ignorant. To her, at that moment,
it did not seem entirely impossible that Edward Morlant
should return from the dead.

"To-day is the third day after his burial," she said softly, breaking the silence.

"So it is!" agreed Betty, starting. "I'd forgotten."

"Splendid!" cried Mr. Knight. "I've come at a lucky
time. I hope the jolly old sport shows up. Next to selling
furniture, I enjoy meeting spooks."

"This is no subject for mirth, young man," said Mr.
Broughton severely. "Miss Elizabeth, I hope you are not
attaching too much importance to this diary. Mr. Edward
must have been ill. The whole thing is impossible and—"

"Why is it impossible, Mr. Broughton?" asked Sally.

"Well—er—Miss Poulter, you do not seriously expect
us to believe—"

Betty turned away from them. Her thoughtful gaze had
rested for a moment on the oil painting over the chimney
piece, and immediately a feeling of vague yet intense discomfort had seized upon her. She could have sworn that
somewhere near at hand, yet hidden from view, someone
was watching everything she did, listening to all she said.

"I'm sick of the whole stupid business!" she cried irritably. "'We won't talk about it any more to-night. I'll lock this
book up in my room, and read the rest of it sometime else."

She crossed to the table beside the door, and lit a candle. Sally rose slowly from her chair, and watched her with frightened eyes.

"Betty," she faltered, "d-don't go alone. It's dark upstairs. Let me come with you."

"Don't be silly," said Betty firmly. "I'm not a child. I'll be back in a minute."

She went out, and they heard her light footsteps crossing the stone-flagged hall. Sally sat down again, biting her lips in anxiety. She was trembling with fear, and she didn't know why; except that, in the irrational, unexplained fashion in which spirit messages came to her, she had received a strong impression that some dreadful thing was about to happen.

The others, too, whether infected by her or on their own account, seemed to be uneasy. Bidgood and the solicitor were grave, and avoided looking at one another. Even Mr. Knight had lost his fatuous grin, and an eager expectancy showed in his earnest face.

No one spoke. The old grandfather clock in the corner ticked out the seconds with maddening monotony. The slow minutes dragged by in strained silence. And then, with sickening abruptness, a shrill scream rang out.

Mr. Broughton sprang to his feet, his broad face pale and drawn.

"My God, that's Miss Elizabeth!" he cried hoarsely. "If anything's happened to her—"

9

THE MAHATMA

The injury to Mr. Clarence Knight's ankle did not prevent him from being first out of the room. He was halfway up the stairs when the others rushed into the hall. By the time they reached the top, he was out of sight.

They hurried along the dark, drafty corridors, holding their candles aloft. The multitude of shadows with which the darkness was peopled confused them, causing them to turn aside into corner after corner in the wake of dim shapes which vanished before the light. It was not until they reached the corridor outside the girls' bedroom that they came upon what they were fearing to find.

Betty's slim figure lay motionless in a crumpled heap on the floor. Mr. Knight knelt beside her, supporting her curly head in his arms.

"Is she ill—hurt?" Sally asked him breathlessly.

By the light of the candles he quickly examined the girl's limp figure. Then he grinned up into their anxious faces.

"The lady has fainted," he announced. "I think she must have seen a Mahatma."

Sally dropped on her knees and indignantly pushed him away.

"You're a fool!" she cried, drawing Betty's head onto her own lap. "A conceited, ignorant fool!"

In nowise abashed, Mr. Knight dragged a big flask from his hip pocket.

"A spot of brandy for the lady," he said, holding it to the unconscious girl's pallid lips. "To counteract the effect of the other spirit."

He rose to his feet and watched, a curious smile, half mocking, half tender, curling his lips. After a while, Betty opened her eyes. She looked up at the anxious group around her, and a little shudder ran through her.

A moment later full memory returned to her, and she sat bolt upright.

"Bidgood!" she asked sharply. "Who else is in the house besides us?"

"N-no one, Missie," faltered the old man.

"Are you sure? No one at all? I want the truth this time. Bidgood, if you've been entertaining friends while the house has been empty, please tell me now, and we'll forget all about it. But if you lie to me—"

"I have no friends in the house, Missie. I never have had. As God is my judge!"

"Then it must have been him!" Betty struggled to her feet. "There's no possible doubt about it. It must—it must have been he!"

"Really, Miss Elizabeth!" Everard Broughton laid a soothing hand on her shoulder. "You are nervous, upset. It is not surprising in this old house with all its shadows and eerie noises. Come, now. Calm yourself. Who else could be in the house?"

Betty shook off his hand impatiently.

"Edward Morlant!" she said.

"Now, now, Miss Elizabeth. You are over-excited. You must know that what you suggest is impossible. Poor Mr. Edward sleeps peacefully in Blackshaw cemetery."

"He does not!" cried Betty fiercely. "He is here! In this house, I tell you! I have just seen him!"

"Then the jolly old sport has kept his word," remarked Mr. Knight. "He has come back as he said he would."

"Tell us about it, Betty," urged Sally, throwing her arms about her friend again. "Tell us what has happened."

"You'll not believe me. You'll think I'm a silly, nervous fool—that I imagined it."

"Of course we'll believe you. You're not the kind of girl to imagine things."

Betty shivered again. She looked at Sally doubtfully for a moment, then her lips trembled into a wan smile.

"I was frightened," she admitted. "Terribly frightened. But I didn't imagine it. It—it happened. . . ."

She glanced into the darkness beyond the circle of candlelight. Her quivering mouth set into a firm line.

"I was not nervous when I came upstairs," she went on. "For some reason or another, I was cross and bad-tempered, but not at all inclined to worry about the shadows. I never gave them a thought. Besides, the lamp in the hall was lighted.

"But as I came into this corridor, I began to feel very creepy and uneasy. I had left the lights behind, and everything about me seemed black and mysterious. Perhaps what we had just been reading had affected me. Anyhow, I don't mind confessing that I was really scared just then. I walked right in the middle of the corridor, expecting at any moment that some ghostly hand might shoot out of the darkness and clutch me.

"I had just passed that bedroom along there when I heard a noise behind me. My heart jumped into my throat. I looked round, and I nearly screamed with fright. For, standing in the doorway was a man. And that man was Edward Morlant!"

"But that is impossible, Miss Elizabeth!" said Broughton quickly. "Quite—"

"Don't keep on saying things are impossible," cried Betty, an angry flush staining her soft cheeks. "I know it all sounds rubbish, and I said you wouldn't believe me. But impossible or not, I tell you I saw him as plainly as I see you."

"How did you know the old boy, lady?" asked Mr. Knight.

"By that painting, of course. No one could mistake those eyes of his. Besides, he told me."

"He told you?" echoed Broughton, as though this were the most astounding event of the evening.

"Yes," Betty flamed. "Are you deaf? If you'd listen instead of interrupting, you'd learn all there is to know.

"I'm sorry to be such a pig," she continued almost immediately. "But, you know, it—it's been rather a shock to me."

"Poor kid!" soothed Sally. "Go on, dear. We won't interrupt again."

"Well, you can imagine my state of mind. I stood there rigid, like a stone statue, frozen to the spot, as they say. Honestly, I couldn't move an inch. I was in a blue funk. The blackness of the corridor seemed to be closing in on me. I could hear all sorts of weird, startling noises. And there in front of me was this white face, the face of a dead man, all blurred and shadowy because I couldn't hold the candle still.

"Nothing happened. After a while I must have stopped trembling because the face grew clearer. I could see now that it was kind and smiling. Some of my fear left me. This ghost, or whatever it was, didn't seem inclined to harm me.

"It took a step towards me with a conciliatory gesture, and then spoke.

"'Dear Elizabeth,' it said, in a quiet, gentle tone as though not wishing to alarm me, 'dear little Elizabeth, please give me the diary.'

"The voice sounded quite normal and natural, and I plucked up some more courage.

"'W-who are you?' I stammered. 'What do you want?'

"'I am Edward Morlant, of course. You know me quite well. I loved your mother, my dear. I want the book you have in your hand.'"

Betty paused, looking round at the interested faces of her listeners as though challenging them to disbelieve her. No one spoke.

"The words and tone were so quiet and matter of fact," she went on, "that I began to grow hot and cold all over. You might have thought that the absence of any attempt to harm me would have kept me cool and collected, but I was now just as frightened as at the beginning. It was all so uncanny. It seemed so funny, so impossible, to be standing there calmly talking to a man who was supposed to be in his grave—like a nightmare.

"'They told me you were dead,' I said.

"'I am dead!' was the soft reply.

"Well, that sent cold shivers running down my back again. I stared at this Thing, and I couldn't think of a word to say.

"'I am dead,' it repeated, in a more animated tone. 'So far as human knowledge goes, Edward Morlant has passed before his Maker. But as you see, his soul still lives upon this earth.'

"A growing excitement flashed in the odd colored eyes, and a wild exultation leaped into the voice.

"'I have trained and perfected my soul. I have attained to the topmost heights. I am an Adept! I am immortal! Edward Morlant is indeed dead. But his soul commences its second incarnation in the same earthly body to-day.'

"'Then the diary is true?' I murmured, hardly knowing what I said.

"'Yes, the diary is true. Please give it to me.'

"'Why do you want it?'

"'To destroy it. It contains much that you should not see, much that you would not understand. For you are not an Adept. Moreover, there is trouble and strife recorded in it, paltry trouble and strife of weak humanity, which ended with Edward Morlant's death.'"

Betty paused again, and Sally noticed for the first time that her hands were empty.

"Why, where is the diary?" she asked.

"I'll tell you in a minute," replied Betty, her lips trembling a little. "I'm coming to the nasty part now. . . .

"I want you to understand that somehow or other I had got past being frightened just at this moment. It was quite clear that I was in no danger, and though I couldn't reckon things up at all, I was very interested and felt as though I were talking to some normal human being.

"'But I want to read the diary,' I said. 'If you are dead, it cannot harm you. You have done so much for me that I want to learn all I can about you, to understand you and to love your memory.'

"'You must not read it, little Elizabeth,' replied Edward Morlant sadly. 'If you know all, you will turn from me as your mother did. You will hate my memory. I have come back for no other purpose than to destroy that diary.'

"I stood wondering. Those oddly colored eyes were glistening with tears, and I've never heard of a ghost crying.

"'I don't believe you're dead at all!' I said suddenly. 'I believe you're just as alive as I am!'

"'In a way, you are right.' A slow wistful smile transformed the pale features into surprising beauty. 'I am more alive than you are, for I can never die. But he whom the world knew as Edward Morlant has been dead six days— buried three.'

"I was still trying to make up my mind what to think about all this when I saw the face in front of me begin to change. The beautiful smile faded, and a most ghastly expression took his place. Oh, it was horrible! It makes me sick even to remember it. The features became drawn and contorted, the eyes staring and terrible.

"It looked like fear to me, deadly paralyzing fear, but it might just as well have been mad, raging fury. I had no time to decide. The candle in my hand went out, leaving me in utter darkness. The book was roughly snatched from my other hand. And then—well, I was all taut and keyed up, I suppose. I screamed and I—I fainted."

"Then you don't know what became of—of Edward Morlant?" asked Sally.

"I know nothing more."

There was a little silence.

"It is a most inexplicable occurrence," said Mr. Broughton, uneasily fingering his mustache. It was obvious that he was very deeply affected by Betty's recital. "I have never heard of anything like it, anything approaching it, in fact. I suppose it is not possible, Miss Elizabeth, that with your overwrought nerves, and some trick of the shadows—"

"Don't be a fool, man!" interrupted Betty wearily. "I'm not a child."

"Besides, the diary is gone," added Sally.

"True," admitted the solicitor thoughtfully. "The diary, as you say, is gone."

Sally squeezed her friend's arm in sympathy.

"I don't know what to think about this," she murmured. "What's your honest opinion, Betty? Do you believe—?"

"I don't know what to believe." There were tears in Betty's voice. The ordeal through which she had passed had shaken her. "Oh, I wish I'd never come to this hateful house! What can I think about it? What can I believe? I saw him. I spoke to him. And he's dead! I've never believed in such things before. But the only other explanation is that he never died. And that won't do." She shivered and clung to Sally's arm. "No, that won't do at all. For he was not an ordinary man. There was something about him . . . he was altogether different from an ordinary man." Her voice took on a higher pitch. "At the end, he was—horrible—and—and—"

"Of course the old boy's not an ordinary man," interposed Mr. Knight cheerfully. "You forget that he's been promoted to a Mahatma."

Whether the effect was intentional or not, his words certainly acted as a cold douche, and brought Betty back from the verge of hysteria, on which she was hovering. Her pale cheeks flushed as she looked at him.

"Your ankle, apparently, is quite recovered," she said coldly. "I see no further reason why you should remain here."

Mr. Knight's leg immediately gave way beneath him.

"On the contrary," he protested, limping around to demonstrate the fact, "it is more painful than ever. I made it worse running up the stairs when you screamed."

"You expect me to believe you?"

"I do, lady. Besides, I don't want to go just now when the fun is starting. I want to stay and see this jolly old friend of yours. I consider he's been very rude to you, and I want to make him come back and apologize."

Again a phrase used during that dreadful episode in the fog! Betty's eyes narrowed as she watched him, trying to read his thoughts. His face still wore its fatuous smile and gave her no information. But now she was sure, sure that it was he who had saved her from the river.

And with her certainty came a strange sense of comfort. It was true that his unexplained presence here suggested that she was still in danger, that the ghoul who had tried once to murder her was in the vicinity and might make another attempt on her life. It seemed, even, that this unknown enemy of hers must be in the house at the moment since Mr. Clarence Knight dare not openly declare himself but had to be content with veiled allusions to their previous meeting. Despite all this, and the apparent foolishness of her protector, she felt that she could rely on him, that he would not fail her.

"I think we'd better have a look round for the old boy," he went on helpfully. "It's not likely that we'll find him if he's developed this magic carpet habit. But we might get a sniff of either brimstone or the odor of sanctity."

He did not seem at all worried or perturbed, but apparently treated the whole business as a joyous adventure. Betty wondered how much he knew. She decided to ask him outright at the first opportunity.

"Yes, we'll make a search," she agreed. "I—I'm sorry I doubted your word."

"You'll not want me any more, then, Missie?" suggested Bidgood, his thin voice faltering a little. "I'll go downstairs and clear away the tea tray."

"Not at all, old chappie, not at all!" protested Mr. Knight. "You come with us. We'll want you to show us round."

Candles in hand, they thoroughly explored the second story, starting at the room where Betty had seen Morlant, the room in which he had slept during life. But their search was entirely fruitless. They did not even get what Mr. Knight called a smell of their quarry.

Their failure, however, did not disturb his serenity.

"Bad luck!" he said cheerfully as they emerged from the last room. "He must have a very magic carpet. But most likely he'll turn up again. Anyhow, we'll hope for the best."

"You are an extremely foolish young man," Broughton rebuked him. "There is not the slightest indication that what Miss Elizabeth saw had any existence except in her—"

Betty was not prepared to listen to any more of this kind of talk.

"Look here, Mr. Broughton," she interrupted angrily, "if you know so much about all this, why don't you—"

A dog's frenzied barking from downstairs cut short her challenge.

"That's Rover," she muttered, startled. "W-what's the matter?"

In a moment, the dog's excited bark changed abruptly to an agonized yelping.

"There's someone down there," said Sally, her eyes wide with apprehension. "And—and Rover's frightened!"

They stood motionless, listening. Sally had put into words the thought that was in the mind of each one of them. What could there be downstairs that would frighten the dog?

A creaking sound came from the direction of the stairs. Mr. Knight rapidly blew out all the candles.

"I say," began the solicitor, "what on earth do you—"

"Be quiet, you fool!"

They stood in the darkness, waiting. Downstairs, the dog was whining uneasily. Apart from this, a dead silence reigned in the old house.

The creaking noise was repeated. A gleam of light appeared at the end of the corridor. Sally's hand found Betty's and gripped it frantically.

The light grew stronger. It was clear that someone was approaching the corner of the corridor, someone walking slowly, carefully, stealthily.

Betty's heart was beating as though it would choke her. She felt that she could not breathe. Her eyes, fixed and staring, gazed at the quivering patch of light as though hypnotized.

Suddenly a figure turned the corner and came into full view. The candle it was carrying lit up a familiar face, a pale, studious face with something odd about the eyes.

Betty could not completely stifle the cry which rose to her throat.

"It's Edward Morlant!" she gasped. "Edward Morlant again!"

10

THE TUNNEL

The mysterious newcomer must have heard Betty's half suppressed exclamation. He cast a startled glance into the shadows where the little search party was standing, then darted into the nearest room, dropping his candle as he did so.

The corridor was plunged in utter darkness. Mr. Broughton's heavy breathing was plainly audible. Sally gripped Betty's hand until it hurt. For a moment, no one moved or spoke.

Then Mr. Knight's groping fingers closed firmly on Bidgood's shoulder.

"Is that your master, old chappie?" he whispered. "Is that Edward Morlant?"

The old man was trembling beyond control.

"Y-yes," he stammered. "That's Mr. Edward."

"You're quite sure? You haven't a doubt about it?"

"It must be him," faltered the servant. "It couldn't be anyone else. Yes, it is him!"

"Then we'll ask for an interview." Mr. Knight struck a match and grinned at the others. "We'd better not all go together, or he might be embarrassed. Suppose you folks stay here while I see if he's in a good temper."

Without waiting for a reply, he blew out the match and tiptoed away.

The seconds passed. Betty could neither see nor hear anything of him, but she guessed that he was listening at the door of the room into which Edward Morlant had disappeared. She was surprised to find that most of her excitement had been displaced by a keen anxiety lest any harm should come to him. The others stood silent and motionless.

A sudden crashing noise startled them. Knight had thrown open the door of the room. They heard the scrape of a match, and his cheery voice rang out.

"Walk up! Walk up! Admission free to the peep-show. But bring your own illumination, please."

They hurried forward as the match flared, lighting up the open doorway. Once inside the room, they halted, uncertain. Sally looked meaningly at Betty. Mr. Knight was seated on the bed, lighting his candle. Apart from him, the room was empty.

"Why!" cried Broughton. "There's no one here!"

"Stated with precision and accuracy," agreed Mr. Knight.

"Well, where is he?" asked Betty. "Where's he gone? He must be somewhere about. A man can't vanish—"

Mr. Knight rose briskly from the bed.

"There's no limit to what a Mahatma can do, lady, he said solemnly. "Miss Poulter will tell you that. But he *might* be hiding in that wardrobe."

He limped across the room to a large wardrobe built into the wall. The others watched in mystified silence. Bidgood edged up to Betty. His dim old eyes were worried, and he fidgeted nervously.

"You'll not want me now, Missie," he suggested. "Shall I go downstairs and clear away—?"

"No!" snapped Betty. She was annoyed with him because it was so apparent that he was somehow mixed up with what was going on. He had tried twice to get away,

offering an excuse that would not bear consideration. He
knew more than he would tell, and he was frightened. Even
as he stood there before her he was trembling with fear. In
a way, she felt sorry for him. But her pity was swamped by
anger because he would not tell what he knew.

"No," she repeated. "You'll stop here with us." The room
was very similar to that in which Betty and Sally had slept
last night, with its massive four-poster bed, thick carpet,
and substantial furniture. It had been Edward Morlant's
bedroom during his lifetime, but there was little to show
this unless the big, modern, double-doored wardrobe was
an indication.

Mr. Knight had flung open the doors of this and was
peering curiously inside.

"Quite a tailor's shop!" he murmured, holding his candle nearer. "But I suppose these magic carpet stunts must
be rather hard on clothes."

There were, as a matter of fact, besides dressing gowns
and overcoats, four suits neatly folded and hung in the
wardrobe. These were of the heavy, good quality broad-
cloth such as old-fashioned country gentlemen frequently wear. There was nothing in any way remarkable about
them except that they were all exactly alike.

To the surprise of everyone, Mr. Knight commenced
removing the clothes from the wardrobe, and piling them
in a neat heap on the floor.

"Whatever are you doing?" asked Betty, leaving the
others to cross towards him.

"Studying, lady," he replied, without pausing in his
task. "I'm an expert in furniture, you know, and this wardrobe interests me. I'll be at your service again in a moment."

When all the clothes were removed, he stepped inside
the wardrobe, and ran his hands carefully over the smooth
surface of its interior. Sally watched him with open eyes.

Betty noticed that both Broughton and Bidgood seemed anxious and ill at ease.

She was growing impatient at the delay herself when Mr. Knight chuckled. Almost immediately, one half of the back of the wardrobe slid silently behind the other, revealing a large black cavity in the wall.

"A simple little spring," said he, turning round with a grin. "Here is a way a Mahatma could take his departure if he didn't want to use his magic carpet."

Betty caught at Bidgood's arm.

"You knew about this, didn't you?" she asked accusingly.

"N-no, Missie," faltered the old man, looking at her with shamed pleading in his dim eyes.

It was fairly obvious that he was lying. But a strange suspicion was growing up in Betty's mind, a suspicion which as yet she would not formulate even to herself. If this were true, the old servant's actions were probably prompted by the highest motives, and she could not blame him. She shrugged her shoulders and climbed into the wardrobe to join Mr. Knight.

"Welcome, lady," he greeted her. "You'd like to see the wheels go round?"

He showed her two small protuberances, no bigger than the heads of small nails, in one corner of the wardrobe. He pressed heavily on one of these and the movable panel slid back into place. Pressure on the other caused it to open again, and he held the candle so that she could see into the cavity.

Just inside was a large and complicated piece of machinery which was evidently well cared for.

"A little old-fashioned," said he, "yet evidently efficient and electrified by means of these two accumulators. Even a Mahatma, you will notice, can't afford to despise a drop of oil and some strong springs. Shall we go down?"

A flight of stone steps led from the hole in the wall to darkness below. As Betty looked down, she could see two luminous pin points of light in the distance, and realized that two small eyes were watching her from the depths.

"Rats," she murmured, with a little shiver. "I hate 'em. Still, we'd better risk it, hadn't we?"

"There'll be lots of 'em, I expect," said Mr. Knight encouragingly. "But I really would like to find the jolly old sport if possible."

"Then we'll all go," whispered Betty. "I'm not going to leave either Mr. Broughton or Bidgood up here. I believe they both knew about this passage. You'd better go first, I suppose. Then Mr. Broughton. Sally next, and Bidgood. And I'll come last to keep an eye on you all."

She turned and communicated her decision to the others.

"But, Miss Elizabeth," protested the solicitor, "surely you do not intend to penetrate into this old passage. It cannot have been used for years. The air is probably poisonous, and I should consider such a project highly dangerous."

"I don't think the air will worry us," replied Betty with a short laugh. "Anyhow, we're going!"

There was nothing more to be said, as Mr. Broughton realized. One by one the little party filed into the wardrobe, and commenced to descend the stairs.

The passage was both narrow and low, so that they had to stoop. Apparently it had been built in the thickness of the wall many years ago, for the mortar between the large stones of which it was constructed was crumbling. The steep steps were littered with dust and accumulated debris, and spiders had woven diligently in every corner.

At the bottom of the flight of stairs, a horizontal, tunnel-like passage led off to the right.

"Travel by subway," grinned Mr. Knight, plunging into this without hesitation. The other had perforce to follow him.

It was an eerie business stumbling along, crouching almost on hands and knees, between the narrow stone walls, accompanied by the flickering shadows thrown by the candles. More than once, Betty caught herself glancing uneasily over her shoulder into the darkness behind. She wished she had been somewhere in the middle of the party. She tried to keep her wandering gaze on Bidgood, who was stolidly plodding along just in front of her. Luckily, she saw no more rats.

Soon the passage opened out into what was almost a room. The roof, composed of stone flags, was supported by beams, and the four walls formed a square some sixteen feet across.

Mr. Knight halted and looked curiously around. The usual grin had left his features, which were now alert and thoughtful.

"Piccadilly Circus," he remarked, "I should think we're just under the hall at present. Suppose it's no use asking you, Bidgood, if there's any direct communication?"

"I—I don't know. No, sir," stammered the servant.

"There doesn't seem to be much you do know, does there? Never mind, old chappie. We'll have a good look round later. In the meantime, we'll follow our Mahatma's probable course. He must find these relics of more turbulent days extremely useful in his profession or whatever you call it."

On the opposite side of the square was another tunnel similar to the one from which they had just emerged. Still keeping the same order, they stooped again, and cautiously proceeded.

Before long the character of the passage changed. The walls became wet and slimy, the floor thick with mud. Betty shivered at the beetles and centipedes which scuttled away from the light. She realized that they were now under the garden.

The air was dank and heavy, and progress over the slippery, uneven floor called for care. It seemed to Betty that they slithered and stumbled for miles, though the actual distance could not have been more than three or four hundred yards, before they came to a halt in a sort of rocky cave, where fresh night air from without dispelled the mustiness of the atmosphere.

"Thank Heaven that's done!" she exclaimed, ruefully surveying her muddied shoes and stockings. "Where are we? And how do we get out of here?"

Mr. Knight was searching round the walls of the cave, poking his candle into every crevice in the rocks.

"Here we are!" he cried jubilantly. "Here's the way we get out. Those of us who can, I mean. It looks as though we'll have to leave Mr. Broughton behind."

There was a natural, perpendicular cleft in the rocks. It was very narrow; and the solicitor had, indeed, considerable trouble in squeezing through. Eventually, however, the exit was safely effected, and they all emerged from the cave and stood looking eagerly about them.

The night was calm and still. The flames of their candles, burning long and steady, did not even flicker. There was no moon, but the frosty starlight enabled them to distinguish their surroundings clearly.

They were standing in a thick shrubbery at the end of the garden. Close behind them rose the grass-covered mound inside which was the cave. The narrow entrance to this was so cleverly concealed by bushes that they could now see no sign of it.

Betty looked across at the black bulk of Hameldon House silhouetted against the jeweled sky.

"It's pretty obvious what happened, isn't it?" she said, a certain relief in her voice. "I'm glad to know that he was a living man and not—anything else. He got into the house by the secret passage, and after I talked to him in the corridor he escaped by the same way. Then, while we were all upstairs, he just walked in by the front door. I think that's the explanation."

"Sounds pretty thin to me, lady," remarked Mr. Knight. "Doesn't seem to explain—but does a Mahatma need any explanation?"

"Do spirits or ghosts need secret passages for their wandering?" asked Betty tartly.

"There's something in that," interposed Sally. "It almost seems that he must have been alive, that—but all the same, Betty, Rover was frightened of him."

"Y-yes. I'd forgotten that."

"And it's so very important, isn't it? If he'd been well, real, surely his own dog would have been delighted to see him. Instead of which—and, you know, dogs are always scared of anything supernatural."

"Oh, dear!" Betty sighed irritably. "I thought I was seeing daylight, and now you've upset everything again. I'd quite decided in my own mind that Mr. Broughton and Bidgood have been conspiring to deceive us, that Edward Morlant never died, but is acting some silly sort of play for reasons best known to himself. But I'd forgotten about the dog. And it is important. It means such a lot. Besides—" her voice trembled a little, "—when I think again it's an impossible idea. It wasn't an ordinary living man I spoke to in the corridor. It wasn't! It wasn't! It's no use trying to convince myself otherwise. No normal man could have acted as he did."

"I assure you, Miss Elizabeth," began the solicitor, "that your suspicions of myself—"

"Oh, yes!" interrupted Sally. "You're above suspicion, aren't you? Quite above it. All the same, you knew—"

"Really, Miss Poulter, I cannot imagine what has caused you to think—"

The two of them entered into a lively altercation, and Betty took the opportunity of turning aside to Mr. Knight, who had moved a little way apart.

"What's your opinion about it all, Mr. Knight?" she asked. "Do you think he was real, or—not?"

His fatuous smile was very pronounced.

"I never think, lady," he responded brightly. "It sends the blood pressure up."

"I wonder why you pretend to be such a fool," she whispered. "I know you're not, really. I'd like to thank you for saving my life two nights ago."

"Nothing to thank me for. Mere selfishness on my part. Pure, undiluted selfishness. It's such a joy to see you living!"

Betty flushed. "Why did you come here?"

"To see you, of course."

"Don't be silly. I wish you'd tell me the truth."

"The truth is, lady," said Mr. Knight solemnly, "that your eyes are very beautiful."

"Oh!"

"Especially when they're angry," he continued, with an appreciative chuckle.

His facetiousness in such circumstances annoyed Betty intensely. She shrugged her shoulders and turned abruptly away. As she moved, she caught sight of a streak of light which had just cut into the black bulk of Hameldon House.

"Look!" she cried. "Look! The door is open!"

They all turned eagerly towards the house. There was no doubt that the door was open, the light from the hall showing clearly through it. As they watched the narrow slit broadened. A dark figure passed quickly across it. Faint yet clear, they could hear the howling of the dog inside. Then the door closed.

"Gosh! We've not finished," murmured Sally. "Someone's either gone in or come out."

"Gone in, I hope," said Mr. Knight cheerfully. "Something seems to tell me we're going to see our Mahatma again soon."

11

The Stranger

A hush fell on the little search party at Mr. Clarence Knight's words. To Betty, in particular, they sounded ominous. After all, she thought, their discovery of the secret passage had led them nowhere. It had, indeed, for a time strengthened her suspicion that what they had been following was nothing more or less than Edward Morlant in the flesh. Then Sally's remark about the dog, and her own recollection of the incident in the corridor had disturbed her so that now she did not know what to think. She could not bring herself to believe that a man could return from the dead in this way, and yet there seemed to be no other explanation. It had been a great relief to her that they had not overtaken their quarry, and she had hoped that they had seen the last of him. It was not particularly pleasant to think that he had returned to the house.

"There's no telling what'll happen now if it is him," she murmured dolefully. "I've half a mind to leave, and let him have the place to himself."

"Oh, don't spoil sport, lady," begged Mr. Knight. "Let's go back. It'd break my heart if I didn't get the chance of meeting him."

It was strange that, ever since he had discovered the secret of the wardrobe, he seemed to have taken command and no one was disposed to question his authority. Even

117

now, despite their reluctance, they all accepted his suggestion without demur, and obediently started off towards
the house.

"Hey! Wait a minute," he cried. "Not all together. We'd
better watch both ways, or we'll be playing peep-bo all
night. You, old chappie," to Bidgood, "take Mr. Broughton
and Miss Poulter to that door; and you, lady," to Betty,
"will perhaps accompany me back by the subway."

They split up as indicated without remark.

"Keep a good watch on the door," he advised Sally.
"And make Mr. Broughton tackle any Mahatma who comes
out. But whatever happens please don't go in until we open
the door for you."

"Right-o!" agreed Sally. "We'll wait for you."

She set off towards the house with her two companions.
Mr. Knight pushed aside the bushes and held them so that
Betty could pass through the crevice into the cave.

"I don't like this a bit," she said, as they retraced their
way into the wet, muddy passage. "Why did you suggest
me coming with you?"

"I thought it would be safer," he replied briefly.

"Safer? Then why send Sally the other way?"

"I don't think Miss Poulter's in any danger." He grinned
back over his shoulder. "Besides, it's your own idea that
Broughton and the old servant chappie should not be left
alone together. They're rather naughty boys, aren't they?
They certainly do tell stories. I'm with you there, lady,
with you all the way. But I think they're quite harmless."

Betty made no reply. It seemed clear to her that Mr.
Knight had ideas very similar to her own. She wished she
knew whether he really believed that Morlant was dead;
but if he didn't want to tell her, she wouldn't ask him
again.

The tunnel under the garden did not appear to be so
long this time. They soon emerged into the open space

under the hall, and stood for a moment listening. Everything in the house above was quiet. They could hear no
sound but a trickle of water in the passage they had just
left.

"Doesn't seem to be much doing," said Mr. Knight,
stooping to enter the second passage. "But come on. We'll
soon know if our friend has returned."

For some reason he appeared to be in a hurry. He pushed
forward at such a rate that Betty could hardly keep up with
him. She wondered if he were expecting something else to
happen, and decided that he must be. She grew breathless
in her determination not to be left behind.

It occurred to her as she followed him that she would
have felt very frightened and miserable if he had not been
in the house. She had an idea that in some mysterious way
danger threatened her, and yet she was not frightened.
Now that she had made up her mind about him, she could
face anything without fear so long as he was near. It was
strange, she thought, that she had come to rely so much
on any man in so short a time. Of course, he had saved
her life two days ago; and the very fact that he thought it
necessary to play the fool indicated that he knew more
than she did. But even taking this into account, she
couldn't understand why his mere presence should be a
comfort to her.

It was such a pity that he wouldn't talk sense. Betty realized that probably he had some very good reason for acting as he did, but she would have given much to know just
what had brought him to the house, and what he thought
of Edward Morlant's apparent return from the dead.

This latter question, as it happened, was answered when
they stepped out of the wardrobe.

"It didn't take you long to tumble to this," remarked
Betty, as Mr. Knight pressed the spring to close the opening.

He turned to her with a slow smile very different from his usual grin.

"Well, you know," he said, almost apologetically, "I don't believe much in magic carpets."

She looked into his steady gray eyes and saw that they were serious.

"You mean that you sought for a matter-of-fact explanation of Edward Morlant's disappearance?" she asked eagerly.

"Just that, Miss Harlan."

"Then you think that he is not dead? That we saw him actually in the flesh—still alive?

"Quite frankly, I do not understand exactly what is happening here," he replied. "There are many things which seem to contradict one another But one thing is sure—I do not believe in any supernatural explanation."

"I'm glad of that," said Betty gratefully "Because I don't—not really. At least, I don't want to. It seems so impossible, doesn't it? But every time I think of that face and the horrible change in it—"

She broke off abruptly, clutching his arm, as a shrill cry echoed through the house, a cry so full of agonized fear that it struck a cold chill to her heart.

For a moment they stood in startled silence, the scream ringing in their ears. Then Mr. Knight hurried to the door, dragging Betty with him.

"It came from downstairs," he muttered. "I hope to God they haven't come in!"

Wild fears for the safety of Sally and her two companions filled Betty's mind as they raced along the dark corridor. She could not imagine what might have happened to them, but it seemed certain that someone was hurt. When they reached the top of the stairs, she could not nerve herself to look down.

"It's not them!" cried Mr. Knight, ignoring grammar in his excitement. "It's a stranger!"

Still holding her arm, he led her more slowly down, she glanced over the stairs. Recovering her courage, she glanced over the banisters. The figure of a man lay sprawled on the stone floor of the hall. She sighed with relief to see that it was no one she knew.

"Who can it be?" she whispered, awe-stricken by this new development. "Is he—dead?"

"Looks like it," he replied laconically. "I don't know him from Adam."

As they neared the bottom of the stairs, the dog, which had been crouched, whimpering, in a distant corner, came running towards them, frisking around in a very ecstasy of delight. Betty caressed him mechanically, her eyes still fixed on the sprawled figure on the floor.

It was that of a man of middle age, who looked as though he had once been a gentleman. His clothes were worn and shabby, but his linen was clean. The bloated face indicated the probable reason for his downfall, and his hands, white and slender as a woman's, showed that he was not acquainted with manual labor. His clean-shaven features might have been pleasant but for the unmistakable ravages of dissipation.

Despite the general unpleasantness of his appearance, Betty felt a warm glow of pity for the man surge through her.

"I wonder who he is?" she asked again. "Is he—dead?"

Mr. Knight looked up from his examination of the limp body and grinned.

"Dead?" he echoed. "No, he's not dead. He's asleep!"

"Asleep?"

"Yes—and drunk."

He rose to his feet and crossed to the door to admit Sally and her companions.

"We've found someone," he announced. "But it's not our Mahatma. Better come and see if you know him."

Apparently no one recognized the newcomer. There was no doubt that both Broughton and Bidgood were as mystified as the others.

"No one knows him?" said Mr. Knight cheerfully. "Well, he's here, undamaged, but gloriously drunk, whoever he is and however he got here."

"Perhaps it was him we saw come in," suggested Sally. "And in that case—"

"You mean perhaps Edward Morlant didn't return to the house," interposed Betty quickly. "I thought of that."

"We heard a most curious noise," began Broughton, glancing round uneasily. "Like a scream or—"

"It was a scream," put in Bidgood, his dim old eyes full of anxiety.

"It must have been this man calling out," observed Sally. "Though it sounded to me—"

"We'll waken the gentleman," said Mr. Knight, shaking the recumbent figure. "Even though this is a free country, we're entitled to some explanation of his presence."

After a little vigorous treatment, the man roused from his stupor. For a moment acute terror showed in his bloodshot eyes, then they became dull and vacant again. His mouth hung slackly open, and he gazed straight in front of him as though unconscious of his surroundings.

"Well, my friend," prompted Mr. Knight, "you've had what is known technically as a skinful, haven't you?"

The stranger spoke with an effort.

"I've been seeing things," he said, his voice hoarse and almost toneless.

"That's hardly surprising, is it? Quite a common result of a skinful. But cheer up. We're all in the same box. We've been seeing things, too. What particular line do your visions take?"

"I've seen a ghost."

"Good! So've we. Who was yours?"

"Edward Morlant!" The man was in deadly earnest, though the dull monotony of his voice showed that he was still dazed. "I've seen the ghost of Edward Morlant."

"Here?"

"Yes."

"You knew him?"

"All my life. I haven't seen him for years. But I heard of his death."

"You've just come in?"

"Yes. I don't know how long since. I rang and rang at the bell. No one answered. I tried the door. It was unfastened. I came in. And he was standing at that door. . . ."

The man's hands twitched, and his voice suddenly rose high and shrill.

"He was standing at that door, I tell you!" he went on, pointing to the library. "I knew him at once. He hadn't altered a bit. And his queer eyes seemed to look through me. Through me, I tell you, not at me! He came towards me with a smile. A smile. Yes, like a devil from Hell! I tried to run away. I couldn't face him, I tell you. I couldn't face that smile. I slipped and fell. And—and—"

"And you remember nothing more, of course. Very appropriate ending—and perhaps as well for you. Well, don't be downhearted. It may console you to know that you're the second person to have that experience to-night. You can regard us as brothers and sisters in distress. Now perhaps you'll tell us who you are, and what you are doing here?"

The fear had vanished from the drunken man's face as he listened to Knight, and a trace of cunning crept into it. He staggered to his feet, and stood swaying dangerously.

"Perhaps you'll tell me who *you* are, and what you are doing in my house?" he hiccoughed, shaking an unsteady finger in the direction of his questioner.

"Is this your house? Oh, pardon me. I didn't know."

"Well, don't you forget it. From now on, this is my house. And I want to know who all these people—"

The man's voice trailed away into silence. His blood-shot eyes had fixed on Betty, and she could see the slow dilatation of the pupils. His face blanched and his jaw dropped.

"Oh, God!" he shrieked suddenly. "Take her away! Take her away!"

They all stared at him in amazement. He covered his face with trembling hands to shut out the light.

"Please go away," he moaned. "Oh, go away! Elizabeth! Elizabeth! I've seen him. And he's dead. And you're dead, to, Elizabeth. You know you are. Don't look at me. Don't come near me. Elizabeth, if you come back, too, I'll go mad. Mad, I tell you! Go away! Go away!"

An almost unbearable nausea swept over Betty. A horrible suspicion had sprung up in her mind and would not be thrust down. She struggled to fight against her faintness. When she could move, she stepped forward with pale cheeks but a firm mouth.

"Look at me!" she cried, pulling the man's hands away from his flabby face. "Look at me! I'm not Elizabeth. I'm her daughter. Who are you?"

He shrank from her, uncomprehending, gazing at her as though fascinated.

"I'm Elizabeth's daughter," she repeated. "Do you understand? Her daughter. Who are you?"

Some intelligence returned to his staring eyes.

"I—I'm Gerald Harlan," he faltered.

Betty drew back as though he had struck her.

"Gerald Harlan?" she echoed. "My father?" And once again: "My father?"

The man had recovered his wits. A slow, cunning leer spread over his bloated features.

"Yes, my dear," he replied. "I am your father."

A short silence followed. Betty's lips were quivering. Her breast rose and fell unevenly. She gazed horrified at the wretched creature before her.

"Oh, you're not!" she cried suddenly, holding out her hands as though to thrust him away from her. "You're not! It can't be true!"

"It is true," he said, trying to take one of her outstretched hands. "I am your father. I have come to look after you."

"A truly touching family reunion!" broke in a harsh, sarcastic voice. "A most affecting example of paternal devotion!"

Startled, they all swung around to see who had spoken. Standing calmly in the library door was the man they had seen in the corridor upstairs, the man with the pale face and the oddly colored eyes.

"Edward Morlant!" gasped Gerald Harlan.

"Our old Mahatma!" exclaimed Mr. Knight. "Well, this is an unexpected pleasure."

12

An Occult Power

The man in the doorway smiled, an evil, vicious smile. Betty remembered the drunkard's description of it as devilish, and understood something of his fear.

She felt Sally touch her arm, and glanced in the direction of her pointing finger. Edward Morlant's dog stood rigid, brown eyes fixed on its master. Its tail draggled between its legs, and its teeth showed in a snarl.

"Look!" whispered Sally, her face flushed and excited. "It's scared to death!"

Betty nodded. Her gaze traveled slowly back from the dog to the drunkard who had just claimed to be her father, and then to the man who was supposed to be dead.

"Yes, I'm Edward Morlant, at your service," he continued, throwing the door wide open. "Come in. I think you'll find it warmer in here."

The situation was bizarre and incredible. No one appeared in any great hurry to accept his invitation. Gerald Harlan, bewildered and still stupefied with drink, stared at the speaker as though doubting the evidence of his senses. Both Broughton and Bidgood were uneasy, casting furtive glances at one another. Sally kept close to Betty, gripping her arm. It was Mr. Knight, cheerful and interested, who set the example and led them into the library in the wake of Morlant. The dog crept in after them, and at once retreated to the furtherest corner of the room.

Betty stood like one stunned. The sudden advent of this man who called himself her father, followed by the equally unexpected reappearance of Edward Morlant, had fired her mind into a whirl of wonder and incredulity, out of which she found it impossible to crystallize any definite opinion. She felt quite incapable of thinking. She looked vacantly round the room, surprised in a vague sort of way to find it just as she had left it less than an hour ago, with the lamps burning steadily, and the remains of tea still on the table.

Morlant seated himself at one side of the hearth, close to the dying fire. She noticed now that he carried the little red diary in his hand.

"Sit down, all of you, sit down!" he chuckled unpleasantly. "You seem to have been running about the house pretty energetically, and I'm sure you're tired."

He looked round at them with a sneer, his oddly colored eyes glinting evilly.

"There are two of you I don't know," he continued, pointing first to Sally. "This, I suppose, is a friend of yours, Elizabeth?"

"Yes, it's Miss Poulter," mumbled Betty, wondering what else she could say.

"And you?" asked Morlant, turning to Mr. Clarence Knight. "Who are you?"

"Oh, I'm just a chance acquaintance," he grinned. "An intruder, in fact. To tell you the truth, I represent the well-known furnishing firm of Lepage, respected all over the world for fair dealing and honest workmanship." He dived into his pocket. "If you could spare the time, I'd like to show you one of our catalogues, and see if I could interest you in—"

"You can save your breath," interrupted Morlant. "Why should I buy furniture?"

"Oh, of course!" Mr. Knight's fatuous grin broadened. "I'd forgotten, for the moment. Mahatmas don't need to buy anything, do they?"

"You dare to scoff?" The other glared at him, and Betty held her breath, fearing some kind of outbreak. Immediately, however, his face cleared. "It's quite evident that your knowledge is confined to furniture," he sneered.

He looked round at their perturbed faces again, and rubbed his hands together.

"A most interesting little gathering," he commented. "An old friend of childhood days, an heiress, a faithful retainer, and an equally faithful solicitor—what could a man who has returned from the grave desire more? Not to speak of a furniture expert and a most charming beauty specialist."

Sally started. "You know who I am?"

"Of course, so soon as I heard your name. There is little concerning my dear Elizabeth that I do not know. There is, indeed, little concerning any of you that I do not know. You, for instance, Broughton: I have learned that you are more of a fool than I thought. I did not ask you to fill my house with a crowd of strangers immediately after my death."

It seemed strange to Betty that the solicitor should attempt to justify himself.

"I—it was not my fault," he stammered, fidgeting nervously with his eyeglasses. "Miss Elizabeth insisted on bringing Miss Poulter from London with her, and this—er—furnishing gentleman is here simply because he has had an accident. As to the other—"

"You are a fool, nevertheless!" snarled Morlant. "Any decent man of affairs would have known how to overcome such small difficulties. Bidgood here would have done better."

He paused, fingering the book in his hands.

"I note that you have all been reading portions of this private diary which I made during life," he went on. "Unluckily, I arrived too late to prevent you. It was you, I suppose, who found it, Elizabeth?"

"Yes," replied Betty. "It—it was quite an accident."

"I know it was. You would never have opened the drawer otherwise. I was foolish not to destroy the diary before I died. But it contained some information which—no matter. Your finding it was an unforeseen occurrence. I will destroy it now."

He placed the open book on the fire, and for a while watched the curling flames lick at the closely written pages.

"I had intended to keep the fact of my immortality secret," he continued. "I had not considered the possibility of any one discovering that secret. Unfortunately, it was necessary for me to recover the diary from your inquisitive hands, and so I had to show myself. This has complicated the situation, and will necessitate an entire change in my plans. The fact that you all know I have returned from the dead is dangerous to me, most dangerous. I cannot leave you here in possession of that knowledge. I hardly know what to do."

There was an ominous tone in his harsh voice that made Betty shudder. It sounded as though he were seriously considering the possibility of killing them all just because they knew his secret. And she felt convinced that, whether he were mortal or not, this strange creature was quite capable of deciding on such an action and carrying it out.

"Well, it's no use crying over spilt milk, he went on. "The harm is done, and we must find some way out of the difficulty. Luckily, your reading of the diary was cut short before you had the opportunity of learning too much from it; otherwise, the situation would have been quite impossible. As it is, nothing will be gained by further mystery. We may as well understand one another. Beginning with you, Harlan—why are you here?"

Gerald Harlan did not reply. Bemused and stupefied, without the slightest comprehension of what was going on, he stared blankly at the speaker, his slack mouth open and awry.

"This is your esteemed father, Elizabeth," sneered Morlant. "This is the—the thing for which your mother left me. I hope you're proud of him."

Betty was silent. It did not occur to her to doubt his words. She felt sure now that the drunkard's claim to be her father was genuine. The knowledge brought a dull pain to her heart. She had always hated his very name because of the way he had treated her mother. And now it was horrible to think that she was the daughter of such a wreck. She loathed the sight of his bloated, dissipated face, and his weak, slack mouth. Yet she was conscious of a deep undercurrent of pity for him, and knew that this pity was a blood tie.

Overshadowing her private troubles, however, her amazement and uneasiness at the present incredible situation increased. Here was a man apparently live and well, who was supposed to be dead. And not only was he supposed to be dead, but he talked as though he were dead, talked of his death and return from the grave in the most matter-of-fact way. His solicitor apologized to him as though he had just been on a journey. Yet his old manservant was in a pitiable state of anxiety and fear. And his own dog sat in the furthest corner of the room, snarling at him! Betty could see no rhyme or reason in it all. She had never believed in spirits or ghosts; but what little she had to guide her at present pointed to the fact that Edward

Morlant had, indeed, achieved the immortality of which he spoke, that she was in the presence of one actually risen from the dead.

He lifted himself slowly from his chair now, and shook the drunkard by the shoulder.

"Come on, Harlan," he said irritably. "Pull yourself together. Why have you come here?"

The man looked up at him with dull, lusterless eyes.

"I heard you were dead," he said.

"You'd be pleased!"

"I was pleased," agreed Harlan listlessly.

Morlant laughed, and Betty thought that his laugh was worse than his smile.

"You can continue being pleased," he said. "For I am still dead." Then, seeing that the dazed man did not understand: "Well, go on," he added sharply. "You heard I was dead. What difference did this make to you? Why did you come here?"

"I knew that you intended to leave your money to Elizabeth," replied Harlan, speaking as though he were repeating a lesson. "And so I—"

"And so, in your own words, you came to protect her?" sneered Morlant. "Well, I can understand that; You always were a worthless sponger, Harlan."

The other made no reply. But a spark of intelligence lit up in his eyes as though the taunt had got home.

"Your daughter is welcome to your protection," Morlant went on scornfully. "But you'll get nothing here more than her dutiful affection. Though I am dead, I can still control my mortal affairs. You stole my greatest treasure, and I do not forget. You'll never have a penny of mine, you dirty, drunken fool!"

The dully glowing spark in Gerald Harlan's eyes flared up into sudden fury. The meaning of the words had penetrated to his sodden brain, and he lurched from his chair with an oath.

"You'll not call me that!" he gasped, his slack mouth working convulsively. "No man can tell me that and live!"

"You braggart! You empty, noisy blusterer!"

"I'll kill you!" Harlan's voice rose to a hysterical scream. "I'll kill you!"

His shaking fingers fastened round the other's throat. Morlant shook him off easily.

"Kill me?" he sneered. "Why, you fool, I'm dead already! I've been buried three days. The worms would be eating me now but for the fact that I am immortal."

Contemptuously he pushed the trembling drunkard back into his chair.

"Kill me?" he went on, his voice full of mocking laughter. "I wonder how you'd do it? Try to do it. Make the attempt. Shoot me dead. Now. At your feet. Strangle me. Poison me. Anything you like. And I'll be back in a few minutes to laugh at you!"

There was a growing frenzy in his tone that held Betty spellbound. She did not see Harlan in his chair and Sally by her side, both watching Morlant with fearful, fascinated eyes. She did not see the furtive glances, full of uneasiness, that passed between Broughton and Bidgood. Only dimly was she aware of the whimpering of the dog in the corner. Her whole attention was focused on the pale, evil face of this strange creature who was making such impossible claims.

"Kill me?" he echoed again, his features horribly drawn and contorted. "No person in the world could kill me. I have risen above humanity. I have conquered death. I am an Adept! I shall live forever!"

"But really, old chappie—" Mr. Knight's cheerful voice broke in. "You don't really expect us to believe that, eh?"

"Believe what, you young fool?" snarled Morlant, turning on him furiously.

"Why, that you're an honest-to-goodness Mahatma? Miss Poulter, you know, says that a Mahatma can do anything, and I don't—"

"You don't believe what I say? You think I lie?"

"Well, you know, old chappie, it's a bit thick, isn't it? I mean—"

Morlant's face was dark with anger, but suddenly he broke into a harsh laugh.

"I'll show you!" he cried, rubbing his hands together in delight. "Yes, it's a good idea!" His evil laugh rang out again. "I'll show you what a Mahatma can do!"

He looked round at the others with a contemptuous sneer.

"I'll need darkness for this experiment," he said. "Dare you risk it?"

No one answered him. Betty felt faint and sick. An unaccountable horror was creeping over her. She knew that something dreadful was about to happen.

Sally crept closer to her side. She, too, was apprehensive. Her hand trembled as she slipped it into Betty's.

"I'm frightened, Betty," she breathed. "There's something wrong. I can feel it. There's evil brewing. Don't let him—"

"Very well," said Morlant. "Apparently no one objects? Then we'll carry on!"

He crossed swiftly to one of the lamps and turned it out. By the other he paused, looking round with a malevolent smile at those watching him.

"Sure you're not scared?" he asked. "All right! Here's a little Journey into the Unknown for you."

He turned out the lamp, and the room was plunged in darkness. Betty gripped Sally's hand tightly and waited, scarcely daring to breathe. Soon she became conscious that Morlant's face, vague and shadowy, had materialized from the blackness in front of her. A chill shudder ran through her. The next moment, she realized the simple explanation. He had returned to the hearth, and his face was faintly visible because of the dim red glow which still came from the ashes of the diary on the fire.

"That won't do," he muttered, looking at the fire. "I must have complete darkness."

He fumbled on the table until he found the hot water jug, and poured the contents on the glowing embers. There was a shrill hiss, a little cloud of steam—and utter darkness.

"That's better," he said, chuckling. "Now I'll show you what a real Mahatma can do."

All Betty's nerves were taut and tense. She stared into the blackness around her, but could distinguish nothing. The unaccountable horror gripped her unmercifully. Her heart was beating as though it would choke her.

What devilry was this strange, unnatural creature planning? What evil doings was he hatching in the darkness? Fear such as she had never known laid an icy hand upon her. She wanted to scream, but she could not make a sound.

"Now I'll show you," repeated Morlant. He was breathing heavily as though exerting himself at his occult task. "Don't move. Don't dare to move if you value your lives. I'll show you something you've never seen before. I'll show you what secret wisdom and power can do when directed by an Adept. I'll conjure a soul from the depths of Hell for you. I'll fill the room with the spirits of the dead and—"

He stopped speaking with a startling abruptness. There was complete silence in the room.

No one moved or spoke. They stood there in the darkness, tense and breathless, waiting for him to resume.

The seconds slipped by, and no further word came from him. Betty was swaying on her feet, and her little teeth

clenched hard in the effort to fight off a threatening faintness.

What was happening in the darkness? What evil thing
was near? What horror would she see in a moment? . . .

"I say, old chappie!" Mr. Knight's voice broke into the
silence. "You shouldn't keep an audience waiting like this."

There was no reply. But from the furthest corner of
the room came a weird, nerve-racking sound, the piercing,
long drawn-out howl of a dog mourning its dead.

A sudden scraping noise. Mr. Knight had struck a
match. As its light flared up, the imprisoned scream broke
from Betty's throat. For on the floor, almost at their feet,
lay the huddled body of Edward Morlant. And the blood-
stained handle of the dagger protruding from his back
showed only too clearly the reason of his silence.

13

THE FUGITIVE

Mr. Knight stared in silence at the huddled figure on the floor until the match burned his fingers.

"Damn!" he exclaimed; and struck another. He lit a lamp and hurriedly knelt to examine the body, taking care not to move it, or to touch the dagger. Then he rose slowly to his feet and looked round at the others.

"Poor old Mahatma!" he murmured. "For all his boasted immortality, he—he's dead!"

For a while no one spoke. They were all shocked by this unexpected and inexplicable ending to Edward Morlant's experiment. Gerald Harlan, now quite sobered, covered his drawn face with twitching hands. Bidgood stood looking down at the corpse with streaming eyes, while uncontrollable sobs shook his frail old frame. Mr. Broughton's broad features showed incredulous horror. Betty and Sally, frankly terrified, clung to one another trembling. Even the irrepressible Mr. Knight seemed affected when Rover crawled from his corner and, whining piteously, lay down beside his dead master.

"Oh, look!" cried Sally hysterically. "Look at the dog! It—it's not frightened of him now!"

"Don't be a baby, Miss Poulter," said Mr. Knight, his voice sharp and cold. "Please try to control yourself."

The rebuke had the intended effect, on Betty as well as
Sally. They both looked at him angrily, but they both lost
some of their fear.

"I've seen that dagger before," he went on almost immediately. "Surely it served the purpose of a paper knife
on the bureau, didn't it, Miss Harlan?"

Betty forced herself to look at the inlaid handle which
projected so gruesomely from Morlant's back.

"Yes, it did," she replied with a little shiver. "I noticed
it this afternoon."

"Can anyone swear to seeing it this evening? After we
all came into the room, for instance?"

No one, apparently, could do this. Mr. Knight's face
regained much of its usual cheerfulness.

"A strange weapon," he remarked. "It wouldn't be very
sharp; paper knives never are. It must have been used with
brutal force to penetrate so deeply."

He removed the cloth from the table and covered up
the body of Edward Morlant.

"We mustn't disturb him, or even touch him; or the
police will be very annoyed."

Everard Broughton uttered a startled exclamation.

"The police?" he echoed, fumbling with the silken cord
of his eyeglasses.

"Of course," rejoined Mr. Knight with his fatuous grin.
"They'll want to know which of us has killed him."

An uncomfortable silence followed this pronouncement.
Betty bit her lips uneasily. Though the fact was so obvious
when stated, it had not occurred to her before that Edward
Morlant must have been killed by one of those standing
about her, that one of them was a brutal murderer.

Which could it be? She glanced round, telling herself
that she was mad to suspect any one of them. Poor old
Bidgood, for instance, weeping over his dead master and

paying no attention to what was going on—it was ridiculous to think that he might be responsible. Mr. Broughton, again—well, on occasions he was a pompous fool, but on the whole she rather liked him; she could not imagine him intentionally harming anyone. Sally, of course, was out of the question. Mr. Knight was a dark horse; but he had saved her life only two nights ago, and she simply would not believe him capable of murder. There remained only Gerald Harlan, the drunkard—her father. . . .

It was a horrible thought, an unnatural thought. Betty shivered again as she looked at him standing there, his weak face still covered by his twitching hands. He was a pitiful, lonely figure, an outcast. But he had evidently borne the dead man a grudge; in their hearing he had threatened to kill him. Of them all, he seemed the only one who could have done it. Yet when Betty saw that the others were eyeing him, obviously with similar thoughts in mind, that warm glow of pity surged through her again, and a curious sense of loyalty to the helpless man sprang up in her.

"Must it have been one of us who killed him?" she murmured, feeling as she spoke that the question was foolish.

Mr. Knight, however, took it quite seriously as though it were worthy of discussion.

"I've heard of daggers being thrown at people," he replied. "But that's impossible in this case. The weapon was driven home by a very heavy blow, and that blow, clearly, must have been struck by someone in the room. No one besides us has been in here. The windows are closely shuttered. If the door had opened while we were in darkness, we should have seen it. By the way, we might as well make sure that no one has put out the light in the hall."

He crossed to the door and opened it. The lamp outside was burning steadily.

"You see," he continued. "No one could have crept in unknown to us. Besides, the idea of any intruder seems impossible to me, quite apart from the fact that there is no one else in the house. Remember the pitch darkness in which the crime was committed. The murderer must have known exactly where his victim was standing." An idea occurred to him. "Er—I suppose none of you have blood on your hands?"

They silently exhibited their hands. All were free from any incriminating stain.

"And that's funny, too," mused Mr. Knight. "With such a blow I should have thought—"

"It couldn't have been suicide?" questioned Betty.

"I'm sure not. No man could have driven a dagger so deeply into any part of his own anatomy, not to speak of his back. And it couldn't possibly have been an accident, either. As I was saying, the murderer must have known exactly where Morlant stood. He must have acted with extraordinary silence and rapidity since none of us heard a sound. I cannot imagine just how it was done. But it must have been done by one of us here."

"I suppose—" suggested Sally, hesitating. "I wonder if there might be some—some supernatural force at work. I—I expect you don't believe in spirits. But I do! I've seen too much to be a skeptic. I know that—that funny things do happen. Impossible things. You all know what Morlant said he was doing. He was calling up evil spirits. It sounds silly, doesn't it? But there have always been people who could do this—or claimed they could do it. And they always have to be very careful to protect themselves by magic circles and so forth. Because sometimes the spirits get out of control and attack the exorciser. I was wondering if perhaps Edward Morlant had been careless, had gone too far; and if, in the darkness, one of the elementals he had conjured up—"

"You really believe what he said?" interrupted Mr. Knight. "I mean, that he had power to do that kind of thing?"

"I don't know," admitted Sally, troubled. I don't know what to believe. It sounds foolish to believe that he really was an Adept, doesn't it? But it seems almost as foolish to think that one of us could have murdered him. And I do know that he was not an ordinary man. I—I could feel it as soon as I saw him. Besides, his dog knew, didn't it? Dogs don't make mistakes about that sort of thing. It knew that there was some change in him."

"There certainly was a difference," Betty chimed in. "Whether what he told us was true or not, there was something strange about him. He made me think of the phrase 'possessed of a devil.' If you talked till Doomsday, you'd never convince me that he was an ordinary man."

"Probably not," agreed Mr. Knight. "He did seem queer, in more ways than one. Personally, I should have said that the old boy's researches into the occult had turned his mind. That's a pretty frequent result of such studies. Anyhow, they didn't give him the immortality he wanted, did they?"

"Then you don't think he was dead before?"

"Without answering that leading question, lady, I would respectfully point out the fact that he is dead now, that he has been murdered by someone in this room, and that we are wasting time instead of informing the police at the earliest possible moment."

"And how shall we do that?" asked Betty. "It's easy to talk about it. But there's no telephone; and I don't suppose anyone feels like walking the six miles into Blackshaw to-night."

"The taxi is coming for me at nine-thirty," suggested Mr. Broughton. "I could tell the police on my way home."

"That's too long to wait," demurred Mr. Knight, looking at the clock. "It's only half-past seven now. We ought to let them know while any possible trail is hot. They might have the whole business cleared up in those two hours. Besides, they'd be sure to want you to come back with them. I think one of us had better take my car and run into Blackshaw at once."

"Your car? I'd no idea you had one."

"I call it a car, lady. You might call it a perambulator."

"Where is it?"

"Just a little way up the road. I hid it this morning in an old disused quarry up there. You see, I didn't want to look too prosperous when I called on you, or you mightn't have bought any furniture."

"You didn't say much about it when you hurt your ankle," mused Betty. "It seems funny to me that, just when we need a car, you should be able to produce one."

"Not at all, lady, not at all. That's the kind of man I am. Anything from a pin to a pantechnicon. It's really part of my business."

"Well, who do you think should go?"

Mr. Knight's glance traveled from Harlan to Bidgood, and then to the solicitor.

"I should think Mr. Broughton," he suggested. "Apart from anything else, he probably knows the police in Blackshaw personally and, as Morlant's executor, can explain matters better than I could. Don't you agree?"

For some reason Betty felt very relieved that Mr. Knight was not going.

"I do," she replied promptly. "I'm sure that's the best plan. Will you go, Mr. Broughton?"

The solicitor hesitated. He opened his mouth to speak several times, and closed it again as though changing his mind. It was clear to everyone that he was vacillating and uncomfortable, that he did not at all relish the task assigned to him.

"Yes, I'll go," he decided reluctantly at last; and added, with the sigh of one who faces a most unpleasant duty: "It'll have to be done. I might as well do it now."

"That's right," approved Mr. Knight. "I'd better come and show you where the car is."

"Can't we come with you, please?" asked Sally, with an oblique glance at the body of Edward Morlant. "I—I don't want to be left here."

"Very well. Come along if you wish to do so. You, Bidgood—and Harlan—will perhaps wait here until we come back."

Betty and Sally, not without some trepidation, ran upstairs to fetch hats and coats. There was nothing in the dark corridors now to frighten them, but they were glad to reach the comparative brightness of the hall again, and follow Mr. Knight and his lantern down the graveled drive.

Once away from the depressing influence of the house, the beauty of the night seemed to soothe and calm them. There was no wind, and the only sound beyond the crunching of their own footsteps was the melodious tinkle of a nearby stream. Under the peaceful serenity of the jeweled sky, the fear that they had experienced inside grew unreal and incredible, taking on the quality of a half-forgotten nightmare.

At the bottom of the drive, they turned into the road in the direction opposite to Blackshaw. Knight and Broughton led the way, with Betty and Sally following behind arm in arm.

No one had much to say. Each was busy with private thoughts, and discussion did not seem profitable.

"There's one thing," whispered Sally, breaking the silence at last. "He was a horrible old man, and I—I'm almost glad he's dead."

"It's a relief to hear you say that," agreed Betty. "Because I've been feeling the same way myself. It's dreadful,

I know. But there really was something very horrible about him. He seemed to have changed altogether since I first saw him. It would have been terrible to think that he—he was going on living."

They came to an old, deeply rutted cart track which led off from the road. After a few yards, this turned abruptly into the bottom of a small hollow cut in the hillside, the remains of a long-deserted quarry. As they walked forward, the light of the lantern was reflected back by the polished nickel work of a small car.

"Here she is!" said Mr. Knight cheerfully. "'Gertrude,' I call her. Not much to look at, but a divil for work. She'll be quite cold, of course. You'd better let me start her up, then you can take her in hand."

After various tinkerings under the hood, he swung the handle vigorously. He seemed surprised when the engine fired at once, the explosions sounding startlingly loud in the confined space of the hollow.

"That's pretty good for Gertrude," he remarked approvingly. "Perhaps I'd better back her out for you. She has her moods, you know, and there's not much room to turn round here."

He jumped in and switched on the lights. The broad beam lit up everything in its path with cold, clear brilliance. Betty, blinking, noticed that Broughton looked very worried, and suddenly felt sorry for him.

The cart track was negotiated without much difficulty beyond a few coughings and splutterings from Gertrude. Out on the road, Mr. Knight gave up his seat to the solicitor.

"You'll be all right now," he said, "if you don't let the engine stop. She'll buzz if you humor her. You should be back in about an hour?"

"Yes, I think so," replied Broughton, putting in the gear. He hesitated a moment, then added: "You—you'll look after Miss Poulter, won't you?"

Without waiting for a reply, he hurriedly pressed down the accelerator and moved off, leaving them wondering what he had meant by his last words.

The darkness of the night seemed more intense now that the lights of the car were withdrawn. They stood watching the red rear lamp until it turned a corner and was lost to sight. It occurred to Betty that their last link with Blackshaw and civilization was gone.

"It's a big risk," murmured Mr. Knight. "But I don't see what else we could have done."

"What's a risk?" asked Betty.

"Letting him go."

"Whatever do you mean?"

"Well, he might be the murderer, you know. In which case, we'll probably never set eyes on him again."

"But surely," began Sally in some indignation, "you don't think that he—"

"I don't think anything, Miss Poulter. As I told Miss Harlan a little while ago, I find it bad for my blood pressure. I like to know. And the only thing I know is that Edward Morlant is dead. Come on. Let's get back to the house."

The brief interlude was over. The atmosphere of suspicion and uncertainty descended again like an impenetrable fog. Knight's words were a reminder that a foul murder had been committed, and that the murderer remained undiscovered.

Neither Betty nor Sally was keen on returning. Out in the pure fresh air of the moorland night there was peace and sanity, while they both felt instinctively that further trouble and sorrow awaited them at Hameldon House.

"I'll never stick it for six months," murmured Betty. "I couldn't do it if my life depended on it. I'm afraid it's back to the studio for me to-morrow, Sally."

They strolled slowly down the road, delaying their return as long as possible, wondering at the velvety blackness of the sky and the unusual brilliance of the stars. Mr. Knight offered his cigarette case, and they smoked in silence.

"I'm glad you didn't go to Blackshaw, Mr. Knight," said Betty in a sudden burst of confidence. "I—I feel more comfortable with you here."

"You honor me, lady. You make me blush with pride."

"I wish you'd drop all that tomfoolery, and tell us who you really are."

"But surely you know?" exclaimed Mr. Knight, his gray eyes twinkling in the lamplight. "Surely I told you that I represent the well-known firm of—"

"Oh, shut up!" exclaimed Betty, annoyed. "If you can't talk sense—"

She stopped abruptly, listening. In the stillness of the night, they could all hear the sound of someone running along the road towards them.

"Who can it be?" she whispered, her voice agitated and apprehensive. "Whatever can anyone be doing up here at this time?"

"Perhaps it's Broughton," suggested Knight. "He may have quarreled with Gertrude."

There was no conviction in his tone, and both girls could see that he was alert and excited. They waited in tense silence, staring into the blackness ahead. The running footsteps rapidly approached. Soon they could hear the sounds of labored breathing. And immediately afterwards a man burst into the circle of light from the lantern.

Betty's heart sank within her as she recognized her father. He looked round at them breathlessly, his dissipated features contorted with terror.

"Thank God!" he gasped. "Oh, thank God you're here."

14

Bidgood is Lost

The man was obviously distraught. Mr. Knight caught him by the shoulder and shook him.

"What are you doing here, Harlan?" he asked. "What's the matter?"

With a great effort, Gerald Harlan managed to control his trembling limbs.

"It's Bidgood," he panted. "The old servant. He's gone!"

"Gone? What do you mean?"

"He's not in the house. He's disappeared. I—I think he's dead."

"All right, now. Don't get worked up again. You're safe enough here. There's nobody to harm you. Have a cigarette and tell us all about it."

Harlan accepted the cigarette, and lit it with twitching fingers. After a few deep inhalations, he grew calmer.

"I'm sorry to appear so excitable," he said, making a pitiful attempt at dignity. "It's not my nature, but my—my nerves are not too good at the moment."

"We know that," said Mr. Knight drily. "Go on."

"There's so little to tell, really. Soon after you left the house, Bidgood commenced to clear the tea table. We had not spoken a word. I was hardly conscious of his existence, being fully occupied with my own thoughts."

"What kind of thoughts?"

"I think you can guess. Though I am, and always have been, a fool, I do not lack a certain elementary intelligence. It was perfectly clear to me that, as soon as the police arrived, their suspicions would fall on me. I had threatened Morlant. In the presence of you all, I had tried to choke him. I could offer no really plausible reason for being in the house, and my past would not bear investigation."

"Had you a good reason for coming to Hameldon House, by the way?"

The eagerness disappeared from Harlan's face.

"I've told you the reason," he said sullenly. "I'm not proud of it, but it's true."

"All right. Perhaps you'll be able to persuade the police to believe it. Go on."

"Well, as I say, Bidgood was moving about, going to and fro between the library and the kitchen, I suppose. I paid no attention to him, being busy trying to think out what I ought to do. But suddenly I realized that he had not been in the room for quite a long time.

"I wondered what he was doing and I grew uneasy. Now that my thoughts were interrupted, I didn't like being left alone with that body on the floor. I went to the door and called.

"There was no reply. I called and called again. The house was silent as the grave. It got on my nerves. I ran into the kitchen. It was empty!

"I began to feel seriously alarmed. It seemed that Bidgood had left the house. As I returned to the hall, I heard a car go down the road."

"That's quite a while ago now."

"I suppose it is. It looks a lifetime to me. As soon as I heard it, I jumped to a conclusion. I thought I could see what was happening. You were all concerned in the murder of Morlant, and now you were making your getaway. The four of you had deceived me by bluffing about sending for the police, and Bidgood had followed when opportunity afforded. You were all in the car, getting clear away, leaving me alone with the dead man, leaving me to take the blame."

"You're not quite sober yet, I'm afraid," said Mr. Knight, not unkindly.

"Perhaps I'm not. I can see now, of course, that I was wrong. But that's what I thought. And it made me panicky straight away. Because if the police came and found me there alone I shouldn't have a dog's chance of clearing myself.

"I didn't dare go back into the library. I was scared silly of Morlant and his threat to return from the dead again. But I was determined to make sure about Bidgood. I fought down my fear, and I searched the house from top to bottom. There wasn't a sign of him anywhere!

"I made up my mind at last. The only thing to do was to get away myself as quickly as possible. I was crossing the hall to the door when I heard a terrible cry, quite near to me. It was unearthly—horrible. I had just searched the house. I knew it was empty except for the dead man. And that cry finished me. I didn't care what happened so long as I got away from the house. I opened the door and ran. And—and that's all."

"And quite enough, too," said Mr. Knight with a short laugh. "I'm not surprised your nerves gave way." He lit another cigarette thoughtfully. "Now I wonder why Bidgood wanted to get away from the house. The obvious inference, of course, is that he killed his master and has now made good his escape."

"That may be obvious to you," demurred Betty indignantly. "But it isn't to me! Didn't you see the poor old man

weeping as though his heart was broken? I'm sure he loved
Edward Morlant. I'll never believe that he had anything to
do with the murder."

"Besides, what about the scream?" added Sally. "I mean
the cry Mr. Harlan heard. Isn't it possible that Bidgood
may—have got into trouble? Mr. Harlan knows nothing
about the secret passage, you know. He wouldn't look there."

"But, my dear Miss Poulter, there's not a soul in the
house to harm Bidgood."

"I know. But there's the body of Edward Morlant. Oh,
it's no use smiling! Screams are not heard without cause."

"As for that—an owl, perhaps. Or an outhouse door
that wants oiling."

"Owl? Outhouse door? Fiddlesticks!" Sally was growing
emphatic. "I've heard that scream once myself! And it's
like nothing on earth."

"Then you think there is some connection between the
cry and Edward Morlant?"

"I don't know. But we heard it just before we saw him
in the library, didn't we? And it wouldn't surprise me a bit
if we found—"

"Poor old Bidgood dead in the passage, and Morlant
returned to life again?"

"Yes!" said Sally defiantly. "Just that!"

To her surprise, Mr. Knight did not laugh.

"You may be right," he said very gravely. "But I hope
you're not."

There was something in his tone that made Betty look
closely at him. In the light of the lamp she could see that
his gray eyes were troubled.

"We'd better go and make another search, hadn't we?"
she suggested.

"Yes," he replied. He hesitated a moment, then added:
"I suppose you wouldn't like to wait here with the lantern
while I go on alone?"

"No, thanks!" said Betty promptly. She knew that he was thinking of their safety, and inwardly she was grateful to him. But she had no intention of allowing him to go into possible danger alone. There was safety in numbers. "We're coming with you, aren't we, Sally?"

"Of course we are," agreed Sally, bravely stifling her own desires. She hated the very thought of returning to the house. "I'd die of fright if you left us up here with no company but a lantern."

Without further remark, Mr. Knight turned and led the way towards Hameldon House. No one spoke to Gerald Harlan, but after a little hesitation he attached himself to the party and returned with them.

They hurried down the road, and up between the stunted trees which shadowed the drive. As they neared the house, however, their progress became slower and they all, as it were instinctively, tried to make as little noise as possible.

The dark bulk of the house slept quietly under the stars. The door was wide open as Harlan had left it, and a broad band of light from the hall swept down the drive. Apart from this, no light showed anywhere; nor could they hear a sound from inside. It seemed that they were on a wild goose chase, hunting trouble in the midst of peace and security.

Nevertheless, Mr. Knight blew out the lantern and led them on the thin strip of turf that fringed the drive, just beyond reach of the light from the door.

"Why all the precautions?" Betty whispered. "What are you frightened of?"

"Don't know, lady," he responded cheerfully. "Just comes natural to me to be careful."

"I wish it came natural to you to be sensible," she retorted, half in earnest.

There was nothing in the hall to alarm them. Once inside the door, they halted, listening. They could hear no sound but the solemn tick-tock of the clock in the library. Yet here again, without any order or caution given, they all walked on tiptoe across the hall towards the library.

The door was open, and Mr. Knight peeped in. After one glance, he turned and grinned encouragement to his companions.

"Come along," he said, entering the room. "Our old Mahatma's still here. He hasn't come to life yet, Miss Poulter."

Sally sighed with relief at the raillery in his voice, and Betty smiled at her in sympathy. They both breathed more easily. They had more than half expected to find something dreadful in the library.

But their fears had been unnecessary. The body of Edward Morlant lay undisturbed on the floor, covered by the white tablecloth. The dog, Rover, still kept faithful vigil by his side. Except that the table had been cleared, the room was just as they had left it.

"Everything seems in order here," said Betty doubtfully. "But we'd better have a look in the passage, hadn't we? I wonder if I could tempt that poor dog away."

She spoke soothingly to Rover, trying to persuade him to move. He looked up at her with soft brown eyes and feebly wagged his tail; but instead of coming to her, he crouched closer to his dead master.

"Poor old fellow," she murmured, giving up the attempt. "We'll have to leave you where you are. It's funny, isn't it?" she added, turning to the others. "You wouldn't think a dog could love such a man as Edward Morlant."

"Dogs and women are notorious, lady, for the foolish manner in which they bestow their affections."

Betty flushed. "We're wasting our time," she said, leading the way out of the room. "We ought to be looking for Bidgood."

They went first to the kitchen to make sure that the old servant had not returned. As soon as they entered, they were met by an appetizing smell of cooking.

The fire was burning brightly. Mr. Knight opened the door of the oven. Inside, two chickens were roasting. On the hob, pans containing vegetables simmered.

"Now, that's rather extraordinary," he said thoughtfully. "It doesn't look as though the old chappie had intended leaving the house. He must have put those chickens in the oven while we were out. But there's no sign of him, is there? We'll take a look upstairs, then see if the tunnel tells us anything."

Their search of the bedrooms and corridors was fruitless. No one was surprised at this, for Gerald Harlan had already covered the ground once. It seemed evident that if they found anything at all it would be in the secret passage.

So far as they could see, no one had entered this since they left it. The suits of clothes lay neatly folded on the floor where Mr. Knight had placed them, and the sliding back of the wardrobe was closed.

He pressed the spring and stood aside to allow the others to pass.

"If you don't mind waiting a moment," he said, "I'd like to try a little experiment here."

After digging into several pockets, he brought out a length of fine thread. He stretched this across the opening, attaching the ends with soft wax taken from the candles.

"There," he murmured, surveying his work with satisfaction. "We shall at least know if anyone uses our subway again."

They descended the narrow stairs to the tunnel, watching carefully for any hint or clew. The uneven floor was so thick with debris that it was quite impossible to distinguish a footprint, and so decide whether anyone had preceded them. In the second half of the tunnel, past Piccadilly Circus, as Mr. Knight called the wide space below the hall, the wet slimy mud was equally destitute of information. They arrived at the cave without making any discovery.

Disappointed and irritated by their failure to solve the mystery, yet relieved that they had not stumbled upon the body of Bidgood, Betty pushed through the crevice into the calm beauty of the night, and took deep breaths of the pure, keen air.

A sensation of gloom and depression was weighing heavily upon her. For some reason, the murder of Edward Morlant had not affected her so powerfully as the disappearance of Bidgood. Despite her knowledge of the fact that the murderer must be among those present at the time, the character of the man who claimed immortality was such that his unquestioned death had brought with it a freedom from doubt that was almost relief, while uncertainty about the fate of the old servant, for whom she had conceived a strong liking, plunged her deep into difficulty again, and worried her with its presage of further trouble.

What shape this further trouble might take she could not imagine. But neither could she forget Mr. Knight's gravity when Sally had suggested that Bidgood's disappearance might be due to the man they had seen dead at their feet. Though she was angry at her folly, she knew that she was frightened lest Edward Morlant should come to life again.

In addition to all this, though as yet she had scarcely had time to think of him, Betty had to wrestle with the problem of her father. The unexpected meeting with him had been a shock, rendered all the more powerful because of his character and the extent of his involvement in the murder. She knew that she would have to find an opportunity for a talk with him before long. At present, however, she could not bring herself to any reasoned consideration of purely personal affairs.

"There's no need to go back that way, is there? she asked, as the others squeezed through the crevice after her. "I'm tired of this silly, useless rushing about. I'm going to sit down in the library and not move again until the police come."

"An excellent idea, lady," approved Mr. Knight. "Most sensible speech I've heard to-day."

The light of his lantern glinted on something in the shrubbery. He stooped quickly and fumbled among the branches.

"By Jove!" he exclaimed. "A most peculiar little bird! I mustn't let this escape."

He rose to his feet, slowly extending a closed hand towards the girls. Suddenly he started, and his hand shot up in a warning gesture.

No one moved or spoke. For a moment, the silence of the night was unbroken. Then, clear and unmistakable, there came from the house the sound of a dog's furious barking.

As they listened, startled and apprehensive, a revolver shot rang out. There was an agonized yelp from the dog. And after this, all was quiet again.

Without a word, Mr. Knight turned and dashed towards the house. The others followed, making every effort to keep up with him. They were close on his hall. They entered the library immediately behind him. And there they stopped abruptly as he did, staring at one another in dazed bewilderment.

For the body of Edward Morlant had disappeared. It had vanished as though the events of the night had been a dream. But in its place, the dog Rover lay sprawled on the

floor, his blood-stained limbs still quivering convulsively
in his death throes.

15

MR. BROUGHTON VANISHES

"He's been shot," panted Betty, falling on her knees beside the faithful animal, and anxiously raising his head. "And the poor fellow's dead. Oh, whoever's done this must be a monster, a devil, a fiend!"

"But who *can* have done it?" cried Sally, wringing her hands in desperation. "We *know* there was no one in the house but a dead man; and he—he's gone!"

"There *must* have been someone alive in the house to shoot this dog! Mr. Knight, you must have made a mistake about Edward Morlant. He *couldn't* have been dead!"

"He was dead, lady. That dagger had pierced his heart. He wouldn't live two seconds after the blow."

Gerald Harlan was gazing at the crumpled tablecloth on the floor with acute terror straining his bloated features.

"He said he'd come back!" he muttered, his slack mouth writhing and twisting. "He told me so!"

Betty rose to her feet, shivering. A cold chill had run through her veins.

"He said he'd come back!" Harlan repeated, his voice shrill and cracked. "He said he couldn't be killed. 'Try it,' he said. 'Shoot me! Poison me! Now, at your feet. And I'll be back in a few minutes to laugh at you!'"

No one spoke. The drunkard's speech conjured up a vision of a pale, distorted face whose odd colored eyes blazed with malevolent fury. It brought to mind and emphasized the fact that the man who had spoken those words had already died once, that he had apparently returned from the grave only to be murdered. It restored and intensified the atmosphere of dread and tension which had been banished for a time.

A strained, uncomfortable silence followed. And suddenly, in this silence, they all heard a laugh; a laugh low and mocking, with a fiendish quality that froze the blood; a laugh that seemed to float up from amongst them, so near it was.

"It's Morlant!" gasped Harlan, covering his face with twitching hands. "My God, it's Morlant! Laughing at us, as he said he would!"

Mr. Knight snatched up the lantern from the floor, and made for the hall.

"Wait here until I come back," he commanded, hurrying out. "Don't move."

He ran swiftly up the stairs without showing any trace of his injury. For a few seconds they heard him moving about above them. Then he came down again and rushed out into the garden, leaving the door wide open.

Sally made a move to follow him, but Betty laid a restraining hand on her arm.

"Let's do as he says," she whispered. "Let's wait until he comes back."

"Oh, I don't want to stay in this horrible place, Betty." Sally's voice was trembling and tearful. "It was b-bad enough before, just to know that there was a murderer among us. But now it's so much worse. It—it's—"

"I know," interrupted Betty gently, trying to thrust aside her own fears in order to calm her friend. "But don't worry, dear. We shall soon find out—"

"We shan't find out! We can't find out! Betty, I'm frightened. Oh, I'm terrified! Because it looks as though he really is immortal, doesn't it? And he's wicked—he's evil itself. He's not an ordinary human being. Remember how scared his dog was of him. And now he's killed it. I expect he's killed Bidgood, too. And if he gets half a chance, he'll kill us. He's not human! He's a creature without a soul! A vampire! A ghoul!"

Betty put her arms round Sally and tried to comfort her.

"I can't believe that he's really come alive again," she said. "I think we shall find some explanation eventually."

"It's so easy to say that! But he must have come to life. What other explanation can there be?"

"I don't know. Let's wait until Mr. Knight comes back. Perhaps he will find something."

"Mr. Knight doesn't know everything. Besides, he's probably mixed up in all this. He didn't come here for nothing. Oh, I wish Mr. Broughton would come back with the police!"

Betty was surprised to find how much she resented the slighting reference to Mr. Knight. An angry retort trembled on her lips. Then she remembered that Sally did not know how he had saved her life in the fog, and forgave her.

For a while, they were silent. Betty glanced at Harlan, and once again was filled with pity for him. He looked so weak and helpless as he stood there with bowed shoulders and face hidden by twitching hands that she almost forgave him the wrong he had done to her mother.

As she watched him, he slowly raised his head and looked across at her.

"He was mad," he muttered. "All his life he was mad."

"You mean Edward Morlant?" she asked.

"Yes. He was subject to attacks of insanity which came on now and again. They were hereditary—in the family; his father before him suffered in the same way."

"I wonder if that explains anything?" asked Sally eagerly. "I mean—about the dog, for instance, and the way he talked."

"It might explain something," admitted Betty. "He certainly talked like a madman. But it doesn't explain him being alive when he's supposed to be dead, does it?" She turned to Harlan again. "Did—my mother know about this?"

"Yes, she knew," he replied. "It was the reason she broke off her engagement to him."

"Then that's the secret he mentioned in the diary. You remember, Sally? He said that Elizabeth had discovered his secret and that he had lost her."

"Yes, I remember." Sally looked curiously at Harlan. "Why do you tell us this now?"

He covered his face with his hands again.

"I—I don't know," he stammered. "I was thinking of it, and it—it just came out."

Again they were silent, pondering over the news.

"I'm sure both Bidgood and Mr. Broughton must have known about this," said Betty reflectively. "Don't you think they ought to have told us? Mr. Broughton said definitely that he didn't know what the secret was."

"And why should he tell us?" cried Sally, immediately on the defensive. "I should have done the same thing in his place. Edward Morlant was dead. He had been good to you, and you respected his memory. Why should his confidential adviser disclose a family skeleton and destroy your respect without cause?"

Betty smiled ruefully. "I'm afraid you're getting rather fond of Mr. Broughton," she said.

Before Sally had time to reply, they were startled by a voice which seemed to come from below their feet.

"Hello, hello!" it called. "Hello, lady! Are you there?"

"That's Mr. Knight," said Betty. "It sounds as though he's in the tunnel." She went towards the hall and called: "Yes, I'm here. Where are you?"

"Down in Piccadilly Circus. Everything all right? No one else vanished?"

"No. We're still waiting for you."

"All right. I'll be with you in a jiffy."

Betty returned to Sally, feeling decidedly more comfortable now that she knew her protector was close at hand.

"He was down in the tunnel," she remarked. "I wonder what he's been doing."

A few moments later, Mr. Knight descended the stairs and came to join them. He cast one glance at their worried faces and assumed a serene cheerfulness.

"I'm afraid we've lost our old Mahatma," he grinned. "He evidently uses only the best quality in magic carpets. Can't see a sign of him anywhere."

"What have you been doing?" asked Betty.

"Taking a little exercise, lady. Did you hear my voice quite plainly?"

"Yes, it sounded very near. Almost at our feet."

"That's what I thought. When I heard that laugh, it occurred to me that our old friend might be using the tunnel. I dashed upstairs to see if the thread in the wardrobe was broken; but it was still there, so he couldn't have gone out that way. Anyhow, I thought I might as well make sure by trying the other end. Assuming that laugh came from under the hall, I knew I could get to the cave by way of the garden much more quickly than he could walk along the passage. I rather expected, as I came back, to meet him about halfway between the cave and Piccadilly Circus. But I was disappointed. Shy and retiring old Johnnie, isn't he?"

"Then you think he's still in the house?"

"Looks like it, doesn't it? He didn't come out of the door, or we should have seen him."

"You—you really believe it was Edward Morlant who laughed, that he—he's come back to life again?" asked Sally, her eyes wide and apprehensive.

"Quite honestly, Miss Poulter, I can't see any other explanation at present for what has happened. Unless—"

"Unless what?"

"I didn't show you the funny little bird I caught in the bushes." Mr. Knight dived into his pocket and extended his hand towards the two girls. "I wonder if you will recognize it?"

They saw a pair of old-fashioned *pince-nez* with a broken end of silk cord attached.

"Why!" cried Sally. "These belong to Mr. Broughton!"

"Spoken with one hundred per cent accuracy, Miss Poulter."

"But what were they doing in the bushes?"

"Ah, that's their secret. They don't tell, do they?"

"It looks as though he lost them while pushing his way through the shrubbery, doesn't it?" suggested Betty.

"There's no doubt about that. The question is—when were they lost?"

"I don't see what you mean?"

"Don't you, lady? The point at issue is really very simple. Mr. Broughton came through the tunnel with us earlier in the evening. Did he lose those glasses then? Or has he been near the cave—alone—since then?"

Both girls were silent for a while, appreciating the importance of this. Gerald Harlan looked on in bewilderment. His sodden mind could not grasp what was happening.

"I—I can't remember him putting them on since we all came through the tunnel together," stammered Sally at last.

"I didn't think you would," said Mr. Knight with a short laugh. "But as a matter of fact I can remember perfectly well. Mr. Broughton was fidgeting with these glasses in this room while Morlant was talking to us."

"Yes," said Betty reluctantly. "I remember, too."

"Even if you do," urged Sally in desperation, "it may mean nothing at all. He perhaps slipped back for something on his way to Blackshaw."

"Through the cave?" Mr. Knight laughed again. "Now that's pretty feeble, isn't it, Miss Poulter? If your friend 'slipped back' for anything—well, both Bidgood and the body of Morlant have vanished."

"But surely you don't think—"

"I don't think. As I've told you before, it's bad for my blood pressure. But consider the facts: Mr. Broughton is supposed to be on the way to Blackshaw; indeed, he ought to be coming back by now. We know that he has passed through the tunnel since he set off in the car. Bidgood is not here. And the body of the murdered man is not here. It must have been plain to anyone that there was some secret between the solicitor and the servant. Surely you noticed it? What was this secret? And have they, between them, removed the dead man?"

"Why should they do that?" asked Betty.

"I don't know. But here's a point that suggests a possible explanation: You can't prove a murder unless you can produce the corpse. Especially if the murdered man is already dead officially. And, you know, I can't believe that anyone of us here at present stabbed Morlant."

"If that's what you think," muttered Sally, "where are they now? Whatever Edward Morlant can do, neither Bidgood nor Mr. Broughton can disappear at will."

"That's true," acknowledged Mr. Knight. "And when we find them we shall have solved the mystery."

"There's another thing," he went on, after a pause, "which may or may not have some bearing on the case. I don't know whether you've noticed that Mr. Broughton is strangely like Edward Morlant in feature, that without his mustache—"

"Yes, we did notice it," said Betty, glancing at the oil painting over the chimney-piece. "But I don't see—"

"Neither do I. Still, it's possible that some scheme of impersonation—"

"That's a most ridiculous assumption," cried Sally angrily. "I'm sure Mr. Broughton—"

"You're not sure, Miss Poulter. You merely think. Anyhow, it's no use quarreling about things which we don't understand. The question will soon answer itself. If Mr. Broughton brings back the police with him—"

"Well?"

"I'll return his glasses and apologize most humbly for my suspicions."

"And if he doesn't?"

"Then I'm very much afraid I've seen the last of Gertrude—and Mr. Broughton."

Betty turned away impatiently.

"Things get worse and worse," she muttered. "Oh, I am tired of all this mystery! And I feel as though I'm responsible. As though it wouldn't have happened if I'd never come here. I wish I hadn't come. I wish I'd stayed at the studio. I wish I'd taken Mr. Broughton's warning—"

She broke off abruptly, realizing the significance of her words after what had just been said. For a while there was silence in the library.

"It's half past eight," said Mr. Knight, a little later. "Time the police were here."

"I've been departing from my rule, lady" he went on. "I've been thinking. It seems to me that underground passage is decidedly too popular just at present. What do you say to blocking it up? The entrance to the cave will be the easiest place."

"All right," agreed Betty, glad of any excuse for action. "Let's go and do it now."

They all went out together and made their way through the garden to the mound which covered the cave. There was a rockery close by and while the girls watched, Mr. Knight, aided by Harlan, carried stones from this and piled them against the opening into the cave until it was completely blocked.

"There!" said he, satisfied, when they had finished. "It'll take any one considerable time and trouble to find a way through that little lot." He held his watch towards the lantern. "Nine o'clock. Mr. Broughton is late, Miss Poulter."

Even as he spoke, the nearby hillside was faintly lit up by a distant light. A few seconds later, they heard the hum of an approaching car.

"I told you so!" cried Sally triumphantly. "Here's Mr. Broughton and the police!"

"I believe you're right," admitted Mr. Knight. "That certainly sounds like Gertrude. And she's traveling some!"

They hurried back towards the house. As they reached the drive, the car came tearing up towards them, and stopped with a squealing of brakes and crunching of gravel.

"Rotten driver!" murmured its owner solicitously. "Hope he's not stripped any gears."

Though blinded by the dazzling headlights, they could see that only one man got out of the car. He advanced towards them, raising his hat.

"I'm Sergeant Kendall of the West Riding Constabulary," he said. "Where's Mr. Broughton?"

16

A Discovery

The simple question fell among the little party like a bombshell. It was such prompt confirmation of their suspicions and fears. They all stared at the newcomer without reply.

He stepped forward into the light of the lamps. They saw a middle-aged man in plain clothes, with a small bristling mustache, and shaggy overhanging eyebrows which gave to his face the appearance of a perpetual frown.

"Where is Mr. Broughton?" he repeated curtly. "Didn't you hear me?"

"Is—isn't he with you?" stammered Sally. "We thought he'd come—"

"He did come," snapped the sergeant. "And evidently he hasn't returned here. Damnation! That's my last hope gone. There'll be the devil to pay when the inspector sees me."

"You seem rather put out, old chappie," suggested Mr. Knight. "Are you very fond of Mr. Broughton?"

"You seem rather a fool, young man. Of course, I'm not fond of him. But I'll get hauled over the coals. I ought never to have let him out of my sight. He was all excited and wound up when he called at my house with a queer tale about murders and ghosts. While I was telephoning headquarters about it, he said he'd run home for something—

I've forgotten what. Not a hundred yards away. Left his car outside my door. I've known him for years, and never suspected anything. But he didn't come back. I went to his house. No one in. No one about had seen him. Obviously he had taken fright and skedaddled."

"Why should he be frightened?" queried Sally. The fact that Mr. Broughton had actually been for the police merely strengthened her conviction of his integrity.

"How should I know? There's been a murder or something, hasn't there?"

"And if he'd had anything to do with it," she said scornfully, "do you think he'd have come for you at all? If he'd wanted to run away, he could have done so without letting you know a word about it."

"Well, he's missing, anyway. I had to go back home to circulate a description of him in case we want him; and then I hurried on here as fast as I could."

"Car run well?" asked Mr. Knight, fingering the mascot on the radiator cap. "She's mine, you know. I call her Gertrude."

"Oh, do you? Of all the— But we're wasting time. Now, what's been happening here? I thought Edward Morlant died about a week ago. Yet Broughton talked about him being murdered to-night."

"He has been murdered to-night."

"Then he wasn't dead before?"

"Now you're asking me something, and I'm not good at riddles. You'd better talk to Miss Harlan. She's the mistress of the house—inherited it."

"You talk like an idiot, young fellow. I can't make head or tail of you." Sergeant Kendall turned to Betty. "You're Miss Harlan, are you? Well, how could you inherit the house if Morlant wasn't dead?"

"It's rather complicated." Betty tried to explain. "You see, for all we know, he was dead."

"Before he was murdered?"

"Yes."

The sergeant grunted. "I don't know whether this is a funny joke, but I'm not laughing. I've been fooled once to-night, and I'm not asking for any more, thank you. Better start at the beginning, young lady, and tell me a proper story."

His tone was offensive, but Betty felt that she could not blame him. Really, he must think he was dealing with a pack of lunatics.

"I'll try to tell you," she said. "But I'm far from clear about everything myself."

"Hadn't we better go into the house?" suggested Mr. Knight. "It'll be a long story, and it's beastly cold out here."

"You'll stay where you are, if you please," said the sergeant tersely. "I want to know something about each one of you before I go in."

"All right, old chappie. No need to snap my head off."

Betty started at the beginning and gave a rough outline of what had happened since Mr. Broughton first visited the studio two nights ago. She had neither the patience nor the time to go into details. Sergeant Kendall listened quietly until she came to the appearance of Edward Morlant in the corridor, when his incredulity burst forth.

"You actually mean to tell me," he snorted, "that you saw him—a man who has been buried three days?"

"We saw him," repeated Betty quietly. "All of us. And we not only saw him, but we talked to him."

"You—what?"

"He was telling us about himself when he was—killed."

"How was he killed?"

It was not difficult for Betty to describe this event, every detail of which was only too clear in her mind.

"So he was stabbed, was he?" mused the sergeant. "And he was standing with you in the darkness when it happened? By crimes! Then one of you must have done it!"

"Just what I said, old chappie," exclaimed Mr. Knight. "One of us must be a jolly old murderer."

"You shut up!" Sergeant Kendall's temper, already worn thin by the way Broughton had eluded him, was beginning to fray. "I'm talking to Miss Harlan. Now, young lady, who was in the room when Morlant was killed?"

"We all were," replied Betty. "The four of us here, and Mr. Broughton and Bidgood."

"Bidgood? You mean the servant? Yes, I know him. A surly, conceited old fellow. Comes to the village without ever a civil word for anyone. I know him—and Broughton. But I don't know any of you. You say you're Edward Morlant's heiress?"

"His will's inside the house."

"H'm. I'll have a look at it later. And you"—turning to Mr. Knight—"who're you?"

"I represent the well-known firm of Lepage, respected all over the world for quality and fair dealing. Our factories are the largest—"

"You can cut all that out. What's your name?"

"Clarence Knight," said he, with a sweeping curtsy. "If you'll let me show you a catalogue—"

"What are you doing here?"

"Trying to sell furniture, my lord. We have some very lovely lines in—"

"Be quiet, will you? I'm not interested in your lovely lines. What I want to know is what you're doing here now. You don't come to sell furniture at this time of night."

"Oh, I came this morning. You see, I sprained my ankle, and Miss Harlan kindly allowed me to remain."

"Sprained your ankle, eh?" The sergeant's shaggy eyebrows contracted into a frown more ferocious than usual. "If you're as lame as your story, you're in a bad way. You don't expect me to believe you?"

"Of course, old chappie."

"Well, I don't! But I'll talk to you again later. Now, who's this other young lady?"

"This is my friend, Miss Poulter," explained Betty. "She came here with me last night because—"

"Because what?"

"Because I was frightened."

"Of what?"

"I—I don't know."

"Oh!" Sergeant Kendall grinned irritably. "Strangely nervous young person, aren't you?"

It was obvious that he was very skeptical about what he heard, that he was suspicious of each one of them. But though his manner grew more offensive each moment, Betty felt that he had every excuse. He must think that they were all lying.

He turned now to the last member of the little party. "And who are you?" he asked with a sneer. "The Grand Cham of Tartary, I suppose?"

"I—I'm Miss Harlan's father," stammered Gerald Harlan, fidgeting uneasily.

"Harlan? Harlan? It sounds familiar, somehow. Here, let me have a look at you." The sergeant suddenly swung the other round so that the headlights of the car fell full on his face. "Harlan? By crimes, I thought so. Ever done time for forgery, Mr. Gerald Harlan?"

The drunkard shrank back, his bloodshot eyes flitting from side to side like those of a cornered rat. Betty realized miserably that the accusation was not without foundation.

"I've got a photograph of you in my desk at home," chuckled Kendall. "Two, in fact; full face and profile. Also some fingerprints. Three years you got, wasn't it? And if my memory doesn't fail me, the Edinburgh police are simply aching to make your acquaintance.

"Well, well," he went on, turning back to the others, "it's quite a jolly party, isn't it? I'm not surprised Morlant was murdered. Rather convenient for you, Miss Harlan, wasn't it? With his will already made? Very convenient, indeed! Now tell me: did this jailbird father of yours kill him? Or one of these accomplices? Or was it my sour old friend, Bidgood? By the way, where is Bidgood?"

"I don't think I like you very much, old chappie," drawled Mr. Knight. "But I'll pass over all your faults if you'll answer that question yourself."

"What do you mean? Don't you know where he is?"

"We do not. He has vanished. Into the *ewigkeit.*"

"You're a fool! I wish you'd keep your mouth shut unless you've something to say. Miss Harlan, perhaps you'll oblige with another fairy tale?"

Betty flushed indignantly. The man had his duty to do, of course, but surely he was overstepping the mark. It almost seemed as though his insolence was studied.

She controlled her rising anger, however, and told him all she could about the disappearance of Bidgood.

"So he was left alone with Harlan, was he?" he commented. "And you never saw him again? Well, well! Gerald, my boy, you're going to have some pretty awkward questions to answer in this department before the Edinburgh police get so much as a smell at you."

An uncomfortable silence followed; for though the words were addressed to Harlan, everyone knew that they referred with equal force to him or herself. Up to the present, perhaps, the importance of the murder had been obscured by the strangeness of its circumstances, and the danger to each one personally overshadowed by the mystery of the situation as a whole. Now, however, the sergeant's threat brought home the possibility that in such hopeless confusion the innocent would not escape unscathed.

"It seems to me," he went on thoughtfully, "that you're all mixed up in this. Broughton has funked it and vamoosed. Bidgood's either done the same, or been put out of the way in case he squealed. Evidently it's a put-up job between all of you, though I can't understand Broughton coming to me. What were you doing out here when I came?"

"Destroying a magic carpet, old chappie," said Mr. Knight with his fatuous grin.

"Destroying a—what?"

Again it fell to Betty to explain about the old passage which connected Edward Morlant's bedroom with the cave in the garden. At the sergeant's request she led him to the mound and showed how they had stopped up the opening with stones.

"So you say that's a tunnel?" he grunted, unconvinced. "It looks to me as it might equally well be a grave. However, that can be investigated later when the inspector comes. In the meantime, I'll have a look at the body of this dead man who's been murdered."

"I—I'm afraid you can't do that," faltered Betty. "It—it's gone."

"Gone? The body?"

"Yes. We left it in the library while we searched the house and the tunnel for Bidgood. And when we got back, it—it wasn't there."

"And there was no one else in the house? No one who could have moved it?"

"No."

"Well, of all the tales! Really, young lady, you must have a very poor opinion of the intelligence of the police force if you expect me to swallow that. But I see your little game. Every murderer tries to get rid of the body of his victim. If he succeeds, he's pretty safe; but it isn't often he

does succeed. You may have hidden that body very cleverly, but we'll find it in the end."

"'You'll never find it!" put in Sally suddenly.

"Oho, Miss Poulter! You're singing rather loudly, aren't
you? What do you know?"

"You'll never find it," repeated Sally. Her face was pale,
but she spoke firmly. "Because it—it's come to life again!"

"Good Lord, girl! Are you raving?"

"It's the only possible explanation of what has happened. Before he was killed, he said he'd come back; and
he has come back! He's discovered the secret of immortality. He told us so. He rose from the grave before. And he's
risen again. That dead body is walking about somewhere
now. It—it laughed at us!"

Sergeant Kendall swore viciously under his breath.

"You must think I'm a fool!" he exclaimed. "If that's
your only explanation of a murder and subsequent disposal of the corpse, by crimes, you're in for a bad time, all of
you! However, I've no time to waste talking about ghosts
and resurrections. The inspector'll be here any minute,
and he doesn't believe in such things—not much! If I can't
have a look at the body, I'll see the place where it was."

They walked towards the house. No one had anything
more to say. Naturally, the sergeant could not be expected
to believe so impossible a story as they had to tell. And his
attitude of distrust and suspicion forbade any attempt at
further explanations.

Mr. Knight opened the door, and stopped short on the
threshold in surprise. The hall was in darkness.

"Now that's funny," he murmured. "Decidedly funny.
The lamp was burning when we went out."

"Oil finished?" asked the sergeant.

"No," replied Knight, stepping forward and shaking
the lamp. "There's plenty in it yet."

"Then there's someone else in the house. You told me there wasn't."

"We said there was no one but Edward Morlant," corrected Sally softly.

"Bah! Dead men don't turn lamps out."

Sergeant Kendall strode to the library door from which a beam of light streamed. Inside the room he halted, turning back towards the others.

"You folks have a dangerous sense of humor," he growled. "It will get you into trouble if you're not careful."

They followed him into the room wondering what was amiss. One glance was sufficient to show them. The body of the dog had been flung aside, and in its place the human corpse lay there as before, neatly covered by the tablecloth.

"It—it wasn't there when we went out," stammered Betty, holding on to Sally.

"It's really a most peculiar corpse, old chappie," said Mr. Knight in corroboration. "It does all sorts of queer things."

"Oh, don't try to fool me any more," snapped the sergeant. "I'm not in the mood for it. Let's have a look at him, anyway."

He pulled away the tablecloth roughly. Sally screamed; and the others stood petrified in amazement and horror. For instead of the body of Edward Morlant, the old servant Bidgood lay there on the floor. And his throat was cut from ear to ear.

17

A Pair of *Pince-Nez*

The old man had been brutally murdered. There was no question of suicide. His head was almost severed from his body. No man, however desperate, could have inflicted such terrible injuries upon himself.

"Well, here's something definite to go on," said Sergeant Kendall grimly. "Whatever's happened to Edward Morlant, here's a body that won't sprout wings and fly away!"

"W-where has—it come from?" stammered Sally, looking round at the others helplessly. "It wasn't there when we went out. And there's nowhere it could have been hidden. We've searched the house from top to bottom."

"Including that underground passage you've mentioned?"

"Yes."

"Well, since you went out, if I'm to believe anything you say, the light in the hall has been turned out, and this body dumped here. Obviously, there's someone else in the house."

"We know that," cried Sally, her voice shrill and high pitched. "We know it only too well. But—"

"Ah, we're getting to something now!" The sergeant turned on her quickly. "You're admitting that there's someone else in this. Who is it?"

"I've told you. Edward Morlant."

"Oh, damn! You mean the other dead man?"

"Yes. But he's not—dead. Not like Bidgood. He's come back to life and—"

"Oh, don't try any more of that stuff on me. It won't do you any good."

Everyone was silent for a while. A physical sickness swept over Betty and she could hardly stand. She had liked Bidgood. Despite the fact that he had lied to her, she had felt that he was loyal and trustworthy. She remembered the tears streaming down his wrinkled old face when Edward Morlant lay murdered at their feet, and she had to dry her own eyes. His humility and evident desire to please her had touched her heart. Surely only a monster—a ghoul— could have killed so harmless and helpless an old man! Surely such brutal, inhuman violence could only be the work of a madman!

A madman! A new fear thrilled through her with the thought. She glanced at Sally, and knew what was passing in her mind. Edward Morlant had been subject to recurrent attacks of insanity. Her own mother had broken her engagement because of them. She thought of his pale, contorted face with its blazing, malevolent eyes, and she shuddered. She could imagine such a man shooting his dog in a fit of mad rage; she could see the owner of just such a face cutting his faithful old servant's throat without remorse.

Had Edward Morlant indeed risen again from the dead? Betty knew that Sally was convinced that this had happened; and she herself began to wonder if so dreadful, so unbelievable a thing were possible. Could it be that, in all the immunity of his immortality, armed with all the terrible power of his occult secrets, he still remained alive in the house, a creature without soul, his very brain rotten

with disease, ready to destroy without compunction anyone who crossed his path?

It was a nerve-racking, a paralyzing thought, but Betty
could not thrust it aside. She glanced round at the others,
and found no comfort in their evident perturbation.

Sally, she knew, was feeling just as frightened as she
was. Gerald Harlan—she could not yet think of him as her
father—was staring as though fascinated at the huddled
figure on the floor, his face twisted and blanched. Even
Mr. Knight's usual composure had deserted him; he paced
about the room in moody silence, whistling softly and
tunelessly. And because she could see that he was deeply
affected, Betty grew more frightened still.

As for the police sergeant, he appeared in no way surprised by the turn events had taken.

"You're a mighty clever gang," he said in reluctant ad-
miration, after a while. "I don't know what your game
is precisely, but you're smart right enough. You're trying
to throw dust in my eyes, and I'll confess that I can't see
everything clearly just yet. But I can see one thing: if
Broughton hadn't squealed, you'd have got away with it."

"Got away with what, old chappie?" asked Mr. Knight,
pausing in his restless walk.

"That's just what I don't know. I can't tell yet what your
game is. But it's pretty clear that, between you, you've
made away with both Morlant and Bidgood. You've buried
Morlant under the stones in the garden, and you'd have
done the same for this old fellow here if I hadn't interrupted you."

This, of course, was ridiculous. But no one felt more
comfortable because it was said. It opened before them a
vista of disturbing possibilities. How could they expect the
sergeant to believe anything else? How could they expect
anyone to believe their story? There seemed to be some

malevolent force at work, implicating each one of them in the double murder, drawing a net closely about them.

The mention of Mr. Broughton's name, too, set them all wondering. Betty looked at Sally again, and caught the trouble in her eyes. She knew that her friend had developed an interest in the solicitor, and felt very sorry for her. For it certainly seemed as though he were somehow mixed up in this mysterious business to such an extent that he dare not face it out.

Had he murdered Bidgood and fled? She could not believe him capable of such a deed. And yet there was the undoubted fact that the two had shared some secret. It had been perfectly clear that they had both known more than they would tell. And Mr. Broughton had returned to the house before setting off for Blackshaw. Had Bidgood been put out of the way because he knew too much? It seemed a reasonable assumption. But if it were so, where had the actual murder taken place? How had his body got here? The solicitor could not be responsible for bringing it into the library, because he must have been in Blackshaw at the time.

It was a hopeless muddle, and Betty could glimpse no suggestion of a clew which might help to clear it up. The only thing which seemed certain was that Morlant had been murdered by one of the little party present at the time. There was no getting away from that fact. Broughton or Bidgood, Sally or herself, Harlan or Knight—one of them had plunged a dagger into a defenseless man's back with the same inhuman ferocity as had characterized the killing of the old servant. This was incontrovertible. Yet in spite of the probability that both deeds had been committed by the same hand, and though she had seen Morlant lying dead at her feet, Betty found herself, despite the dictates of her reason, inclining more and more to the conviction that the madman was still alive, that he had murdered Bidgood as he had shot the dog.

Sergeant Kendall carefully replaced the tablecloth over the dead body.

"I wish the inspector would come," he muttered. "This job looks like being a bit big for me."

He straightened himself after a moment's thought, and faced the others with a grim smile.

"This question of the murderer is narrowing down a bit," he said. "When Morlant was killed—assuming he was killed—there were six possibilities. Now Broughton and Bidgood are out of it, and there are only four of you to choose from."

"Like the jolly little nigger boys, isn't it?" grinned Mr. Knight from the hearthrug. "But, you know, old chappie, you've forgotten one possibility."

"What's that?"

"That your friend Mr. Broughton committed both murders."

"'More dust!" said the sergeant dryly. "'And it doesn't sound any more convincing than the rest of your story. It's possible, of course, that Broughton might have had a hand in the first job, but not in the second."

"Why?"

"Because he was in Blackshaw at the time. According to your own story, Bidgood was killed after he left."

"But Broughton came back to the house after leaving us."

"The devil he did!" Kendall was visibly startled. "How do you know that?"

Mr. Knight showed him the eyeglasses, and explained where they had been found.

"You see, old chappie," he said severely, "one can't be too careful in a case like this."

"That's true," responded the sergeant, nettled. "And I might pass the same advice along to all of you. Somehow, I don't see a jury paying much attention to any yarn about eyeglasses. I fancy they'll be more interested in one of you four. You, Harlan, for instance. You were left alone in the house with Bidgood, weren't you?"

Gerald Harlan glanced at him furtively, then turned away again, moistening his dry lips with his tongue.

"Yes," he replied sullenly.

"Well, you know, we've already got one or two black marks against you, and—"

"Oh, I know!" The drunkard swung round on him in sudden, impotent rage. "I know what will happen. I've met your kind before. Just because my sheet's not clean, you'll try to make it worse. You'll blacken it until a jury will believe anything. You'll twist everything about in your own devilish way until you manage to fix this job on me. I know you!"

"Conscience troubling you, evidently, Gerald," observed Kendall, quite unmoved by the hysterical outburst. "Confession is good for the soul."

"Conscience!" Harlan glared at him with bloodshot eyes. "Confession! I've nothing to confess. I didn't kill him. I didn't, I tell you! I heard him scream—"

"Ah, you heard that? You were somewhere about when it happened? Where was he when he screamed?"

"I don't know. He wasn't here with me. I was alone in this room."

"Bah! You're lying!" The sergeant caught him by the shoulders and shook him. "Come on, now! Let's have the truth! Tell us how you killed him."

Before this definite accusation, Gerald Harlan wilted entirely. A fit of trembling seized him, and his slack mouth writhed and twisted in his effort to find words to defend himself.

"I didn't do it!" he cried in abject terror. "I didn't kill him, I tell you! I've been a forger. I've been a thief. I'm confessing it openly. I'm not trying to hide it. But I've never been a murderer!"

"You killed both Morlant and Bidgood at the instigation of your daughter here."

"I didn't! She knows nothing about it. She knows nothing about me. She didn't even know I was alive. I haven't seen her for years."

"That's true, sergeant," interposed Betty. "He's not lying. Until to-day, I thought he was dead. I've always been told so."

"Honor among thieves," sneered Kendall. "That's a likely story, isn't it?"

"But it is true," protested Harlan eagerly. "I've spent most of my life abroad. The last five years, I've been—crooked. I never intended her to know anything about me and—"

"Then why did you come here?"

The question was too direct to be avoided. Gerald Harlan evidently realized that prevarication would be useless. He hesitated for a moment, then slowly drew a crumpled sheet of paper from his pocket.

"I came because of that," he said, handing the paper to the sergeant.

It was a telegram addressed to *"Tomlinson, 5a Horley Mansions, N. W."* and dated the previous day.

"'Tomlinson'?" queried Kendall. "That the name you were passing under?"

"Yes."

"Well, that's worth knowing, to begin with. *'Your daughter inherited Hameldon House. Introduce yourself immediately. I shall be there to-morrow. X.'* Who's X?"

"Sounds like a co-respondent in a divorce case," suggested Mr. Knight from the hearthrug.

"You shut up," snapped the sergeant. "Now, Harlan. No more lies. Who's X?"

"I—I don't know."

"No lies, I said! Come on. Out with it. Who is he?"

The drunkard shrank back, his bloodshot eyes quailing, one arm raised as though to ward off a blow.

"I—I don't dare tell you," he stammered.

Kendall caught him by the shoulder and roughly swung him round so that their faces were almost touching.

"You'll tell me!" he snarled. "You'll tell me or I'll break you in two!"

Betty took a step forward. Harlan might be everything that was bad, but he was her father. His terror was pitiful to see, and she felt that she could listen no more.

Before she had time to interfere, however, Mr. Knight's pleasant voice broke in again.

"I say, old chappie, you might tell me: you haven't arrested him, have you?"

"Not yet," said the sergeant significantly. "Why?"

"Well, then, you mustn't bully him, you know. Either arrest him and warn him, or leave him alone."

Mr. Knight crossed over to Harlan and laid a reassuring hand on his arm.

"You needn't take a bit of notice of him if you don't want to," he said kindly. "He's acting very illegally, and he knows it. Don't be bullied into answering his question if it incriminates you in any way."

"Oh, I'll tell him," moaned the drunkard. "He'll make it worse for me if I don't. I'll tell him all I can."

"Just as you like." Mr. Knight seemed annoyed, and commenced walking about the room again, while the sergeant looked at him in silent triumph.

"I can't tell you much," continued Harlan. "Because I don't know much. I've never seen him. I don't know his name. All I know is that I've done several jobs for him—"

"What sort of jobs? Forgery?"

"Yes. And I've always been well paid. I've tried to get to know who he is, but never succeeded. His orders always came by letter or through some third person. He's clever.

He does things in a big way. He's the leader of a gang, so I've been told, each an expert in his own particular line. They're all frightened to breathe a word about him. They say he's a devil in human form. They call him 'The Ghoul.'"

"'The Ghoul'?" Sergeant Kendall started, and clutched Harlan's shoulder again. "Did you say 'The Ghoul'?"

"That's what they call him."

"I've heard of him. My God, is there a police station in England that hasn't heard of him? 'A devil in human form,' you say? That just about fits him. He's wanted for I don't know how many murders."

The sergeant seemed very worried and uneasy over this new development.

"I wish the inspector would come," he muttered. "If 'The Ghoul's' here, it's too big a job for me."

He carefully folded up the telegram, and placed it in his pocket. As he did so, an idea occurred to him.

"By crimes!" he exclaimed. *"I shall be there tomorrow!"* Then one of you must be 'The Ghoul'!"

No one spoke. They were all staring at him in apprehension.

"It's neither Broughton nor Bidgood," he went on, "for I've known both of 'em for years. Nor yet the two girls. He said in the wire he'd be here to-morrow. That's to-day. And there's just two of you who've arrived at the house to-day. You"—with a contemptuous glance at Harlan,—"you're not 'The Ghoul'. It must be—"

He looked round in search of Mr. Knight. And suddenly raised his clenched fists on high.

"Hell and damnation!" he cried, tearing his hair. "The cunning devil's gone!"

18

The Face at the Door

Hardly able to breathe in her agitation, Betty glanced quickly round the room. The sergeant's words, so ominous yet so assured, had struck a cold chill to her heart. And they were true! Mr. Knight had vanished! He had gone without a sound, probably slipping unobserved through the open door while they had been discussing "The Ghoul."

There was a moment of hesitation while the significance of this timely disappearance became apparent to everyone. Then Sergeant Kendall swore forcibly, and dashed from the room.

Gerald Harlan sank into a chair, whispering to himself. His hands were twitching violently, and his bloodshot eyes stared vacantly at the door.

"He's 'The Ghoul'!" he muttered, fingering his slack mouth. "God in Heaven. He's 'The Ghoul'!"

Seeing her distress, Sally ran to her friend and flung comforting arms around her. Betty tried in vain to control her trembling limbs.

"He—he's not 'The Ghoul'!" she faltered. "He can't be! It's impossible!"

"Of course, he's not," agreed Sally, soothingly. "He'll be turning up again with his silly grin in a minute."

They stood looking at the huddled body on the floor in silence for a while before Betty spoke again.

"I wish you'd tell me the truth, Sally," she pleaded. "Everything seems so—complicated. I'm all—upset and muddled. I wish you'd tell me what you think."

"I don't know what to think. Honestly, Betty, I don't. I'd like to assure you that he's all right, but I—I don't know. You see, he's the only person here without apparent cause, isn't he? I mean, you don't believe that he really came this morning to sell furniture, do you?"

"No, I don't."

"And he didn't want Harlan to mention 'The Ghoul.' It looks suspicious. You remember how he tried to stop him?"

"Yes."

"And there was something queer right at the beginning," Sally went on thoughtfully. "I'd forgotten about it until just now. I mean before lunch, when he disappeared out of this room just as you were coming in."

"He was in the garden. I don't think it was he I heard in here."

"You think it was—"

"Edward Morlant. Yes."

"I see. Well, it may be so. We can't tell, can we? But there's no doubt that he's been playing some sort of game. He's not such a fool as he's been pretending."

"You're right there, Sally," said Betty suddenly. "He's not a fool. And I'm going to believe in him, to trust him. What you've just said has helped me to understand how necessary it is that I should trust him. You know, he was with us when Bidgood was killed, so he couldn't have had anything to do with that. And there's something I ought to have told you before, but I don't seem to have had the chance. The drunken young man who appeared in the fog the night before last was—"

"Not Mr. Knight?"

"Yes. He saved my life then, and I think he's trying to do the same thing again."

"I don't see what you mean."

"Well, I'll tell you what has just occurred to me as being the probable explanation of it all." Betty shivered, but set her lips together firmly. "I believe the man who attacked me in the fog was 'The Ghoul.' The cold-blooded, relentless way in which he tried to push me into the water was just what you'd expect from such a criminal. I believe he wants to get rid of me for some reason connected with the inheritance."

"Gosh!" exclaimed Sally, wide-eyed. "You really think he's after you?"

"I do. And I think Mr. Knight's after him. That's my explanation. He must have found out in some way that 'The Ghoul' was coming here, and followed him."

"Why hasn't he told you so?"

"I don't think he dare. He doesn't want anyone to suspect that he's not what he pretends to be. Though he has tried indirectly to make me understand. You don't remember what he said when he slipped and sprained his ankle?"

"I don't. Except that he made some sort of silly joke."

"He said: 'It's very wrong to be drunk so early in the day.' He had used those words when he saved my life in the fog. Later, he repeated another similar phrase. It couldn't have been coincidence. I'm sure he was trying to warn me without giving himself away to anyone else."

Sally was silent for a while.

"It looks as though you might be right," she said slowly at last. "And if you are— Look here, Betty. If Mr. Knight had to be so careful, then 'The Ghoul' must have been somewhere about at the time."

"Y-yes."

"Well, in the house there were you and I, Bidgood and your father, and—Mr. Broughton. Betty, it looks as though— You surely don't think Mr. Broughton is 'The Ghoul'?"

"Oh, I don't know, Sally," cried Betty miserably. "I liked him, and I know you— But what else can one think? There was that false mustache which we found after the attempt on my life. He was with us when Edward Morlant was killed. He came back to the house about the time Bidgood was murdered. And now he's gone—vanished."

"Yes, he's gone," muttered Sally. "But so has Mr. Knight."

Again they were silent. It seemed to them that a net of tragedy was closing in on them, that inevitably they would find themselves still further involved in its meshes. The discovery of the fact that so desperate a criminal as 'The Ghoul' was somewhere near was terrifying. If Betty were right in her surmise that it was he who had tried to kill her in the fog, then it was apparent that they were in grave personal danger. And this danger was intensified enormously because they did not know his identity.

"Well," said Sally, with sudden decision, "you can put your trust in Mr. Knight. I'm going to do the same with Mr. Broughton. I'll never believe he could be a cold-blooded murderer." Her voice sank into a whisper. "I'll tell you what I've been wondering, Betty. Can Edward Morlant be 'The Ghoul'?"

"Sally?"

"Just think about it. It sounds absurd, I know. But remember his contorted face. Remember his evil eyes. Remember that hideous laugh of his. Isn't he just the sort of man to commit such inhuman crimes?"

"He—he was very kind to me."

"Yes, when he was sane. But when he was mad . . . ? Suppose what your mother found out was that he became a dangerous criminal in his madness."

"That may be so. But, anyhow, he's dead, Sally."

"We only think so. And we thought so before. How can we be sure that he's dead? His body's gone. And if he can come to life once, he can come to life again."

"Oh, it isn't possible. It can't be so."

"It *is* possible, Betty! It has happened before. You've heard of vampires, haven't you? Evil spirits that take possession of the bodies of human beings who have died, and use them for their own devilish purposes?"

"Yes, I've heard of them. But you surely don't believe in their existence?"

"Why not? Why shouldn't we believe in them? Betty, I've seen so many queer things! I *know* that spirits can show and manifest themselves to us. I've seen them. Talked to them. Most of them are harmless, but some—are not. And how else can you account for Edward Morlant's immortality?"

"We don't know that he's—immortal, Sally. We only thought he was dead before. Obviously, we were mistaken, and he had some reason for deceiving us. He hasn't come to life again since we actually saw him killed."

"I believe he has, Betty. I believe he's somewhere about at this moment. Remember that mocking laugh we heard when we found Bidgood. I'm firmly convinced that we shall see Edward Morlant again!"

Betty shuddered. She knew that Sally was in earnest, and, despite her own skepticism, she could not help being moved. It was bad enough to have to deal with a human criminal. But if they had to face the supernatural. . . .

"You can't be right, Sally!" she cried. "You can't! It's impossible that he should have come to life. And I don't see how he can be 'The Ghoul,' either. Remember how he was stabbed. In the back. He couldn't do that himself. One of us in the room must have done it. And that one must be 'The Ghoul.'"

She paused, feeling utterly helpless, realizing how much worse everything seemed without the comforting presence of Mr. Knight.

"Oh, it's horrible, horrible!" She tried to stifle the sob in her throat. "And it's all due to me. If I hadn't come here, all these dreadful things wouldn't have happened. I wish I was back at the studio, Sally. It seems so safe—and so far away. Oh, I wish I'd never left it!"

"Well, let's go back," suggested Sally eagerly. "Let's go now. There's nothing to stop us if we hurry away while the sergeant's out of sight. He wouldn't set off for Blackshaw after us. We can walk."

"We can't do that now," said Betty mournfully. "It's too late. The harm's done. Besides, it would look as though we were guilty and were trying to escape. No, I think we'd better wait. The rest of the police will soon be here, and everything will be cleared up."

"Not if they've the mentality of Sergeant Kendall, my dear. Of all the blundering, asinine, conceited—"

Sally's strictures were cut short by the entry of the sergeant himself. He looked very angry, and his shaggy eyebrows were contracted into a ferocious frown.

"There's not a sign of him!" he announced, stamping his feet. "He's got clear away. By crimes, I there was a telephone here! Imagine me letting him escape like that. I'll get it hot when the Inspector comes."

"I thought he was a fool," he went on bitterly. "He took me in completely. Who'd ever think of 'The Ghoul' carrying on like a half-baked lunatic, with his 'old chappie' this, and his 'old chappie' that? I could kick myself. Still, I've stopped his little game. And I've got three members of his gang. So that's something."

Betty felt a wild impulse to laugh. In the midst of all this worry and bewilderment, the sergeant's insistence on a wrong trail struck a ludicrous note.

"A little less than something," she murmured, "as you will find out eventually. I'm afraid you're hopelessly in the dark, Sergeant. You're just as lost as we are."

"Perhaps I am, young lady," he replied. "Anyhow, I'm running no risk of you two getting away. I'm going to lock you up."

He looked at Harlan who was still sitting with his head buried in his hands.

"You'll stop here until I come back, Harlan," he commanded. "If you move, it'll be all the worse for you."

"All right," stammered the other, without raising his head. "I—I won't move."

"He hasn't the pluck," said Kendall contemptuously. "He's safe enough. Come on. Before I fasten you in your room you can show me the opening of that underground passage. It's my last chance of finding 'The Ghoul.'"

He led the way upstairs, keeping a wary eye on the two girls. Betty showed him how to work the sliding back of the wardrobe in Morlant's room, noticing as she did so that the thread placed there by Mr. Knight remained intact.

The sergeant peered down the narrow steps into the darkness of the tunnel.

"Looks fairly promising," he muttered. "An ideal place for him to hide in. I'll have you two out of the way in case there's some shooting. Where's your bedroom?"

He accompanied them to their room and, after satisfying himself that they could not escape by the window, locked them in and left them.

"I'll come back for you as soon as the inspector arrives," he shouted through the door. "In the meantime, you can be composing some more fairy stories."

For quite a while after he had gone, neither of the girls spoke. Reaction from the excitement of the night was setting in, and they both felt tired and miserable. Each was wondering what had become of the man in whom she had placed her trust, and realizing that there must be more than coincidence in the fact that, except for Harlan and the police sergeant, they were now unprotected.

"Well," said Sally, voicing her thoughts at last, "I suppose we're safe in here, at any rate."

Betty did not feel at all safe. The disappearance of Mr. Knight had shaken her nerve more than anything else. It seemed a presage of further mystery and horror. And a locked door was not much protection against the kind of thing that was happening at Hameldon House. But she made no reply.

"I don't know what we'll do when bedtime comes," Sally went on with a little shiver. "I just simply dare not pass another night in this horrible place."

"You needn't worry about that," said Betty laughing shortly. "We'll probably pass it in a police cell."

Sally grimaced and lit a cigarette.

"Better than this," she said, looking round the shadow-haunted room in disgust.

"I say!" she continued after a while. "That wardrobe's very like the one in the other room. I wonder if— You don't suppose there's a back door to every bedroom, do you?"

"That hardly seems possible, does it? Still, we'll look if you like."

They took up their candles and carefully examined the interior of the wardrobe. If there was a hidden sliding panel, they failed to discover it. But they did find a bunch of rusty old keys hanging on a nail.

"Looks as though one of these would fit the door," murmured Sally. "Let's try 'em."

She fitted the keys one by one into the old-fashioned lock of the door, and eventually was rewarded by a click.

"That's done it," she said. "We can get out if we want to. But I think we're as well here as anywhere else, aren't we?"

"Yes," agreed Betty. "Until the rest of the police come."

They sat down to finish their cigarettes. A moment later they both sprang hurriedly to their feet, tense and alert. From downstairs had come the sound of a loud, high-pitched voice, raised in fear.

"It's Mr. Harlan!" whispered Sally, her face pale and frightened. "Your father! Something's happening!"

Staring at one another in apprehension, they listened. They could not distinguish any words. But from the tone of the distant voice it was evident that Harlan was terrified, protesting against something, screaming for help.

For a few seconds they stood there, chilled by the terror in his voice. Then:

"Come on!" said Betty suddenly. "Let's go!"

With shaking hands they opened the door and stole out into the corridor. As they did so, the voice ceased abruptly, leaving a silence that seemed to palpitate.

"'The Ghoul's' got him!" breathed Sally. "Oh, God! Come back, Betty. Come back!"

"No! We're going to see. We can't leave him to—"

"But if 'The Ghoul's' there—come back to life—"

"I *must* go, Sally. Are you coming with me?"

"Yes."

They extinguished their candles and groped their way along the dark corridor. Except for the creaking of the boards under their feet, not a sound disturbed the stillness of the house. They crept forward in silence, not daring to speak again.

When they neared the top of the stairs and the welcome light from the hall, Betty breathed more freely. But as she looked over the banisters, she started violently and clutched Sally's arm in a wordless command to stop.

Down below in the stone-flagged hall, a figure stood peering out of the half open door, a familiar figure that brought a cold dread to their hearts.

"Oh, look, Betty!" gasped Sally, catching sight of it. "Look at his back!"

Under the man's left shoulder, his coat showed a gaping, blood-stained rent, a rent which they knew had been made by a dagger. Betty stared at it in unbelieving horror. And as she watched, the man turned slowly from the door, disclosing the pallid, evil face of Edward Morlant!

19

In the Library

Sally gripped Betty's hand in a paroxysm of fear. She was shaking from head to foot.

"He's come back!" she whispered hoarsely. "Come back to life again! I knew he would; I could feel it. Betty, he's 'The Ghoul.' And we can't do anything. He'll kill us all!"

Betty did not speak. Her mouth was dry and parched, and her tongue seemed useless. She could not remove her fascinated gaze from the ominous figure in the hall.

Sally was right, after all! Sally had been right all the time. The impossible had happened. All the laws of Nature were broken. Edward Morlant, murdered before their very eyes, had come back to life as he had boasted!

What could one think in the face of such an incredible happening? What could one do? She felt utterly bewildered and helpless, as though in the grip of a nightmare. And a paralyzing dread was clutching at her heart. For this Thing, whatever it might be, was no harmless phantom. It was an entity malevolent and murderous, endowed with supernatural power to wreak its hatred on them.

She had not believed that such things could be. She had considered warlocks and vampires—all the legendary inhabitants of the occult world—to be the creations of diseased imaginations. But here was proof that could not be gainsaid—the evidence of her own eyes. Had she been alone, she might, perhaps, have doubted her sanity. It was certain that both she and Sally could not be deceived.

The two girls waited, stupefied, dreading what might happen next. Morlant, apparently, had not heard their approach. As they watched him, a sardonic grin twisted his thin lips. After another glance out into the night, he commenced to ascend the stairs towards them.

They stood in frozen terror, unable to move. Each slow, soundless step on the thickly carpeted staircase brought a nameless horror closer to them, yet they could not turn to flee. Wide-eyed and tremulous, they awaited their fate as the hypnotized bird awaits the snake.

Betty's face grew paler. The rising surge of her pulses throbbed until she almost choked. Her stifling panic increased until she felt that she must scream or die. And she could not scream. She could not think. Oh, if only Mr. Knight were here! He would know how to deal with this Thing. . .

Morlant was nearly at the top of the stairs. They could hear him muttering to himself. Another few steps, and he would reach them. They held their breath as he advanced. And then, when discovery seemed inevitable, Sally's candlestick slipped from her nerveless grasp and clattered noisily on the floor almost at his feet.

Even to their numbed minds it was clear that he was startled. For a fraction of a second he glared into the darkness ahead, trying to read its secret.

Then, turning, he ran swiftly down the stairs, and disappeared into the library.

"Oh, thank God!" gasped Sally, almost fainting. "Thank God he's gone!"

The tension was snapped. The warm blood flowed back into Betty's soft cheeks. The sense of utter helplessness left her. She was still terribly afraid, but the fear now was such as she could fight.

She took Sally's trembling form into her arms, and tried to soothe and comfort her. But Sally had reached the limit of her endurance.

"He's 'The Ghoul'!" she kept on moaning feebly. "He's come back to life! He's 'The Ghoul' and he'll kill us all!"

Betty's efforts to calm her were of little avail. After a while, she gave up the attempt.

"I'm going down," she said. "I must know—"

Sally clung to her, whimpering like a child.

"Oh, you mustn't, Betty!" she cried. "For God's sake, don't leave me. Don't go down. Don't—"

"I must go, Sally! I must know what has happened to Mr.—my father."

"He's dead. He's dead, I tell you. And you'll be dead, too, if you—"

"Sally!" Betty caught her fiercely by the shoulder. "Sally! Listen! Edward Morlant was frightened. He didn't know what the noise you made was, and he ran away! He didn't dare face whatever he suspected might be waiting in the darkness. He was *frightened!* Don't you understand? Don't you see what it means? He can't have all those wonderful powers which you attribute to him. He can't—or he wouldn't be frightened. I don't believe he's anything more than an ordinary man. I don't believe he can harm us at all. Anyhow, I'm going down if you're game enough to come with me. Are you?"

The challenge succeeded where softer measures had failed. Sally got a grip on her overwrought nerves, and mastered the threatening hysteria.

"Yes, I'll come with you, Betty," she said more quietly. "Thanks for—oh, I'm a baby, I know, to give way like that! But to see him—it—walking upstairs to us! . . . Oh, I'll shut up. And I'll come with you. Anywhere you like. Lead on, Macduff. But it's no use pretending that I'm not in a blue funk. Because I am!"

"So am I," admitted Betty frankly. "And I don't see how anyone could blame us. But—there's my father; I feel I ought to make sure—"

"Then don't let's wait any longer. Let's go now. Or I'll be running away."

They crept cautiously down the stairs, pausing frequently to listen. The old house was abnormally silent; not a creak or a murmur disturbed its stillness. The patter of their footsteps on the stone flags of the hall sounded tremendous to them, though in fact it was barely audible.

Outside the door of the library they stopped, hand in hand. They could hear no sound or movement in the room; but for all they knew, 'The Ghoul' was lying in wait for them inside, and they hesitated to enter.

At last Betty summoned up all her courage, and cautiously peered round the half open door. Her heart sank within her when she saw that the room was empty; for surely there must be something of the supernatural about the man who had entered it only a minute or two ago.

"He's not here," she said slowly. "And—and my father's gone, too."

Sally pushed the door wide open and stood looking round, while fear showed again in her staring eyes.

"He—he was right," she faltered, hardly knowing what she said. "He spoke the truth. He was not lying. He has discovered the hidden secrets of the Wisdom Religion. He is an Adept. He can overcome the laws of Nature. He can disappear at will."

Betty did not reply. Her frightened gaze had rested on the still body under the tablecloth, and a horrible suspicion had come to her mind.

Overcoming her repugnance, she advanced towards the huddled figure. Had another substitution been effected? Would she find her father dead beneath the cloth? Stooping, she slowly drew the cover back. A sigh of relief escaped her when she saw the thin, grizzled hair of the old manservant.

"Oh, I'm glad!" she exclaimed, quickly replacing the cloth. "It's still Bidgood. I thought, perhaps—"

"It might just as well have been Mr. Harlan," cried Sally hysterically. "Because he's dead. 'The Ghoul's' killed him."

"Oh, don't talk like that, Sally! We don't know—"

"Of course, we know! Betty, can't you see it? Can't you see what's happening? He's getting us one by one! One after the other! We're all to be killed, and he's taking us in turn. Just think. First Bidgood, then Mr. Broughton—"

"But Mr. Broughton is not dead."

"How do we know? 'The Ghoul' can reach him any-where. Even in Blackshaw. I think he is dead. If he wasn't, he'd have come back here."

Betty was startled. It had not occurred to her before that the absence of either Broughton or Knight might be due to anything but his own free will.

"And Mr. Knight?" she suggested quickly. "Surely you don't think that he—"

"Yes, he's dead, too. Don't ask me how 'The Ghoul' got him, because I don't know. But he's gone. So has Mr. Har-lan. And it'll be our turn next!"

Sally's nerve was failing again, and her panic infected Betty. She imagined Mr. Knight lying still and cold some-where in the darkness outside, and a fit of trembling seized her.

"T-there's the police," she stammered. "They'll not let him—they'll protect—"

"What good are the police against an Adept? How has this sergeant protected Mr. Harlan?" Sally clutched Betty's arm in desperation. "Let's go, Betty!" she urged eagerly. "Let's escape while we can. This house is doomed and every one in it. If we stay here, 'The Ghoul' will get us.

Let's slip out now. The door is open, and the sergeant's down in the tunnel. We can walk to Blackshaw. And see people again, Betty. Ordinary, human people. Come on! Don't stay here—just to be killed."

The thought that Mr. Knight might be dead had terrified Betty more than all else.

"All right," she agreed. "Let's hurry!"

They had barely taken a step towards the door when they halted again. Someone was crossing the stone-flagged hall towards the library.

Was it Edward Morlant returning? Or the police sergeant? They waited in breathless anxiety. It was a great relief to them, despite the fact that their flight was cut off, when Sergeant Kendall appeared in the doorway.

His shaggy eyebrows shot up at sight of them.

"What the devil!" he exclaimed. "How did you two get here? And where's Harlan!"

"'The Ghoul's' got him," said Sally.

"'The Ghoul's'—what? Look here, young woman, just tell me a proper tale. Start at the beginning. How did you escape from your room?"

"We found a key," explained Betty. We didn't intend coming out, but we heard Mr. Harlan calling for help. As we came downstairs, we—we saw 'The Ghoul' in the hall."

"The devil you did!" The sergeant started, and glanced at her keenly. "Wonder if I hunted him out of the secret passage?" he added, after a moment.

"I don't mean Mr. Knight. He's not 'The Ghoul.' I mean Edward Morlant."

"Morlant? The man who was murdered?"

"Yes. He was coming upstairs, but took fright because we made a noise. He ran into here. And when we came after him, there was no one in the room."

Sergeant Kendall burst into a roar of laughter.

"Same old tale," he chuckled. "Still trying to throw dust in my eyes. You'll be telling me next you've seen old Bidgood here walking about. You must think I'm a fool."

"And perhaps I am," he went on, sobering. "Perhaps I am. I've let you two twist me around your little fingers, haven't I? You're devilish smart, both of you. You've managed to get rid of Harlan somehow. A mighty clever move—he was quite likely to squeal, wasn't he? I ought never to have left you. But I had to make sure whether 'The Ghoul' was hiding in that passage. Anyhow, I'll not let you out of my sight again."

Betty looked at him despairingly.

"Oh, why won't you understand?" she cried, unnerved again by the knowledge that his obsession rendered him worse than useless as a protector. "Why can't we make you see that you're wrong in suspecting us? We don't know anything about Mr. Harlan. He was calling for help. Don't you understand? Screaming for help. 'The Ghoul' was killing him!"

Whether because he glimpsed truth in her statement, or because he could not help admiring what he considered her cleverness, the sergeant's attitude changed.

"Well, I'll keep an open mind about you a bit longer," he said. "Though I'm afraid I can't do anything to verify your statements until the Inspector comes. Curse his damned leisurely ways! He should have been here long ago. And I'll tell him so when he does come if he starts ragging me for what has happened."

He noticed Betty shivering.

"You're cold, Miss Harlan? I'm not surprised. It's not too tropical to-night. We'll get the fire going again. And perhaps make a cup of tea, eh? It'll pass the time away, and take your mind off things a bit. Come on. Let's see what we can dig up in the kitchen."

Both Betty and Sally found the idea attractive. It seemed ages since they had had tea, just before discovering Edward Morlant's diary.

They followed Kendall into the kitchen. As soon as they opened the door, they were met by a strong smell of burning. Betty remembered the chickens which poor old Bidgood had been cooking; they were still in the oven, dry, charred and useless, though the fire was dead.

"That's a pity," commented the sergeant, closing the oven door. "I could just have tackled a couple of wings. Our luck's out. Suppose you ladies see if you can find something to eat while I get the library fire going."

He departed with a shovelful of coal and some wood. The two girls set about preparing a simple meal. Now that the subject had been mentioned, they both found that they were hungry.

Betty foraged in the cupboard, and brought out some potted meat and savories.

"How's this, Sally?" she asked. "Some sandwiches?"

"Yes," replied Sally, putting the kettle on the oil stove. "Lots of 'em!"

They set to work with a will. The opportunity of performing an everyday task had temporarily driven their troubles away. And when Sally found some China tea in the caddy, they became quite cheerful.

"That kettle's a long time boiling," said Betty, wistfully regarding the pile of daintily cut sandwiches that represented her share of the work. "I'm just dying for a cup of tea."

"It won't be long now. That is, if you don't watch it."

"Then I'll carry the tray in, and draw that little table up to the fire—if Sergeant Kendall's managed to light it."

There was a big fire blazing in the library. Betty could hear the crackling of the wood as she passed through the hall. It sounded quite bright and cheery.

In the doorway she stopped abruptly. A sickly fear crept back to her heart. For once again the room was empty.

She laid the tray down on the table beside the door, and stood looking round, hesitating and apprehensive. Where was Sergeant Kendall? What had happened to him?

Suddenly acute terror swept over her like a tidal wave. She remembered Sally's words: "One by one; one after the other." "The Ghoul" was taking them one by one. Had the sergeant been spirited away? Had he, in his turn, fallen a victim to this relentless enemy?

Breathless with fright at the thought, she turned to flee. A movement in the room caught her eye. She looked again, and her heart seemed to stop beating. The body under the tablecloth had moved!

It was only a few minutes since she had seen the corpse of Bidgood there. And now it was moving, coming to life! A scream rose to her throat. Before she had time to utter it, a hand was pressed roughly over her mouth and nose. Someone who had stepped from behind the door held her so that she could not move.

She tried to kick, to wriggle from the restraining arms. Her struggles were of no avail. The suffocating hand did not relax its pressure. She had a momentary impression of two evil, odd-colored eyes glaring into hers. Then black, star-spangled oblivion descended upon her.

20

THE SPIDER AND THE FLIES

The kettle boiled at last. Sally warmed the teapot and mashed the tea with care. There must be nothing wrong with this all-important part of the commissariat. Satisfied with the fragrant aroma that resulted, she picked up a tray and hurried out of the kitchen.

The lamp in the hall was burning low, and the cold, drafty place was full of shadows. She stopped to adjust the wick of the lamp. It occurred to her that the house was very quiet.

She stood for a moment, listening. In the unnatural silence, she could hear the ticking of the clock and the crackling of the fire in the library. But there was no sound of movement or conversation such as she had expected. A presentiment of disaster arose.

Anxiously she hurried into the library. Even as she entered the door, she knew the worst. Except for the huddled figure under the tablecloth, there was no one in the room. The tray dropped from her hands and crashed upon the floor.

"Betty! Betty!" she called shrilly, turning in every direction. "Betty! Where are you?"

Her voice rang through the old house. Its hollow echoes died away into a silence that seemed more profound than before. But there was no reply.

"He's got them!" moaned Sally, beating her hands together. "He's got Betty and the sergeant!"

She was alone. One by one, the others had fallen victims to the murderous lust of the soulless Thing that haunted the house. One by one they had been caught up into its evil clutches. One by one they had vanished from human ken. She was alone!

She screamed loudly as full realization came to her. She was alone in the house with "The Ghoul"! Alone with this murderous Thing, this vampire! There could be no escape for her. It would be her turn next!

Soul-destroying terror seized upon her. She ran wildly about the room. In her frenzy, she sought a place to hide, though she knew full well that there could be no concealment from "The Ghoul."

Suddenly she stopped, and screamed again. The body under the tablecloth was moving. Half fainting, she clung to a chair, gazing spellbound at this new horror.

As she watched, the figure struggled up into a sitting position. Slowly and painfully, it disentangled itself from its covering. And then, when Sally felt that her racing heart must burst, she found herself looking into the clouded, vacant eyes of Mr. Clarence Knight.

She swayed on her feet, almost overturning the chair. Forgetting her terror for the moment, she stared at him, open-mouthed. What could be the meaning of this? How could he possibly have got here, under the tablecloth which only a few minutes ago had covered the mutilated body of poor Bidgood? And what had happened to the old servant?

Mr. Knight seemed unaware of her presence. He was gingerly feeling at his head.

"That 'Ghoul' of ours," he muttered indistinctly, "he's got a heavy hand."

Sally was bewildered. The events of the evening were entirely beyond her comprehension. She felt lost and helpless. But she could not help remembering that this man had fallen under suspicion, that he must have been in the room when the sergeant and Betty were spirited away.

He looked at her again, and a gleam of recognition lit up in his gray eyes.

"It's Miss Poulter, isn't it?" he asked, grinning feebly. "What are you singing for, Miss Poulter?"

There was comfort in his foolish question. Sally suddenly saw that he was dazed, that he did not understand what was happening. He did not even realize that she had been screaming. Surely it was ridiculous to imagine that he might be "The Ghoul."

Her relief brought a flood of tears. She fell on her knees beside him.

"He's got her!" she sobbed. "He's got her!"

"You were not singing, evidently," he pondered. "I could have sworn I heard you. But it did sound rather queer. Now I wonder who has got whom?"

"Oh, don't you understand?" cried Sally, shaking him. "It's 'The Ghoul'! He's got Betty!"

The vacant expression slowly cleared away from Mr. Knight's face.

"Betty?" he echoed. "'The Ghoul's' got Betty?"

"Yes! And the sergeant, too!"

"My God!" Mr. Knight stiffened as complete recollection came to him. He rose to his feet, tottering. "If he harms a hair of her head. . . . Oh, Lord, I'm done in!"

He collapsed on the floor again. Sally ran for the water jug, and bathed his face. At the side of his head she found a large, ragged scalp wound, and attended to it as well as she could.

In a few moments he recovered consciousness.

"Where is he?" he asked feebly.

"Where is who?"

"'The Ghoul'? That sergeant fellow?"

"But he's not 'The Ghoul.'"

"Yes, he is."

"He can't be," wailed Sally. "Oh, he can't be! For God's sake, don't get on the wrong track now. Don't make a mistake when there's so much depending on it. You don't know everything that's happened. Edward Morlant's 'The Ghoul.' We've seen him! Seen him—walking about! He's come to life again. First he got Mr. Harlan; we heard him screaming for help while we were upstairs. Then he got the sergeant. And now Betty."

"You—you've seen Edward Morlant again?"

"Yes. In the hall. He came in here, then disappeared."

"Miss Poulter! Surely you must be mistaken?"

"I'm not mistaken. Both Betty and I saw him. He was within a yard of us. And there was a big hole in his coat where—where the dagger had been in."

Mr. Knight tried to sit up again and failed.

"Oh, damn!" he muttered. "It's beyond me. Utterly beyond me. And just when I'm wanted, I'm helpless as a baby. That devil Kendall will be back any minute. He thinks I'm dead, and he'll come back for you. We *must* collar him when he comes. It's our only chance of saving Betty. Because despite what you say about Edward Morlant, I *know* that this pretended sergeant is 'The Ghoul.'"

"You think he'll come back for me?" asked Sally, impressed by his distress.

"Of course he will! And we can't do a thing for Betty until he does. God knows where she is. He's spirited her away through some secret passage which we might be days in discovering. If we found her at all, it would be—too late. Our only hope is to surprise him when he returns, overpower him, and compel him to lead us to wherever he has hidden her."

The truth of this was evident. Sally finished bandaging the wound in silence.

"Oh, if only he keeps away long enough for you to re-cover your strength," she murmured after a while.

"There's a brandy flask in my hip pocket," he suggested. "If you don't mind . . ."

She found the flask and held it to his lips. She listened fearfully for any sound which might herald the return of the sergeant, but the old house was silent as the grave.

"Do you know who—who he is?" she asked softly.

Mr. Knight nodded. "I'm sorry—yes," he replied.

"Not—not Mr. Broughton?" she faltered, shrinking from the pity in his gray eyes.

"Yes, Miss Poulter. There's no doubt about it. My suspicions were first aroused when we discovered those eye-glasses near the opening of the cave. And later I found more definite proof."

"It must be a mistake. I can't believe it. Mr. Broughton is not a murderer."

"I wish I could think so. I do, honestly." Mr. Knight took another sip at the brandy. "But listen: why is it, do you think, that the inspector of whom the sergeant has talked so much is not here?"

"I—I don't know."

"I'll tell you. When this man who calls himself Kend-all drove up, I happened to put my hand on the radiator of the car. It's my car, you know, Miss Poulter, so I'm not drawing conclusions from guesswork. Well, the radiator was almost cold, and I knew at once that the car had not been driven from Blackshaw. There was only one possible explanation. When Broughton left us—and he didn't want to fetch the police, if you remember—he drove down the road a little way past the house, and hid the car. He came back to the house, through the tunnel, dropping his eyeglasses on the way. He killed Bidgood before Harlan left, and was still somewhere in the house when we all came back. He removed the body of Morlant, shot the dog, laughed at us—you remember?—and substituted the body of Bidgood in Morlant's place while we were out blocking the opening of the cave. Then he extinguished the lamp in the hall so that we should not see the door open, and slipped out, returning disguised as the sergeant a little later."

"You're wrong," muttered Sally, still clinging to her faith. "You must be wrong, though it seems to fit in."

"I told him about the eyeglasses to test him," pursued Mr. Knight unevenly. "And you'll remember that he was disturbed. When Harlan started talking about 'The Ghoul,' I knew that I was on the right track. I tried to stop him saying anything definite, because I didn't want you girls to be more scared."

He tried again to sit up, and this time was successful.

"You see," he continued, "I know a thing or two about 'The Ghoul.' As a matter of fact, I've been trailing him for the last week or so."

Sally gazed at him in surprise. "You're a detective?" she exclaimed.

"More or less. No official connection, you know. I was engaged to look after the interests of some people whom 'The Ghoul' was blackmailing. I've been following him about—"

"Then it was he who attacked Betty in the fog, and you who saved her?"

"Exactly. Though that was just a lucky accident, and I'm claiming no credit. I'd no idea then that he was interested in Miss Harlan. As I've said, I was after him for quite another matter."

"But surely, if you know so much about him, you ought to have recognized him at once?"

"I've never seen him, Miss Poulter. Not in his true self. Whenever I've managed to catch a glimpse of his face, he's been disguised. And he's a master at that game, I can tell you. I haven't the faintest idea what he actually looks like."

"And so you came here, not because of us, but just because you were following him?"

"That's right. He was making some guarded inquiries about Hameldon House in Blackshaw late last night, so I took a risk and came straight out this morning, hoping to get here first. I was hanging around for a long time before I came to the house, and no one turned up but Mr. Broughton. I began to think 'The Ghoul' had given me the slip. But I guessed I was on the right track as soon as I met Miss Harlan, though I was very surprised to see her. I recognized her as my lady of the fog; and I felt sure 'The Ghoul' would be somewhere near. I had to act the fool because he might be listening to every word I said. For the same reason I didn't dare to openly disclose my identity to Miss Harlan. I made an excuse for stopping. And, thank Heaven, I'm still here!"

Mr. Knight managed to get to his feet. He took a few steps, then plumped down into the nearest chair.

"But mighty little use to any one yet, I'm afraid," he muttered, frowning. "If 'The Ghoul' returns just now, he'll make mincemeat of me."

"Haven't you a—a weapon of some sort?"

"I've a revolver."

"I hope you'll kill him! Oh, I hope you'll kill him!"

Sally thought of Betty, perhaps even at this moment facing "The Ghoul" in some secret hiding place, and shivered. But the fact that her companion's faintness was passing away gave her courage.

"Where have you been the last half hour or so?" she inquired. "Why did you slip away?"

"There were two reasons. One was to gain a little time. Things were getting pretty awkward for me, weren't they? The only way I could prove that I wasn't 'The Ghoul'

was by unmasking this pretended police sergeant. And I
wanted to make some provision for the future before I did
that.”

“Provision for the future?”

“Yes. That was the second reason. Do you remember
Broughton saying, earlier in the evening, that he had
arranged for the taxi to come from Blackshaw at nine-
thirty? It occurred to me that he was probably speaking
the truth. So I slipped out and walked down the road to
meet the car. It turned up all right, and I sent the driver
back with a note to the real police.”

“Oh, how splendid! You’re sure they’ll come?”

“They’ll not be long. I happen to know the official
S.O.S. code, and they’ll act on my message without delay.
But I asked them to collect a few men. ‘The Ghoul’s’ not
the sort of Johnnie to trifle with.”

“Oh, they must get here in time!”

Even in her anxiety, Sally was wondering about Mr.
Broughton. It seemed foolish to doubt Mr. Knight’s evidence that the self-styled police sergeant was “The Ghoul”;
every little bit of it fitted in so perfectly. But she could
not bring herself to believe in the solicitor’s guilt.

“There’s Edward Morlant, too,” she murmured, thinking aloud. “You’re not taking him into consideration. And
if you’d seen him, returned to life with all his mad lust for
killing intensified. . . . Oh, he’s evil—utterly evil! I’m sure
he’s the murderer! I’m sure he’s ‘The Ghoul’!”

“Yes, there’s Edward Morlant,” agreed Mr. Knight,
frowning. “I can’t offer any explanation of his return. I
can’t understand it at all. There’s no doubt about the fact
that he was dead. I can swear to that. It looks impossible
that he . . . Anyhow, it wasn’t he who knocked me out. It
was the sergeant.”

“When you came in?”

"Yes. It can't be very long ago. I heard you and Miss Harlan talking in the kitchen. I came in here quietly, and was surprised to see that the body of Bidgood had disappeared. The sergeant was calmly poking the fire. I was wondering what to do about him when he turned and saw me. I don't know whether he guessed what I'd been up to or not, but he acted without the slightest delay. Before I had an inkling of his purpose, he had raised the poker and—I was out!

"I think I owe my life to you, Miss Poulter. His first blow knocked me senseless. I know 'The Ghoul' well enough to be certain that others would have followed. Probably, however, he heard you coming from the kitchen. He had only just time to throw the tablecloth over me and—"

"It must have been Betty who interrupted him. She came in before me."

"Then she saved my life. How long were you in the kitchen after she left you?"

"Only two or three minutes. It doesn't seem possible for him to have carried her away—"

"Only two or three minutes? Then it's absolutely certain that there's some secret way out of this room." Mr. Knight rose from his chair and took a few paces round. He was still unsteady on his legs. "Lord, if only there was something we could do! I expected the police before this."

They were silent for a while, listening. With returning strength Mr. Knight was growing fidgety and impatient.

"I can't stand doing nothing," he muttered at last. "Will you keep an eye open for the sergeant, Miss Poulter, while I look for any sign of that secret opening?"

He walked slowly round, scrutinizing the book-lined walls.

"There's no possible outlet unless some of these shelves move," he murmured. "It means taking out every book. If we had any sort of clew—" He stopped abruptly. "By Jove!" he exclaimed, stumbling to the hearth. "I wonder—"

He fell on his knees beside the fire, and turned back the hearthrug.

"Whatever are you doing?" asked Sally.

"I've just remembered," he replied, rising to his feet again. He showed her some sheets of damp scorched paper. "Part of Edward Morlant's diary. It may tell us—"

"I thought it had been burned."

"Most of it was. But you remember Morlant pouring water on the fire to put it out just before he was murdered? While Harlan was telling us about 'The Ghoul,' it occurred to me that some of the diary might have escaped complete destruction. Examining the fireplace while you were all intent on the telegram, I noticed that there were a few pages left, not entirely burned away. I didn't dare stoop to pick them up at the time. I managed to get them out of the fireplace with my foot, and slide them under the rug. I'd forgotten them until we mentioned the possibility of a secret exit."

"Why?" cried Sally, watching with a growing excitement as he separated the pages. "Do you think—"

"Well, Morlant was very keen that we shouldn't see this diary, wasn't he? He took a big risk in order to recover and destroy it. There must be something in it that—oh, and by Jiminy, there is!" Mr. Knight's voice shook with triumph. "Miss Poulter, we've won! There is a secret way out of the room! And here's a complete plan and—"

"Oh, let me look! Please let me look!"

"Don't let's waste any more time now there's something we can do. If we can disappear before Kendall shows up, it will be all to the good. Count up four shelves in that bookcase by the side of the fire, and pull out the end volume."

Sally obeyed. She was trembling so much that she dropped the book.

"Now put your hand to the back of the shelf," instructed Mr. Knight, reading from the paper. "Feel anything?"

"There's a sort of tiny knob."

"Press it."

Sally did so, and then jumped back in surprise. Without a sound, one section of the big bookcase had turned on a central pivot, disclosing an aperture in the wall, half as wide and fully as long as an ordinary doorway.

Cramming the scorched papers into his pocket for further investigation later, Mr. Knight ran to her side.

"We'll soon get to the bottom of all this mystery now," he cried, jubilantly. "'The Ghoul' can't have any idea that we've found this way out. We'll rescue Betty and—"

"Won't you walk into my parlor?" invited a sneering voice from the blackness beyond the aperture. "No, on second thoughts, don't move. I have you both covered."

The next moment Sergeant Kendall appeared in the opening, a deadly-looking automatic in his hand.

"Just in time, evidently," he continued. "You've got a pretty thick skull, Knight. I thought you were asleep for good."

Mr. Knight grinned at him amicably.

"The game's up, Broughton," he said, holding out his hand. "You might as well give me that gun. The house is surrounded by police. It'll be swarming with 'em in a minute."

The sergeant laughed harshly.

"Bluff!" he sneered. "If they were within hearing, I'd still have plenty of time to dispose of you before they could reach us. You fool!"

A sudden fury shook him, and his eyes blazed.

"You damned idiot! To imagine 'The Ghoul' could be caught by a trick like that. You've not an idea—"

Words failed him, and he trembled with uncontrolled passion.

"You think I'm Broughton," he went on. "A mealy-mouthed solicitor! Look!" His voice rose into a hideous shriek of rage. He tore at his mustache and eyebrows which came away in his hand.

"Damn you! Look at me!"

Sally screamed and Mr. Knight staggered back in amazement. For the evil contorted face thus disclosed was that of Edward Morlant!

21

The Oven

It was several seconds before Mr. Knight recovered his aplomb sufficiently to force his usual fatuous grin.

"Well!" he exclaimed, as though delighted with the meeting. "If it isn't our old Mahatma!"

"You can drop that talk now," snarled Morlant. "It fooled me once, but it won't do it again. You needn't act the lunatic any longer."

"Just as you like, old chappie," agreed Mr. Knight pleasantly. "But you mustn't expect me to be anything different from what Nature has made me."

He spoke easily enough, but in truth he was feeling utterly dumfounded and bewildered. Up to a moment ago, he had regarded the situation as being well in hand. With the identity of "The Ghoul" determined, the secret way out of the library discovered, and the police on their way to the house, it had seemed to him that the resolution of their troubles was only a matter of minutes. And he had not been unduly anxious about Betty's safety because he felt sure that Broughton's plan, whatever its motive might be, would be to hold her prisoner without harming her.

The unexpected revelation that Broughton was not "The Ghoul" had been a great shock to him. All the clews he had picked up pointed so definitely in this direction that, despite Sally's story of seeing Edward Morlant, he had not wavered in his conviction that he was on the right track.

And now it seemed that the impossible had happened again. This man, whom he had seen stone dead with a dagger in his heart, had kept his boasted promise. He had come back to life to carry out some unfathomable plan of murder and destruction which evidently included Betty in its scope.

It was incredible—beyond human understanding! For there was not the slightest doubt that Morlant had been murdered. Yet he was real enough now. He was no creature of the imagination. He was living, breathing—and filled with inexplicable hatred.

Mr. Knight's courage failed him as he realized that the situation was much worse than he had thought. If Betty were not already dead, she was in the gravest possible danger. She was in the power of this Thing, this sadistic enigma. And he was helpless to aid her. The automatic was leveled at his heart. He knew enough of "The Ghoul" to be sure that it would spit instant death if he moved.

He was caught, trapped in the moment of success! He glanced at Sally, wondering desperately if any assistance could be expected from her. But one look at her pale, bewildered face was enough to tell him that Sally was a broken reed. She had crumpled up entirely before this new menace.

The poor girl was, indeed, in a state of deepest distress and despair. The definite proof that Edward Morlant was "The Ghoul" had added the last straw to her troubles. She had given up hope. It was foolish to expect to save Betty from his murderous lust. With his immortality and his occult powers, the foul creature was invulnerable. The end of all of them could be nothing less than a horrible death at his hands.

She shrank even from looking at his evil, passion-twisted face. He was a thing apart from humanity and normal life, a veritable ghoul, with power to escape from the hell to which he belonged. She shivered as she remembered that the legendary vampires returned from the grave to feast on the blood of their victims. Oh, God! Surely it could not be that Betty—and she herself!

"So you're a Sherlock Holmes, a private detective?" Morlant continued, his yellow teeth showing between his snarling lips. "It's you who's been following me about for the past few weeks, making a damned nuisance of yourself?"

"You've got good ears, old chappie," observed Mr. Knight. "I'd have been more careful what I said if I'd known you were listening."

"You'd have been more careful if you'd kept away from here altogether. I've a reckoning with you which shall be paid in full. You followed me to my dear Elizabeth's studio when I intended removing her without any fuss; and because of your interference, I had the mortification of seeing Broughton get there before me and so upset all my arrangements. You followed me in the fog, and again prevented me from killing her. Damn you, you've put me to no end of trouble! All would have been so simple and easy with her out of the way. Instead of which, I've had to scheme and plan afresh. But I've got her now and—"

"And if you harm her in the slightest degree," said Mr. Knight gently but with the utmost assurance, "I'll kill you myself."

"Kill me? Bah!" Morlant laughed horribly. "You've already tried that once, and you can see the result. You can't kill me. No one can kill me. I'm immortal. Besides, in a few minutes you'll be dead yourself. Both of you," with a side glance at Sally.

"You forget the police are coming."

"I forget nothing. At least, I—well, I must admit that I forgot about that taxi. I also overlooked the question of the cold radiator. It was a foolish oversight. But it makes no odds; there's no harm done. As for the police, what can they do? They are powerless against me. Truncheons or bullets—by the way, before we part, I'd like to know who it was that stabbed me in the back. Can either of you tell me?"

The incongruity of the astounding question asked in so matter of fact a way held both Sally and Mr. Knight silent.

"No matter," said Morlant, shrugging. "It is of no importance. Whoever it was will not escape me, for I've got you all."

He was speaking more calmly now, with a leering triumph in his voice.

"I've prepared a little reception for you—quite a warm reception, in fact. There is plenty of time before the police come for me to explain the situation so that you can appreciate it to the full.

"Downstairs, there is a nice, quiet room, built of good solid stone, and hidden away so carefully that it is a perfect retreat from the strife and trouble of the world. In olden days, it was known as the Priest Chamber and in it my devout ancestors used to conceal any fugitive clerics who were fleeing from persecution. Good old days those must have been, eh? In our family records are particulars of at least twenty priests who were given free board and lodging in this reception room. And never once was the hiding place discovered, though the house was searched from top to bottom times without number.

"These secret passages which my forbears built have always been very useful to me. Not until to-night, however, have I fully appreciated their value. They will enable me to dispose of you so easily—and so effectively. I'm going to take you down now and fasten you up in the Priest Chamber. Such a nice little room, so solidly constructed of good honest stone!"

"You might almost be describing your future home," murmured Mr. Knight. "In the condemned cell."

"I'm describing your last home," snarled Morlant, "the grave from which you will not return."

"You'd leave us there to starve?" cried Sally, aghast.

"Oh, dear me, no! I shall have far too great a regard for your comfort. I shall take every precaution to ensure that you are well cared for. For instance, being built of stone, your little home will doubtless be cold. I had decided to sacrifice even my house for your comfort. As soon as you are safely installed in your new abode, I shall return up here and empty a few tins of paraffin about. A match here and there, and—well, you know how these old houses burn!"

Full realization of his devilish intention came to Sally and set her trembling. The horror of the fate reserved for her numbed her mind. Anything—anything but that! She swayed unsteadily on her feet. But for Mr. Knight's outstretched hand she would have fallen.

"Oh, no!" she cried wildly, pleading in desperation. "You can't do that! Please don't do that. Kill me now. Shoot me where I am. Don't leave me to burn to death!"

"Burn?" echoed Morlant, the mad frenzy returning to his voice. "My dear young lady, you'll not burn! Recollect the good solid stone of which the little room is built. You can't burn in there. At first, indeed, there will be nothing but a slight smell to show you that the house is alight. You'll feel safe and secure. Later, of course, the heat will begin to tell. The stones of your walls will begin to grow hot as the fire rages about them. Just like an oven, you know, just like an oven. Oh, you needn't fear that you will burn to death! But you'll roast, damn you, you'll roast!"

He burst into a roar of mocking laughter which echoed through the silent house.

"You'll roast!" he repeated. "Like the two chickens in the kitchen!"

Mr. Knight measured the distance between them with a rapid glance. He saw only too clearly that "The Ghoul" was right. Once in the secret chamber, there could be no escape. At any risk, he must make an attempt to disarm this murderous fiend.

Bracing himself for the effort, he suddenly sprang forward. Sally screamed as the automatic spat twice, and he staggered back with a broken shoulder.

Beyond pressing the trigger, Morlant had not moved a muscle.

"I could have shot you through the heart," he said calmly. "But I'd rather save you for the oven."

There was nothing more to be done. Resigning himself to his fate, Mr. Knight tried to stanch the flow of blood from his wound with a handkerchief. He abandoned any thought of attacking "The Ghoul" again. He was helpless, beaten, and he knew it. He could do nothing to rescue Betty. He could not even protect Sally. Their only hope now was that the police might arrive in time to save them before they were imprisoned.

"If the police do happen to come before I get clear away," continued "The Ghoul" as though reading his thoughts, "well, here I am, Edward Morlant, the owner of the house. The reports of my death,"—he grinned—"have been greatly exaggerated. As a matter of fact, I have been the victim of a gang of crooks playing a very deep game which I have managed to thwart. They have just left after killing my faithful servant and setting fire to my house in their chagrin. I can give a very complete description of each one of them. I don't know who sent for the police, but it's a good job they've come to help put this fire out.

"And they will help, you know. Whether I'm here or not, they'll put out the fire eventually. But I'm afraid it will be too late to interest you. And they'll never find you in your cozy, warm oven. Because, except for myself, there's not a soul in the world who even knows of its existence."

Sally had recovered some of her nerve and ceased sobbing. She recognized fully that what "The Ghoul" said was correct. They could expect nothing from the police. All hope was gone, and a dreadful death awaited them. But she was determined not to give way again. Mr. Knight was accepting his fate with seeming nonchalance, and she also must try to put on a brave face. She longed to ask Morlant what had become of Betty, but she would not give him the opportunity for further gloating.

"Come along, now," he said, stepping to one side. "We've wasted enough time. Miss Poulter, you'd better take a candle from the table. Our sagacious detective is fully occupied nursing his shoulder."

Sally slowly crossed to the table by the door and lit a candle. She noticed that the automatic was hovering between her and Mr. Knight, ready to bark at the slightest excuse. It was no use making any attempt at escape.

"You can lead the way," continued Morlant when she returned, "and light the footsteps of the invalid. I'll bring up the rear with my artillery."

There was nothing for it but to obey. Sally passed through the opening, and found herself at the bottom of a short flight of steps which led up to the left. The others followed. "The Ghoul" pressed a spring somewhere in the wall, and the bookcase silently revolved back into position.

The steps terminated in a small landing from which a longer flight led down again. Sally guessed that they were standing above the library fireplace, and Morlant confirmed her supposition.

"We're just behind my portrait now," he chuckled. "An ingenious little arrangement, that. A touch on a button here opens the eyes of the painting so that everything that goes on in the room can be both seen and heard. Quite a recent innovation which has proved most useful to me. Carry on, Miss Poulter. 'Facilis descensus—' You know the rest."

Sally did know the rest; and as she slowly descended the steep, dusty stairs, she felt that she was, indeed, making her last journey, a journey from which there could be no return. She looked back at Mr. Knight, wondering what was in his mind, and saw from his pale face and vacant eyes that he was almost on the point of collapse. The wound in his shoulder was bleeding freely.

"You can help him down," said Morlant, noticing her backward glance. "I think he'll last until we reach the oven. If not, I'll have to cut his throat—always a messy business, though very efficacious."

The steps went down until Sally realized that they must have reached the level of the square under the hall which Mr. Knight had christened Piccadilly Circus. At the bottom was a passage very similar to that which they had discovered earlier in the evening, except that it was both higher and wider.

Urged forward by repeated digs of the automatic in her back, she reluctantly struggled along, supporting the almost unconscious form of Mr. Knight as well as she could. Before she had gone far, she stopped short with an involuntary cry of horror. The body of a man lay across the passage, completely blocking it.

A moment later, she recognized Gerald Harlan, bound hand and foot, and with a handkerchief gagging his mouth. Morlant pushed forward and stooped to unfasten his bonds, afterwards dragging him to his feet.

"I want you now, Harlan," he said brusquely. "I've a little job for you. Don't play the fool or—or I'll manage without you!"

Ignoring the half-stupefied man, he turned to one side and pressed heavily on a stone. A section of the wall swung away, disclosing a black cavity.

"Here's your little home!" he chuckled. "So secluded and cozy! In you go! And don't waste any time looking for the door. It doesn't work from inside."

Sally hung back terrified. With an oath, he caught her roughly in his arms and pushed her through the opening, extinguishing the candle as he did so. He flashed an electric torch, then pushed Mr. Knight through after her.

"Sorry I shan't have the opportunity of seeing you again," he said, with his horrible mocking laugh. "You'll both look well when you're nicely browned!"

Sally stood motionless, supporting the limp body of Mr. Knight. The light flashed in on her for a moment. Then the section of wall swung back with a muffled crash, leaving her in utter darkness and silence.

22

A Glimpse at the Truth

For a few seconds she remained standing, staring into the darkness, numbed and dazed. The sound of the closing wall still echoed in her ears like a knell of doom. But as yet her shocked mind was too full of the wonder and dread caused by Edward Morlant's return to life to comprehend clearly what had happened.

With a soft, fluttering sigh, Mr. Knight's body slid from her nerveless grasp and collapsed helplessly on the floor. The movement roused her from her stupor. Full realization of the situation flashed upon her with blinding force. She was caught in a trap, a death trap from which there could be no escape; alone with a wounded, perhaps dying, man!

A blind terror seized her. Stumbling and panting, she battered upon the wall until her hands were bruised and bleeding, searching for a door which she knew she would not find. Screaming hoarsely, she called to the mocking silence for help, though she knew that none was there.

After a while she became calmer. She remembered the wounded man on the floor, probably bleeding to death, and shame for her weakness replaced some of her fear. At least she must do what she could for him.

In her panic she had dropped the candle. She groped about on the stone flags until she found it, then searched Mr. Knight's pockets for matches.

Suddenly she stopped, holding her breath. From somewhere in the darkness behind had come a soft, rustling sound, a sound which must have been made by someone or something moving about very near to her.

Terror gripped her again. What new danger lurked in the impenetrable blackness? What grisly Thing could be preparing to pounce on her?

At all costs she must have a light. Frenziedly continuing her search, she came across the matches and struck one. In the flaring up of the light, she received a momentary impression of the wall through which she had entered, built of large, heavy blocks of stone, carefully and closely fitted together.

Lighting the candle, she turned quickly to face whatever the darkness might hold. A gasp of horror escaped her as the dim light revealed three bodies stretched out in a corner.

The candle burned up more brightly, and she saw that one of the motionless figures was a girl. A dreadful, soul-searing certainty surged over her. It must be Betty! Betty! Killed by "The Ghoul!"

With her heart in her throat she slowly approached and held the light closer. The first figure was that of Bidgood, his horrible wound mercifully hidden from view. She held her breath as she leaned over the second figure.

It was Betty! But a quick thrill of joy ran through Sally at sight of the open eyes, the gagged mouth, and the foot that was moving among the straw. Falling on her knees beside the helpless form of her friend, she rapidly unfastened the cords that bound her.

"Oh, Betty!" she sobbed, half laughing, half crying. "Oh, Betty! Thank Heaven he's not killed you!"

Betty at up, wincing with the pain of movement, and straightened her disarranged clothing.

"He's nearly cut through my wrists with that rope," she said practically. "Sally, you're a darling to rescue me like this! I thought I was done for. But where are we? What has happened? How have you got here?"

"We're shut up in the Priest Chamber. By 'The Ghoul.' Don't you know?"

"I don't know anything. The last thing I remember is being half suffocated by someone in the library. Sally, I'm sure it was Edward Morlant. I saw his eyes! And I'm sure he's 'The Ghoul,' who tried to murder me in the fog."

"He is! We've seen him again."

"You've seen him again? Why, how—" Betty stopped abruptly as she caught sight of her two prostrate companions and her face paled. "Oh, w-who are these?"

"One's Bidgood," said Sally briefly. "And the other—"

She held the candle over the third figure, and started back with a cry of surprise.

"Mr. Broughton!" she cried.

And Mr. Broughton it certainly was, mud-stained and disheveled, trussed up like a turkey. The girls had great difficulty in loosening his bonds, and while they struggled with them Sally told what had happened in the library.

Betty listened with growing concern. She glanced across at the silent form of Mr. Knight lying in the shadows, overlooked until now, and her lips trembled.

"Oh, Sally!" she murmured reproachfully, scrambling to her feet. "Why didn't you tell me before that he was hurt?"

She stumbled towards him, and tenderly gathered his head into her lap.

"I'm sorry, Betty," explained Sally. "I was just going to attend to him when you moved and scared the wits out of me."

Mr. Broughton's bonds were tight, and it was some time before he was freed from them. Even then his muscles

refused to move, and he lay helpless while Sally rubbed
back the circulation into his cramped limbs.

"Whatever have you been doing? And how did you get
here?" she asked eagerly.

The solicitor's broad face was grave and troubled.

"I'll tell you in a minute," he replied. "When the others
are ready. I want you all to hear, and I'd better start at the
beginning because I've a lot to get off my chest."

There was a change in his speech and manner that
rather puzzled Sally even while it pleased her. The pompous tone and the glib phrase had disappeared, and were
replaced by a rough sincerity. She made no comment, however, but continued her massage.

"How is Knight, Miss Elizabeth?" asked Broughton
after a while. "Is he seriously hurt?"

"I don't think he's very bad," replied Betty, looking up
from her task of improvising a dressing for the wound.
"But he's lost a lot of blood, I suppose, and he's fainted."

"He had a flask of brandy in his hip pocket," recollect-
ed Sally. "Why not try a little of that?"

Broughton struggled to his feet and, with Sally's assistance, hobbled across. He stood watching anxiously while
Betty found the flask and applied it to the unconscious
man's lips.

The effect of the potent spirit was rapid. In a few seconds Mr. Knight opened his eyes. He looked round vacantly for a while, frowning with pain. Then, as his gaze
rested on Betty's curly head, a smile of recognition spread
over his pale features.

"Hello, lady!" he murmured feebly. "I thought our old
Mahatma had got you."

Betty said nothing, but her face was very tender.

"Your eyes are beautiful," he continued, still smiling
up at her. "I used to think them most wonderful when they
were angry, but I like 'em best as they are now."

"You mustn't talk just yet," murmured Betty, turning away to hide her flushed cheeks. "Have another drink."

It was not long before Mr. Knight was sufficiently recovered to sit up. He caught sight of the solicitor and grinned ruefully.

"I have to apologize to you, old man," he said. "I've been blackening your character to Miss Poulter."

"I know," replied Broughton. "And I'm not surprised you thought I was 'The Ghoul.' I've acted queerly and—I wish I'd known you were a detective."

"I'm not a detective. I'm a rank failure!" Mr. Knight tried to rise to his feet, but found himself too weak to stand. "I was too pigheadedly sure of myself! Right in details and wrong in essentials."

As he sat down again, he sniffed.

"Smell it?" he enquired softly. "Our old Mahatma's keeping his word." And he hurriedly explained what were "The Ghoul's" intentions.

The excitement caused by the unexpected meeting and reunion faded. The smell of burning became more distinct. It emphasized in the minds of all the horrible death that awaited them. The solicitor hobbled to the wall and thumped on it energetically.

"It's no good," said Mr. Knight, shaking his head. "I saw how it worked, and you couldn't possibly get the necessary leverage from this side. There's no chance of escaping that way unless someone lets us out. Still, you might as well have a look round to make certain there's no other way out."

He sat quiet while the others made a tour of the walls. They examined every stone without result. The smell of burning grew stronger, and a few wisps of smoke drifted in through unseen crevices.

"There's ventilation, evidently," he said when they returned with downcast faces. "And that's about all! Well, ladies and gentlemen, we know now where we are. We're in a devil of a mess!"

"And it's all my fault!" cried Broughton savagely. "God! When I think what a fool I've been . . . If it hadn't been for me . . . Miss Poulter! Miss Elizabeth! Can you ever forgive me?"

"I don't suppose you've done anything very dreadful," said Betty, trying to keep her voice steady. She wanted to know what he had to say. Anything to distract her thoughts from the fire that was creeping near to them. "Suppose you tell us all about it?"

"I will! I will! It has been worrying me more than I can say. I want to tell you everything. In the first place, I lied to you when I told you that Edward Morlant was buried in Blackshaw cemetery. At that time, he was not dead."

No one seemed unduly surprised at this statement. Mr. Knight even smiled.

"We knew that," he remarked. "At least, I did."

"You knew it? How?"

"Well, perhaps it would be more correct to say I guessed it. I think we all had our suspicions. It was pretty obvious, wasn't it? There was a little plot of some sort? Both you and Bidgood were in it?"

"Yes, that's right. But I ought to tell you first that Mr. Edward was not quite normal. He was subject to recurrent attacks of insanity—"

"We know that, too. Harlan told us."

"Then that makes it easier for me. His madness, Miss Elizabeth, was the reason why he wouldn't bring you to live with him in the first place. Just lately, however, he talked about this a lot. He said that some day he wanted to pretend to be dead, to bring you to the house as his heiress, and see how a sudden access of wealth would affect you, whether it would spoil you. It was to be a kind of test. Eventually, I suppose, he intended to disclose himself, and then act according to whether he approved of your conduct or not."

"Pretty feeble sort of joke, it seems to me," murmured Mr. Knight.

"I thought so myself," agreed Broughton sorrowfully. "And I told him so. I wish to Heaven I'd had the sense. . . . But, after all, there didn't seem to be any harm in it, and he was very persistent.

"One day, about a month ago, he came home—he used to be away a good deal—and told me that he was determined to carry out his plan whether I liked it or not. I knew him well enough to be sure that he would find some way of arranging it even if I refused to help him. And with his—his disability in mind, I decided that it would be better to fall in with his wishes, if only so that I could keep an eye on things.

"I hope you'll remember that at this time I'd no idea of the evil side to his nature. His mental disease must have been made worse by his occult studies. But I thought he was improving. He always seemed to be gentleness itself.

"Well, the details of the scheme were simple to carry out. We had no difficulty in arranging things. You see, we knew we couldn't do the thing properly. I mean, we couldn't pretend to have a real burial. There was no question of forging a death certificate or hoodwinking the cemetery authorities. We simply put an announcement in the London papers of the death of Edward Morlant of Hameldon House, so that it could be cited as evidence if any enquiries were made. Miss Elizabeth, of course, accepted my word without question."

"I never dreamed of doing anything else," cried Betty, interested in spite of the circumstances. "Why should I think— And you showed me a photograph of his tombstone!"

"Yes, it was a fake. It has been made, of course, but it still remains in the sculptors' yard."

"It will not be wasted," remarked Mr. Knight dryly. "How about neighbors, friends? Did no one expect an invitation to the funeral?"

"There are no neighbors and there are no friends. If any questions were asked in Blackshaw, I said my information was that Mr. Edward had died abroad, and had been buried where he died. It would have been easy, later, to explain that a mistake had been made."

"It certainly was easy. I'd no idea dying was such a simple matter. What was Morlant doing while you lied about him?"

Broughton flushed. "He was living here. We had furnished a small hut in a secluded ravine on the moor in case of need. He could get out at any time by the passage to the cave—"

"Ah, then you did know about that?" exclaimed Betty.

"Yes. But I didn't know about this Priest Chamber or the secret way out of the library. Morlant never told me anything about it. Bidgood must have known, of course. He's been with the family for years. I expect that was why he was killed when his master's mind gave way."

"You knew that he was murdered? You saw it done?"

"I heard it," replied Broughton, shuddering.

They were silent for a while. The smell of burning grew definitely stronger, and the smoke made a perceptible haze in the stone walled chamber.

"Oh, if only we could do something!" cried Sally, wringing her hands. "To have to wait here while—"

"Well, that explains a good deal," interrupted Betty hurriedly, trying to force her mind away from any consideration of what the future held. "It explains the noises Sally and I heard, and why Bidgood was wandering about in the night. It explains poor Rover's excitement in the library, and the sudden disappearance of the intruder who I thought was Mr. Knight. It also explains your rather queer conduct at first, Mr. Broughton. It was clear that you and Bidgood had some secret between you. No wonder you were embarrassed!"

"I'm thoroughly ashamed of myself," muttered the solicitor.

"Oh, I can't understand it all," he added miserably. "I can't think what has come over him. I felt quite sure, when I agreed to his plan, that I was doing no harm. Although his mind was affected, he was always kind and gentle. I can't believe that he was playing a part, that he was living a Jekyll and Hyde existence, at one time the harmless student, at another 'The Ghoul.' And as for the way he has returned from the dead. . . ."

"There's a lot we can't understand yet," said Mr. Knight gently. "Much, I'm afraid, that we shall never have the opportunity of understanding. Tell us how you got here."

"That's quite simple. I set off in the car feeling pretty rotten because I knew I should have to confess my part in the plot to the police. Soon after passing the house, I came across a man lying in the middle of the road. I had to stop, of course, and as soon as I did, he jumped up and stuck a pistol into my ribs. I was utterly dumfounded to see that it was Edward Morlant. I couldn't believe my eyes. Because I was quite sure that he was dead when we left him in the library.

"I thought I must be crazy. I was too amazed by his resurrection to wonder why he should be threatening me with a pistol. I couldn't offer the slightest resistance. I remembered his boast that he would return from the dead. At the time, I had looked upon this as a symptom of his disease. But now, I—I was frightened.

"He made me drive the car off the road into a side track, and walk back to the house. With his pistol at my back, I was forced to enter the cave and stumble along the passage. Halfway through, he stopped and blindfolded me.

In the part you christened Piccadilly Circus, he turned me round so that I lost all sense of direction. I thought he was bringing me up through the wardrobe, but evidently there is another way.

"We had just entered the second passage, when someone uttered a startled exclamation immediately in front of us. The next moment Bidgood's terrified voice rang out.

"'Mr. Edward!' he wailed. 'Oh, my God! You're—'

"Morlant darted forward with a yell of rage. Before I could tear at the bandage over my eyes there was a horrible scream of pain, and—and I knew that Bidgood was dead. . . .

"I can't understand it at all. The man—or whatever he is—is a devil, a fiend! He laughed as he pushed me forward. He was still laughing when he shut me up in here after fastening me so that I could move neither hand nor foot. I have spent the time since then praying that none of you would hear him laugh."

"Oh, we've heard him laugh, all right!" muttered Mr. Knight. "All of us! And I'm afraid he's had the last laugh. It's quite evident that he's a madman. What I can't understand is—Broughton, was it you who stabbed him?"

"No. I swear it!"

"Then it must have been Bidgood. Bidgood evidently knew a good deal more than we thought. And yet, remembering his distress— Oh, what an unholy mess it all is! What can be the idea behind it all? Morlant may be mad, but even a madman must have some motive for his actions."

"He's killing us all," said Sally listlessly, "because we've discovered about his immortality. Don't you remember him saying, before he was stabbed, that he couldn't leave us with that knowledge?"

"Yes, I remember that. But there's something else. There's some secret which we haven't even glimpsed yet.

I simply will not believe that a man can be murdered and come back to life. It looks almost as though—"

A faint crackling sound overhead became audible. More acrid smoke filtered into the chamber, setting the occupants coughing. Betty was sure she felt a wave of hot air on her cheeks.

"The fire is getting nearer," she murmured, gripping her hands to keep her voice steady. "And the smoke—we'll be suffocated first."

No one spoke. Suddenly, in the distance, sounding far away, two tiny reports like the cracks of miniature whips stabbed the silence.

"Revolver shots," said Mr. Knight softly. "I wonder if that's the police?"

23

Trapped

The supposition sent a little thrill of hope through the listeners. Surely if the police were actually in the house there must be a chance of rescue.

As though it had been arranged beforehand, they all joined in a loud and long sustained call for help. Almost immediately, however, the hope fled as they realized the impossibility of escape.

"They can't hear us," muttered Sally, putting the thoughts of all into words, "with a fire raging in between. And if they did, they couldn't find us. He'll be able to deceive them with some sort of tale. They'll never dream of looking for a secret way out of the library. Why should they? Even if they knew about that, they couldn't find this place. It's no good thinking about it."

The truth of this was self-evident; there was not the slightest chance of rescue. No one had anything more to say. Failing a miracle, they were all doomed to a dreadful death.

Mr. Knight's hand reached out and closed over Betty's. She looked at him in enquiring silence.

"You've the most beautiful eyes in the world, lady," he said softly.

She neither turned her head away nor withdrew her hand from his. Instead, her lips parted in a shy smile and she met his ardent gaze bravely.

Another wave of smoke and heat eddied into the chamber, setting them all coughing. They were resigned to their fate. Sally and Broughton moved a little way apart, and stood looking at one another without speaking.

"Betty!" whispered Mr. Knight, drawing her towards him. "Betty! I love you!"

In the circumstances it seemed quite natural that he should say this. Betty felt that she had known it a long time. She forgot that she had known him only one day. She made no pretense at resistance. Yielding to his arms, she raised her flushed face to his.

"My dear!" she murmured, returning his kiss. "And—and I love you!"

The crackling sound of the approaching fire grew louder. The heat increased until perspiration stood out on the faces of all of them. The smoke thickened, swirling about them dense and suffocating. Their eyes were reddened and smarting. Their pulses throbbed painfully. Their breathing gradually became more rapid and labored.

"The Ghoul" was smiling evilly as he followed Gerald Harlan into the library, and swung to the bookcase which closed the opening of the secret passage.

"Now," he chuckled, "after a taste of what might happen to you, I think you'll not argue with me anymore?"

Harlan said nothing. He was nervous and trembling, fearfully watching this man who had been murdered before his eyes, yet who still lived.

"Come now!" snapped Morlant. "Your last chance. You know why I sent for you. You know the document I want you to copy. Will you do it?"

"Y-yes."

"Good! I thought you'd come to your senses. Here it is. You'll find pens and paper on the bureau. You can get to work while I attend to the wants of our friends down below."

Thoroughly cowed, Harlan seated himself at the bureau and obeyed. "The Ghoul" hurried from the room, quickly returning with two large tins. They contained paraffin which he commenced to sprinkle freely about the carpet and walls.

The forger completed his work and looked up. His bloated face blanched when he saw what was happening.

"W-what are you doing?" he stammered.

"Heating the oven!" laughed Morlant, splashing the bureau with paraffin. "I'm going to roast 'em!"

Harlan sprang to his feet, overturning the chair. He was trembling in every limb.

"You're not!" he quavered. "You can't do *that!* Oh, God! I won't—"

Morlant whipped out the automatic.

"Sit down!" he snarled. "I'll have no nonsense from you. Sit down, I say!"

"That's better," he continued as Harlan, quailing before the menace of the automatic, collapsed in his chair. "I've no further use for you just at present, and if you value your life, you'll keep quiet."

He picked up the papers from the bureau and stuffed them in his pocket. Then, striking match after match, he fired the paraffin-soaked furnishings in a dozen different places.

In a few moments the room was filled with smoke. Flames leaped up everywhere, licking the tapestries and woodwork with hissing glee. "The Ghoul" flung back the shutters and opened the windows.

"Air!" he exulted madly. "More air! We'll have a proper fire! We'll roast 'em to a turn!"

Gerald Harlan sat cringing in his chair, watching the evil figure that danced about the room, vanishing and reappearing in the smoke like a veritable devil from hell. In his drink-sodden mind, the last vestiges of common humanity were stirring. Down below, four people were being done to death. And one of them his daughter. His daughter—and Elizabeth's. So like Elizabeth that when he first saw her he had thought. . . . Yet he dare not intervene. He dare not move a finger to attempt to save her. Morlant's blazing eyes warned him that any open interference would be fatal. And how could anyone hope to outwit this fiendish creature with his supernatural powers? How could anyone fight a vampire to whom death was but empty phrase?

The flames crackled and roared. It was impossible to stay longer in the room. "The Ghoul" caught Harlan by the arm and dragged him into the hall.

"It burns merrily," he chuckled. "No fear of this dying out. The house will be razed to the ground. Our friends will be lost beneath it. And even if they are found, they'll be nothing but ashes. Come on!"

He turned towards the door, but Harlan hung back. The relics of a former decency in him were raising their shamed heads. Weak, spineless criminal though he might be, he could not be a party to this wholesale murder.

"No, I—I can't leave them," he stammered, his slack mouth writhing and twisting. "My daughter."

"Your daughter!" Morlant threw back his head and laughed loudly. "Your daughter is roasting. You'll do the same if you don't get a move on."

"I won't go!" Harlan's voice rose to a scream. "You devil! I won't leave them to—"

"We'll see!" "The Ghoul" leveled his automatic again. "We'll see how much your parental affection is worth."

He flung the door wide open. The rush of air into the blazing room behind him set the flames roaring more fiercely.

"Now!" he sneered. "Either you come out to safety with me, or you go down to Hell alone. Which shall it be? You've one minute to decide."

"I won't go!" quavered Harlan. "I can't go!"

"You'll change your mind before the minute is up," laughed Morlant. "If it wasn't for the fact that you may be useful to me again, you'd get no second chance. And if you're not out of this house in less—"

He stopped abruptly. Out in the night, the headlights of a distant car lit up the sky.

There was no time to waste. Without the slightest hesitation, he pulled the trigger of the automatic. Two shots rang out, and Harlan dropped like a stone.

"You fool!" snarled "The Ghoul," kicking the prostrate form. "I might have used you yet. But I couldn't let the police see you in that state."

He placed the automatic on the floor beside the body, and calmly walked out of the house. At the top of the drive he stood waiting. The hum of the approaching car became audible. As it turned into the drive, he smiled evilly.

"More fools!" he chuckled. "They're much too late."

As soon as the headlights of the car fell on him, he assumed a state of intense agitation and ran forward to meet it. Before it stopped, half a dozen men hurriedly tumbled out. Three were uniformed constables, the others in plain clothes.

"Oh, thank God you've come at last!" he cried. "You've been a long time. Have you seen them?"

One of the men in plain clothes stepped towards him.

"I'm Inspector Helliwell, sir," he replied. "We've seen no one. But we had a message that a notorious criminal known as 'The Ghoul' was—"

"Yes, that's right! That's right! There was a whole gang of them. I shot one. The others have only just gone. They set fire to the house."

"So I see, sir. We'd better try what we can do with that, and leave explanations for a while. Come on, men! There may be a chance of putting it out."

They all hurried into the house. The inspector frowned as he glanced into the library.

"It's got a good hold," he grunted. "Still, do your best. Get some buckets from the kitchen, and pass them along as quickly as you can."

After directing his men to their stations, he returned to Morlant.

"There's been a rumor in the village that you were dead, sir," he said. "I was quite surprised to see you. Now will you tell me what's been happening? If 'The Ghoul's' really been here, you're lucky to be alive. The message we received was signed by a well-known private detective. Where's he got to?"

"He's gone after the crooks," explained Morlant with a great show of eagerness. "They tied him up and left one man to guard him—the man I shot."

"Ah, yes." The inspector caught sight of Harlan's body behind the open door. "That's him, I suppose?"

"Yes. I winged him as he was escaping. His name's Harlan. From what the others said, I gathered that he was a forger."

"Harlan? I've heard of him. He's one of 'The Ghoul's' gang all right. I'll just have a look through his pockets."

The inspector crossed the hall and leaned over the prostrate figure. With a sneering laugh "The Ghoul" turned to watch the progress of the fire fighting. The men were putting forth every effort, but as yet their attack had made little impression.

He stood smiling at the fiercely leaping flames.

"Another few minutes and they'll be roasted!" he chuckled. "They won't talk. Harlan's dead. Every one gone but old Edward Morlant. Wonderful old Edward Morlant! No one can say that—"

He broke off with a snarl of rage. Someone had seized his arms from behind. Before he had time to move, he felt the cold pressure of steel round his wrists, and knew that he was handcuffed.

Turning furiously, he found himself looking into his own automatic, and behind it the troubled face of Inspector Helliwell.

"What the devil's the meaning of this?" he stormed.

"I don't quite know," admitted the inspector mildly. "I may be letting myself in for trouble. But Harlan says you're 'The Ghoul.' And considering what was in the message we got, I daren't take any risks."

Morlant glared at the motionless figure behind the door and swore viciously.

"You're an idiot!" he raged. "Isn't he dead, then?"

"Not quite. But he's nearly done in. Luckily for him, he had the sense to lie still after you shot him. And now we'll see if what he says is true."

Calling one of his men to guard Morlant, the inspector returned to Harlan.

"Where are these people you mentioned?" he asked. "Can you tell me?"

The wounded man raised himself on one arm with an effort.

"They're down in the Priest Chamber," he groaned. "But you can't find it. It has a secret opening. I can't explain; and they'll be smothered—burned to death!"

"You'll have to show us." Inspector Helliwell passed an arm round his shoulders and helped him to his feet. "Hey, Shackleton, give us a hand here!"

A burly constable in uniform came running in response to his call. Between them, they supported Harlan to the door of the library.

He could not stand unaided. He seemed on the point of collapse, but his features, drawn with pain, were determined.

"That first bookcase," he muttered, pointing. "I saw him work it. There's a catch somewhere."

By now the bookcase was a mass of smoldering ruin. It was hopeless to look for any button or spring. Picking up a chair, the inspector ran through the flames and smoke, and dashed it time after time against the shelves. Sparks flew freely; and before long the blows broke through the charred wood and leather, disclosing the opening in the wall behind.

Willing hands joined in the work, and soon there was room to pass through. The constable lifted Harlan in his arms, and ran with him across the room, into the opening.

"Well, you're right so far, Harlan," said Inspector Helliwell, joining them. "I'm beginning to believe your tale. I hope to Heaven we'll be in time."

He turned back to the room again and handed the automatic to one of the plain clothes men.

"Keep a careful eye on Morlant," he advised. "Unless I'm much mistaken, he's a dangerous criminal—and a cunning devil! If he makes the slightest move to escape—well, don't let him!"

The stairs and the passage were negotiated without much difficulty, though Harlan was now nearly unconscious. Helliwell and the constable had to carry him most of the way. Outside the Priest Chamber, he had just sufficient strength to point out the secret of the wall before collapsing entirely.

The inspector pressed on the stone which was almost hot enough to burn his hands.

"Hello! Hello!" he cried anxiously, as soon as the wall swung open. "Are you there, Mr. Grendon?"

"Hello, old chappie!" a feeble voice replied. "I don't know who you are, but you're as welcome as the flowers in spring!"

"I'm Inspector Helliwell of the West Riding Constabulary."

"Splendid fellow! Have you got 'The Ghoul?'"

"Yes, we've got him."

"Well, don't be too sure about it. He's a Mahatma, you know; a most elusive individual."

Helliwell pushed his way through the opening, and helped the prisoners out one by one. All showed signs of the ordeal through which they had passed. The two girls, in particular, could hardly murmur.

Even in the passage the heat was stifling, and the inspector mopped his brow.

"Let's get out of here," he said. "We can talk afterwards. The fire's too near for my fancy."

"There's another of 'The Ghoul's' victims in the Chamber," said Mr. Knight. "Poor old Bidgood. But he's dead."

"Then we'll come back for him later. It's dangerous to stay here. My men are doing what they can, but—"

From somewhere above their heads came the muffled yet unmistakable reports of three revolver shots in quick succession.

"Damn!" muttered Helliwell. "There's trouble upstairs!"

He hurried them towards the flight of steps. They were still a few yards away when someone came tumbling down. It was the plain clothes man who had been left to guard Morlant.

"Thought I'd better let you know," he panted. "He tried to escape. Fought like a hellcat. Snatched at the pistol. It went off. Three bullets in his head."

"Damn!" muttered Helliwell again. "He's dead?"

"Yes."

"Well, there'll be trouble about that, I expect. But it's not your fault. I take responsibility and—"

There was a rending crash overhead. They all jumped back just in time. A portion of the roof of the passage fell on the bottom of the stairs, together with a large flaming beam which completely blocked the way. The heat almost scorched their faces.

"My God, that finishes us!" exclaimed the inspector. "We're trapped!"

"There's another way out," said Mr. Knight rapidly. "I'm sure of it. Don't waste any precious time over that block. We've only a few minutes at the most before some more comes down. Let's try to find the other exit."

They turned and hurried in the opposite direction, carrying Harlan as best they could. Before long, the passage narrowed and took a sharp twist.

Mr. Knight was first round the corner.

"There's a door!" he cried jubilantly, holding the candle aloft. "There's a door! We're sav—"

He broke off abruptly, staring along the passage. Startled by his attitude, the others crowded about him, peering into the gloom ahead.

The passage was a *cul de sac*. At the end there was, indeed, a door. But beside the door stood a shadowy figure, grim and menacing. And the candlelight flickered on the grinning, sardonic features of Edward Morlant, and glinted coldly on the dagger in his hand.

24

CLARENCE KNIGHT EXPLAINS

An awed silence fell on the party, and a cold, hopeless despair seized them. Surely it was useless to attempt to escape the murderous lust of this grisly creature who broke the laws of Nature as he broke the laws of man. Only a few minutes had elapsed since he was shot dead. Yet here he stood again, remorseless and implacable, barring their escape from the inferno of fire that raged behind them.

After the first gasp of surprise, no one moved or spoke. Morlant himself stood like a graven image, not a muscle of his face or limbs stirring.

The seconds passed. Suddenly Mr. Knight uttered an exclamation and sprang forward.

Betty screamed.

"Come back!" she cried. "Come back! He'll kill you!"

Mr. Knight did not pause. While the others watched in fascinated dread, he stepped briskly up to the motionless man, and laid a hand on his shoulder.

And then a peculiar thing happened. The figure of Morlant fell stiffly to the floor like an overturned statue, and the dagger clattered noisily on the stones.

The inspector swore under his breath and clung to Mr. Broughton.

"He's dead," said Mr. Knight. "He's been dead a couple of hours or more."

He stooped and turned the body over. In the back, below the left shoulder, the clothes were torn and blood-
stained.

"I think," he murmured quietly, straightening himself,
"I begin to see daylight now."

Without another word, he turned his attention to the
door. This was quite modern and offered no difficulty.
Beyond it was a blank wall, and a few trials disclosed an
opening similar to that into the Priest Chamber.

Thankful to escape the heat, they all hurried through
and found themselves, as Mr. Knight had surmised, in
Piccadilly Circus. When he swung to the section of wall
through which they had passed, no trace of an opening
remained.

"If we'd looked for this when we first came down here—
" he began.

"Well?" prompted Betty, puzzled.

"We probably shouldn't have found it," he concluded
with a grin. "This house was just made for a Mahatma!"

He was very cheerful as he led the way through the passage and up the steps to the wardrobe. The others followed
in silence. It seemed that he had made some discovery that
pleased him, but for them the fog of uncertainty remained
as thick as ever.

And they were to receive still another surprise. They
were only just in time to get down the stairs before the
spreading fire made them impassable. When they reached
the hall, they found the remainder of the police, their
hopeless fight against the fire abandoned, standing round
something on the floor near to the door. As they approached, the men drew aside, and they saw lying there,
still handcuffed, the body of "The Ghoul."

"Yes," said Mr. Knight, smiling contentedly. "I begin
to see daylight now."

It was not until two or three hours later that an opportunity for a quiet talk occurred. Betty and Sally were seated before a blazing fire in Mr. Broughton's comfortable house in Blackshaw. They sipped their tea, and felt like purring because all was well. The men had not yet come in from the police station.

"I wish they'd be quick," murmured Betty. "I'm dying to know just what has happened."

"I don't suppose they'll be long now," said Sally. "Everard told me that—"

She broke off, blushing, as Betty smiled at her.

"Well," she continued defiantly, "you've done the same! You've nothing to talk about."

"I know," agreed Betty, her voice soft and tender. "But much to be thankful for."

Knight and Broughton came in immediately afterwards. Both were smiling and cheerful, though Knight's arm was in a sling.

"Good news, Miss Elizabeth," began the solicitor. "The doctor says your father will live."

"Oh, I'm so glad! I—I wish you'd let me go to him."

"Not to-night, please." Mr. Knight intervened gently. "I've just been talking to him. He asked me to give you a message. He says he's learned something this evening. If it's not too late, he intends trying to make a fresh start. He wants to take his punishment like a man. And then— and not till then— he'll come and ask you to forgive him."

Betty's blue eyes were misty.

"He saved our lives," she murmured.

"He certainly did! If it hadn't been for him, we should all have been dead by now. And you may be sure that this will be taken into account when he stands his trial. I don't think you need worry about him, little lady. It won't be long before you can have him with you."

Broughton was busying himself with decanters and glasses at the sideboard.

"I wish you'd sit down in that chair, Knight, or whatever your name is," he said, "and tell us your explanation of what's been going on in that confounded house. I must confess that I can't make head or tail of it."

Mr. Knight smiled as he accepted the proffered glass and emptied it.

"I've got rather an advantage over you," he said, "because of the few pages of the diary I found. I've been reading them over with Inspector Helliwell. There was quite a lot of information in them; and together with what we have discovered for ourselves, they enabled me to piece together a story which is probably not far from the truth. It satisfied the police, anyhow."

"Oh, do tell us!" begged Sally. "We just must know!"

"Very well. What do you want to know?"

"Good heavens! I want to know everything!"

"All right." Mr. Knight grinned, and settled himself in a chair. "I'll tell you the whole story as I've worked it out. But you must remember that some of it is conjecture.

"It begins some fifty odd years ago, with the birth of Edward Morlant. For Edward was a sociable soul. He couldn't bear to be born alone. He was accompanied by a twin brother, James, as like to him as the proverbial pea.

"If James had died at birth, all would have been well. But James did not die. He flourished as the wicked do. In time he ran away from home, and set up in business for himself as a first-class criminal.

"Edward, as you know, had inherited a dreadful legacy. In this legacy James, presumably, had his full share. But whereas Edward, even in his fits of insanity, was kind and gentle, the effect on his brother was very different. Aided to a great extent by his madness, James built up for himself an almost international reputation as 'The Ghoul.'

"I don't think anyone knew about this twin except the old family servant, and—"

"I certainly never heard a word about him," interrupted Broughton earnestly.

"I don't suppose you did. Even Bidgood, as I figure it out, had no idea what had become of him. But Edward knew all about him. A brother like James is not an un-mixed blessing. He kept a careful eye on him—from a distance. And when a little fortune came his way, a fortune which his brother, in all likelihood, would have tried to blackmail him out of, he took steps to have James certified as insane and put away in a lunatic asylum.

"As you will imagine, it didn't take long for James, with all his resources, to make his escape. And now Edward's life became a torture to him. He lived in constant dread lest his brother should discover not only about the fortune, but also the identity of the person who had sent him to the asylum."

"That was what he mentioned in the diary?" asked Betty. "About being frightened of James, I mean? And none of us knew who James might be?"

"Yes. Eventually, of course, James did find out. He learned the whole story. And that's been the cause of all the trouble.

"Edward received word of the catastrophe in some way, and was terror-stricken. He knew his brother only too well. Unless he could think of some method of deceiving him, his life was not worth the toss of a coin.

"The idea of faking his death came to him, and seemed to offer what he wanted. I don't believe he ever dreamed for a moment, little lady, that you would be involved in James's vengeance. He was quite a decent old sort himself, and would not have harmed you for the world. I think the only reason he insisted that you should stay at Hameldon House was to give color to his deception. Seeing you installed as mistress, James would not be likely to suspect that he was being fooled.

"James, however, as you may have noticed, has a strain of perseverance in his nature. If he couldn't have the pleasure of killing this traitorous brother of his, at least he could gather in his wealth. As soon as he saw the death notices in the papers—inserted, of course, entirely for his benefit—he instituted enquiries at Blackshaw, and discovered that Miss Betty Harlan was the sole legatee.

"Now he happened to know Miss Harlan. For her father, under another name, had frequently been employed by him, and he naturally made it his business to know all about his employees. It seemed to him a very simple matter to clear the ground by putting Miss Harlan out of the way.

"He paid her a visit, somewhat delayed, I am thankful to say, by the fact that I was following him. He has told us himself that he was very annoyed to find Mr. Broughton there before him, but of course I knew nothing about all this at the time. I didn't see Broughton myself, though we waited on the landing and the stairs until he had gone."

"Then 'The Ghoul' dropped the false mustache we found?" exclaimed Sally.

"I expect so. I daresay he came disguised as Broughton, intending to lure Betty away with some concocted story. Anyhow, he had to change his plans. And I was lucky enough to prevent the attempted murder in the fog.

"The next day he traveled up to Blackshaw and I traveled with him. But I've already told you all about that, and how surprised I was to find my unknown lady of the fog here. We'll switch over to Edward now.

"Edward, of course, was living in the house, and feeling so safe that he was rather careless. The old passages which he had had modernized were of the greatest assistance to him. He could see what was going on, and could move about at will. Bidgood looked after all his wants;

and Mr. Broughton was there to explain away any noises you girls might hear."

"I—I thought I was acting for the best," muttered Broughton. "If I'd confessed at first—"

"It probably wouldn't have made much difference. You didn't know enough. Now if Bidgood had told all he knew . . . But Bidgood was loyal, too.

"Anyhow, let's get on with the story. I think everything is clear now up to this evening. From the time we finished tea—it looks ages ago, doesn't it?—matters begin to grow a little more complicated.

"Imagine Edward Morlant, behind his portrait over the chimney piece, watching you discover the diary he had inadvertently left behind. It upset him considerably, I'll be bound, because it contained the secret of his hiding place. He would realize at once that he must obtain possession of it somehow; and when you read out that half-forgotten rubbish about immortality, written during his demented periods, he clutched at the opportunity of getting it back by pretending to return from the dead.

"He saw you take the book upstairs, and chased round by underground to intercept you. You know what happened then. Unfortunately for everybody James chose this moment to appear on the scene. You must remember that he would know all about the secret passages in this old house where he had spent his childhood days. He had come in through the cave to spy out the land.

"Can you wonder that poor old Edward was terrified when he saw his enemy silently creeping up behind you? It was lucky for you, little lady, that you fainted, or Heaven knows what would have happened. I take it that Edward fled panic-stricken, and that James, after snatching the diary, followed him.

"The chase continued down to Piccadilly Circus, then through to the Priest Chamber. Here James caught Edward and fastened him up. There was no need for any questions. He would guess at once how he had been deceived.

"The experienced criminal's first impulse is to arrange for his retreat. Before he killed his brother, James wanted to be sure that he could get away without trouble whatever happened. Probably he had had a little difficulty with the new wardrobe, and thought it wise to ensure that he knew how to work the secret way into the library in case of need.

"I think he had already conceived the plan of impersonating his brother. He would hear some of your conversation in the corridor, and the situation was bound to appeal to his abnormal mind. By pretending to be Edward, returned from the dead, he could carry out his schemes with ease."

"What were his schemes?" asked Betty. "I can't think what he expected to gain."

"They're not altogether clear," admitted Mr. Knight, "because we have to guess at them. But we can assume that he was after the money, and there were many ways in which he could achieve this object. Probably his original idea was to get you and Broughton out of the way, then make Harlan forge another will. There's no other reason why he should send for your father to come here. When he discovered that Edward was not dead, of course, he would alter his plans. Most likely he decided that impersonation would be his best card. You must remember that he had the diary with its variety of useful information.

"Anyhow, his first care was to make sure of his ground. He dragged his brother up through the passage, and made him show how the opening into the library worked, both from inside and from out.

"It occurred to him, then, that he would want clothes similar to those Edward wore; and as no one was about, he thought he'd risk coming upstairs for one of the suits he had seen in the wardrobe. Incidentally, I might remark that I first suspected there might be some question of impersonation when I counted four similar suits in the wardrobe. It seemed to me rather a significant number. If a man was ordering so many, he would probably order the round half dozen. Edward Morlant himself was wearing the fifth. Who could be wearing the sixth?

"But that's by the way. It didn't help me to guess at the truth, though perhaps it ought to have done so.

"As James was crossing the hall—you must remember that I am reconstructing this without definite knowledge—the dog saw him. At first it was deceived by his resemblance to its master, and fussed round him joyfully. We heard it barking a welcome. He viciously kicked it out of the way, and its joy turned to puzzled fear.

"He came cautiously upstairs, knowing that we were searching somewhere near at hand. But because all was in darkness, he never suspected our presence in the corridor. When he heard us, he had just time to dash into the bedroom and escape through the wardrobe, snatching up one of the suits as he went."

"Then it wasn't Edward we saw the second time?" asked Betty.

"No. Not if my theory is right. While we were exploring underground, our quarry was changing his clothes and having a few words with Edward whom he had trussed up near the opening into the library. He heard the doorbell ringing, and came out to investigate. He found Harlan in the hall; and Harlan promptly collapsed at sight of what he took to be a ghost.

"Having no urgent need of his underling at the moment, James left him there as a little surprise for us. Going back through the library, he noticed the paper knife on the bureau. Just the thing for his brother! Might be used by anyone! He picked it up, walked through into the passage, and deliberately stabbed Edward to the heart there and then!"

25

A Strange Disappearance

Betty laid a protesting hand on Mr. Knight's arm. "But surely you must be wrong there," she said. "Why, he was stabbed while we were all standing round him."

"I think not, little lady," he replied, gently patting her hand. "You never saw him again after meeting him in the corridor. In fact, you were the only one of us who did see him."

"I don't understand—"

"Well, let me explain. I repeat that James stabbed Edward in the passage. We heard him scream, if you remember, just before we came down and found your father."

"Yes, I remember," Betty shivered. "Then the man who came to the library door while we were all in the hall was—"

"James Morlant. Precisely. It's the only way what happened afterwards can be explained. And you will recollect that the dog was frightened of him."

"He had read the diary and was now quite *au fait* with the situation. He could see that we were puzzled, and he played his part for all it was worth.

"I think, perhaps, he was annoyed because I refused to treat him seriously. He decided to mystify us still further. It was a kind of joke which appealed strongly to his diseased imagination. Incidentally, it probably led to the failure of his schemes because, in his desire for complete darkness, he forgot the half-burned diary on the fire.

"While we stood waiting there, unable to see a thing, he pressed the spring of the secret opening and dragged out the body of his brother with the dagger still in position. He left it there at our feet, while he himself retired into the passage, and watched the effect from behind the portrait."

"Gosh!" muttered Sally, edging closer to Mr. Broughton. "What an idea!"

"I suppose no one but a madman could have thought of it. Anyhow it worked; we were all deceived. But it led to further complications for him. First, there was the question of the police. He didn't want them here. And when we decided that Broughton should fetch them, he saw immediately that this must be stopped. You already know how he kidnaped our friend here.

"Then there was the question of Bidgood. I feel sure that the old servant had begun to suspect the truth; the Morlant we had spoken to in the library was not the kind, gentle master he had known. But fearful of giving the secret away unnecessarily, he ventured into the passages to investigate for himself instead of telling us. And there he met his death.

"Later happenings are pretty clear and straight-forward. You will understand, without further explanation, how James juggled with the bodies of his brother and Bidgood, shot the dog—in fact did everything which I accused Mr. Broughton of doing. His idea of putting Edward, dagger in hand, to guard the door into Piccadilly Circus can be regarded only as a lunatic's impression of a joke.

"Flushed with his success in frightening us, he assumed the character of the police sergeant. This served the double purpose of allowing him to move about freely, and also of giving him more time before we began to realize the police weren't coming.

"My temporary disappearance afforded him the opportunity he wanted of splitting up the party. He locked you girls in your room, intending to come back later. So far as I can see, his idea was to terrify you, in the person of Edward Morlant, to such an extent that you would be ready to sign any document he placed before you, thus transferring your interest in the property to him.

"In furtherance of this idea, he put on the torn and bloodstained coat of his brother, knowing that it would strengthen your conviction that he was returned from the dead. But here again his plans went awry. He wanted first to put Harlan safely away in the passage. And Harlan was so terrified of him that his cries and screams brought you downstairs.

"I flatter myself that James was a little uneasy about me. He didn't quite know what to make of me. I shouldn't be surprised if he half guessed who I was. Anyhow, when the noise you made on the stairs startled him, he dashed back into the secret passage, and reassumed his safest disguise, that of Sergeant Kendall.

"As you were now in the library, he had to return by way of the bedroom. Thinking I was somewhere about, he decided to carry you off to the Priest Chamber, where he would be free from interruption. And—but there's no need for me to go into all this. You all know what happened."

"Yes," said Betty slowly, "I think I can follow everything now. I can see what he was after. But what I can't understand is why he did all these dreadful unnecessary things, such as changing the bodies about."

"I'm afraid I can't tell you anything definite about that," said Mr. Knight. "We have to remember that he was mad. Moreover, there's another point to bear in mind; the

more he frightened you, the easier it would be to persuade
you to do what he wanted."

"But shutting us all up in the Priest Chamber! To burn
to death!"

"Well, of course, that was a different matter. As soon
as he discovered that I had managed to communicate with
the police, the situation was altered entirely. He had to get
us out of the way before the police came, and the Priest
Chamber was admirable for his purpose. Just what he
intended to do afterwards, I don't know. Perhaps disappear for a while, and then claim his brother's property; or
perhaps face the police, still pretending to be Edward. We
found in his pocket a document forged by Harlan which
would have helped him to do either. And in either case he
was quite safe, so long as we were out of the way. But for
your father's unexpected revolt and the quick intelligence
of the police inspector, he would have won in the end."

"Yes, I see." Betty smiled. "You're rather modest for a
furniture salesman, aren't you? Personally, I should have
thought a certain amount of credit for our escape might
be given to the man who realized something of what was
happening, and took considerable risks in order to send
for the police."

"I second that vote of thanks," said Broughton grinning. "Even though he did think I was 'The Ghoul'!"

"I don't think I'll ever forgive him for that," remarked
Sally. Then, unaccountably, she blushed.

"And there's another thing," Betty went on severely.
"You've been deceiving us all. Helping us under false pre-
tenses, so to speak. The inspector addressed you by another
name."

Mr. Knight rose from his chair and crossed to the sideboard. He tried to mix himself another drink, but his in-
jured arm was a handicap. Betty flew to his assistance,
softly scolding him for trying to use it.

"What is your real name?" she asked, as she splashed soda water into his glass.

"Paul Grendon."

"Paul Grendon!" She murmured the name once or twice. "I—I think I like it better than the other." Her blue eyes grew tender and her voice sank to a caress. "Though you've been a very perfect knight to me."

He looked at her sharply; then put down his glass and caught her hand.

"In the Priest Chamber," he began, forcing himself to speak deliberately, "when we were facing death together, you told me you loved me. Because of the circumstances, I have not dared to build on—"

She stopped him with a quick little gesture.

"I tell you again now," she said, her cheeks aflame, "I love you!"

"Betty! Darling!"

His uninjured arm encircled her waist and ardently drew her to him.

"Oh, no!" she whispered, struggling. "You mustn't, dear! Not now! The others—"

He glanced round the room and laughed happily. For Sally and Broughton had disappeared.

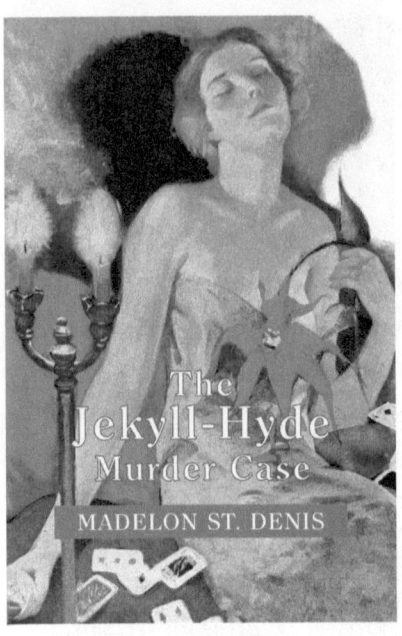

Coachwhip Publications

CoachwhipBooks.com

Coachwhip Publications

CoachwhipBooks.com

FULL CRASH DIVE
ALLAN R. BOSWORTH

GRIMM DEATH

LADY IN LILAC
SUSANNAH SHANE

MURDER IN THE WPA
ALEXANDER WILLIAMS

Coachwhip Publications

CoachwhipBooks.com

WHISPER
MURDER!

VERA KELSEY

DEATH
DOWN EAST

Eleanor Blake

LATE
for the
FUNERAL

Douglas and Dorothy
Stapleton

The Railroad
Murder Case
R. M. LAURENSON

Coachwhip Publications

CoachwhipBooks.com

Coachwhip Publications

CoachwhipBooks.com

MURDER
À LA RICHELIEU
THE ADELAIDE ADAMS MYSTERIES
ANITA BLACKMON

MARIAN GALLAGHER SCOTT

TALL MAN WALKING

THE ATTIC ROOM

THE CRIME,
THE PLACE,
AND THE GIRL

DOUGLAS AND
DOROTHY STAPLETON

CRIME IN
CORN-WEATHER

MARY MEIGS ATWATER

Coachwhip Publications
CoachwhipBooks.com

Jack Dolph

MURDER
MAKES
THE MARE GO

THE CASEBOOK OF
MR. CARRINGTON
SIMON
CARRINGTON'S CASES
J. STORER CLOUSTON

THE
THING
IN THE
BRO K

PETER STORME

HIDE AND GO SEEK
with, GOING TO ST. IVES

HOTEL

COLVER HARRIS

Coachwhip Publications
CoachwhipBooks.com

The Hollow Tree Mystery

MADELON ST. DENIS

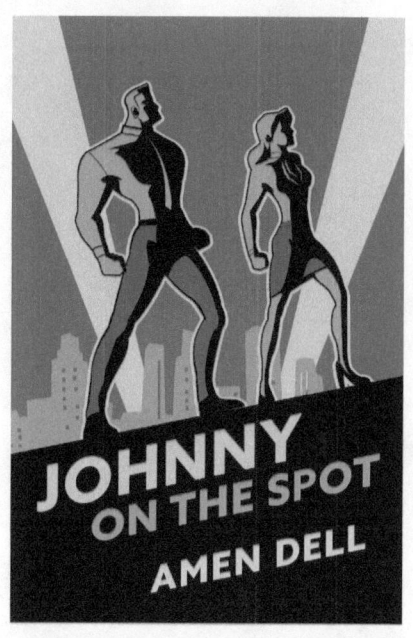

JOHNNY ON THE SPOT

AMEN DELL

VULTURES IN THE SKY

A HUGH RENNERT MYSTERY

TODD DOWNING

SAMUEL ROGERS

YOU'LL BE SORRY!

YOU LEAVE ME COLD!

Coachwhip Publications

CoachwhipBooks.com

THE
SARA ELIZABETH
MASON
MYSTERIES

MURDER RENTS A ROOM

THE CRIMSON FEATHER

DEATH
ON THE CAMPUS
ADDISON
SIMMONS

FEAR OF FEAR

FLORENCE RYERSON
COLIN CLEMENTS

VIRGINIA RATH

FERRYMAN,
TAKE HIM ACROSS!

Coachwhip Publications

CoachwhipBooks.com

THOMAS KINDON

MURDER
IN THE
MOOR

THE SEVEN BLACK
CHESSMEN
John Huntingdon

MURDER
AT SEA

RICHARD CONNELL

SMOKE
SCREEN

Lawrence Saunders

Coachwhip Publications

CoachwhipBooks.com

www.ingramcontent.com/pod-product-compliance
Lightning Source LLC
Chambersburg PA
CBHW050400260626
47156CB00003B/815